W9-BED-206

LINDA HOWARD

Whether she's reading them or writing them, books have long played a profound role in Linda Howard's life. She cut her teeth on Margaret Mitchell and from then on continued to read widely and eagerly. Eventually her interest settled on romance fiction, because she's "easily bored by murder, mayhem and politics." After twenty-one years of penning stories for her own enjoyment, Ms. Howard finally worked up the courage to submit a novel for publication—and is now a multi-*New York Times* bestselling author!

PAULA DETMER RIGGS

discovers material for her writing in her varied life experiences. During her first five years of marriage to a naval officer, she lived in nineteen different locations on the West Coast, gaining familiarity with places as diverse as San Diego and Seattle. She writes romances because "I think we all need escape from the high-tech pressures that face us every day, and I believe in happy endings. Isn't that why we keep trying, in spite of the roadblocks and disappointments along the way?" A five-time nominee for the RITA Award, Paula has won numerous awards, including a Lifetime Achievement Award, two Reviewer's Choice Awards and one Career Achievement Award from *Romantic Times Magazine*.

STELLA BAGWELL

has written more than thirty novels for Silhouette. She always loved reading romances, but it wasn't until an allergic reaction to hair spray ended her career as a hairdresser that she found the urge to write one. Stella married her high school sweetheart at the age of seventeen and has one son. She and her husband live in the beautiful mountains of southeastern Oklahoma, and after nearly thirty years of marriage, Stella feels love is the thing that makes life most precious and worthwhile.

LINDA HOWARD

Paula Detmer Riggs
Stella Bagwell

A Bouquet of Babies

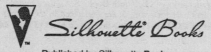

Published by Silhouette Books

America's Publisher of Contemporary Romance

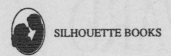 SILHOUETTE BOOKS

A BOUQUET OF BABIES

Copyright © 2000 by Harlequin Books S.A.

ISBN 0-373-48405-4

The publisher acknowledges the copyright holders of the individual works as follows:

THE WAY HOME
Copyright © 1991 by Linda Howington

FAMILY BY FATE
Copyright © 2000 by Paula Detmer Riggs

BABY ON HER DOORSTEP
Copyright © 2000 by Stella Bagwell

CONTENTS

Dear Reader,

Mother's Day is just one day on the calendar. I don't know that it was ever really that important to my mother; she enjoyed more all the other days in the year, the ordinary days, the visits for no special reason. We shopped together, or would meet for breakfast. We occasionally did errands together, not because a calendar said "Pay attention to your mother today" but because we enjoyed each other's company. We were mother and daughter, but when I became an adult we also became friends. As joyful as my childhood was, it was that later friendship that I valued the most, and I think she did, too.

What fun we had! When we talk about her now, it's almost always with a laugh, a tale of something she did or said, and though I'll always miss her, I still enjoy her life. She was what a mother should be, and if I had one wish for the world, it would be that everyone could have such a mother. Not perfect, not a saint, not a neatnik, but a warm, loving woman who made friends wherever she went. She still makes me smile.

Ogida Howard

The Way Home

Linda Howard

Prologue

The Beginning

Saxon Malone didn't look at her as he said, "This won't work. You can be either my secretary or my mistress, but you can't be both. Choose."

Anna Sharp paused, her nimble fingers poised in suspended animation over the stack of papers she had been sorting in search of the contract he had requested. His request had come out of the blue, and she felt as if the breath had been knocked out of her. *Choose,* he'd said. It was one or the other. Saxon always said exactly what he meant and backed up what he'd said.

In a flash of clarity she saw precisely how it would

be, depending on which answer she gave. If she chose to be his secretary, he would never again make any move toward her that could be construed as personal. She knew Saxon well, knew his iron will and how completely he could compartmentalize his life. His personal life never bled over into business, or vice versa. If she chose to be his lover—no, his *mistress*—he would expect to completely support her, just as sugar daddies had traditionally done over the centuries, and in exchange she would be sexually available to him whenever he had the time or inclination to visit. She would be expected to give him total fidelity while he promised nothing in return, neither faithfulness nor a future.

Common sense and self-respect demanded that she choose the upright position of secretary as opposed to the horizontal position of mistress, yet still she hesitated. She had been Saxon's secretary for a year, and had loved him for most of that time. If she chose her job, he would never allow her to get any closer to him than she was right now. As his mistress, at least she would have the freedom to express her love in her own way and the hours spent in his arms as a talisman against a future without him, which she would eventually have to face. Saxon wasn't a staying man, one with whom a woman could plan a life. He didn't tolerate any ties.

She said, her voice low, "If I choose to be your mistress, then what?"

He finally looked up, and his dark green eyes were piercing. "Then I get a new secretary," he said flatly. "And don't expect me to ever offer marriage, because I won't. Under any circumstances."

She took a deep breath. He couldn't have stated it any plainer than that. The wildfire physical attraction that had overtaken them the night before would never become anything stronger, at least not for him. He wouldn't permit it.

She wondered how he could remain so impassive after the hours of fierce lovemaking they had shared on the very carpet beneath her feet. If it had been one hasty mating, perhaps they would have been able to ignore it as an aberration, but the fact was that they had made love over and over again in a prolonged frenzy, and there was no pretending otherwise. His office was permeated with sexual memories; he had taken her on the floor, on the couch, on the desk that was now covered with contracts and proposals; they had even made love in his washroom. He hadn't been a gentle lover; he'd been demanding, fierce, almost out of control, but generous in the way he had made certain she'd been as satisfied as he by each encounter. The thought of never again knowing that degree of passion made her heart squeeze painfully.

She was twenty-seven and had never loved before—never even, as a teenager, had the usual assortment of crushes or gone steady. If she passed up this chance she might never have another, and certainly never another with Saxon.

So, in full possession of her faculties, she took the step that would make her Saxon Malone's kept woman. "I choose to be your mistress," she said softly. "On one condition."

There was a hot flare in his deep-set eyes that just as quickly cooled at her last words. "No conditions."

"There has to be this one," she insisted. "I'm not naive enough to think this relationship—"

"It isn't a relationship. It's an arrangement."

"—this *arrangement* will last forever. I want to have the security of supporting myself, earning my own way, so I won't suddenly find myself without a place to live or the means of making a living."

"*I'll* support you, and believe me, you'll earn every penny of it," he said, his eyes moving down her body in a way that made her feel suddenly naked, her flesh too hot and too tight. "I'll set up a stock portfolio for you, but I don't want you working, and that's final."

She hated it that he would put their relationship— for it *was* a relationship, despite his insistence to the contrary—on such a mercenary basis, but she knew it was the only basis he could agree to. She, on the other hand, would take him on any basis he desired.

"All right," she said, automatically searching for

the words he could accept and understand, words that lacked any hint of emotion. "It's a deal."

He stared at her in silence for a long minute, his face as unreadable as usual. Only the heat in his eyes gave him away. Then he rose deliberately to his feet and walked to the door, which he closed and locked, even though it was after quitting time and they were alone. When he turned back to her, Anna could plainly see his arousal, and her entire body tightened in response. Her breath was already coming fast and shallow as he reached for her.

"Then you might as well begin now," he said, and drew her to him.

Chapter 1

Two years later

Anna heard his key in the door and sat up straight on the sofa, her heart suddenly beating faster. He was back a day earlier than he'd told her, and of course he hadn't called; he never called her when he was gone on a trip, because that would be too much like acknowledging a relationship, just as he insisted, even after two years, on maintaining separate residences. He still had to go home every morning to change clothes before he went to work.

She didn't jump up to run into his arms; that, too, was something that would make him uncomfortable. By now, she knew the man she loved very well. He couldn't accept anything that resembled caring, though she didn't know why. He was very careful never to appear to be rushing to see her; he never called her by a pet name, never gave her any fleeting, casual caresses, never whispered love words to her even during the most intense lovemaking. What he said to her in bed were always words of sexual need and excitement, his voice guttural with tension, but he was a sensual, giving lover. She loved making love with him, not only because of the satisfaction he always gave her, but because under the guise of physical desire she was able to give him all the affection he couldn't accept outside of bed.

When they were making love she had a reason for touching him, kissing him, holding him close, and during those moments he was free with his own caresses. During the long, dark nights he was insatiable, not just for sex but for the closeness of her; she slept every night in his arms, and if for some reason she moved away from him during the night he would wake and reach for her, settling her against him once more. Come morning, he would withdraw back into his solitary shell, but during the nights he was completely hers. Sometimes she felt that he needed the nights as intensely as she did, and for the same reasons. They were the only times when he allowed himself to give and accept love in any form.

So she forced herself to sit still, and kept the book she'd been reading open on her lap. It wasn't until the door had opened and she heard the thump of his suitcase hitting the floor that she allowed herself to look up and smile. Her heart leaped at the first sight of him, just as it had been doing for three years, and pain squeezed her insides at the thought of never seeing him again. She had one more night with him, one more chance, and then she would have to end it.

He looked tired; there were dark shadows under his eyes, and the grooves bracketing his beautiful mouth were deeper. Even so, not for the first time, she was struck by how incredibly good-looking he was, with his olive-toned skin, dark hair and the pure, dark green of his eyes. He had never mentioned his parents, and now she wondered about them, about the combination of genes that had produced such striking coloring, but that was another thing she couldn't ask.

He took off his suit jacket and hung it neatly in the closet, and while he was doing that, Anna went over to the small bar and poured him two fingers of Scotch, neat. He took the drink from her with a sigh of appreciation, and sipped it while he began loosening the knot of his tie. Anna stepped back, not wanting to crowd him, but her eyes lingered on his wide, muscled chest, and her body began to quicken in that familiar way.

"Did the trip go all right?" she asked. Business was always a safe topic.

"Yeah. Carlucci was overextended, just like you said." He finished the drink with a quick toss of his wrist, then set the glass aside and put his hands on her waist. Anna tilted her head back, surprise in her eyes. What was he doing? He always followed a pattern when he returned from a trip: he would shower while she prepared a light meal; they would eat; he would read the newspaper, or they would talk about his trip; and finally they would go to bed. Only then would he unleash his sensuality, and they would make love for hours. He had done that for two years, so why was he breaking his own pattern by reaching for her almost as soon as he was in the door?

She couldn't read the expression in his green eyes; they were too shuttered, but were glittering oddly. His fingers bit into her waist.

"Is something wrong?" she asked, anxiety creeping into her tone.

He gave a harsh, strained laugh. "No, nothing's wrong. It was a bitch of a trip, that's all." Even as he spoke, he was moving them toward the bedroom. Once there, he turned her around and began undressing her, pulling at her clothes in his impatience. She stood docilely, her gaze locked on his face. Was it her imagination, or did a flicker of relief cross his face when at last she was nude and he pulled her against him? He wrapped his arms tightly around her, almost crushing her. His shirt buttons dug into her breasts, and she squirmed a little, docility giving way to a growing arousal. Her response to him was always strong and immediate, rising to meet his.

She tugged at his shirt. "Don't you think you'd be better off without this?" she whispered. "And this?" She slipped her hands between them and began unbuckling his belt.

He was breathing harder, his body heat burning her even through his clothes. Instead of stepping back so he could undress, he tightened his arms around her and lifted her off her feet, then carried her to the bed. He let himself fall backward, with her still in his arms, then rolled so that she was beneath him. She made a tight little sound in her throat when he used his muscular thigh to spread her legs, and his hips settled into the notch he'd just made.

"Anna." Her name was a groan coming from deep in his chest. He caught her face between his hands and ground his mouth against hers, then reached down between their bodies to open his pants. He was in a frenzy, and she didn't know why, but she sensed his desperate need of her and held herself still for him. He entered her with a heavy surge that made her arch off the bed. She wasn't ready, and his entry was painful, but she pushed her fingers into his hair and clasped his head, trying to give him what comfort she could, though she didn't know what was wrong.

Once he was inside her, however, the desperation faded from his eyes and she felt the tension in his muscles subside. He sank against her with a muted groan of pleasure, his heavy weight crushing her into the bed. After a moment he propped himself on his elbows. ''I'm sorry,'' he whispered. ''I didn't mean to hurt you.''

She gave him a gentle smile and smoothed his hair. ''I know,'' she replied, applying pressure to his head to force him down within kissing range. Her body had accustomed itself to him, and the pain of his rough entry was gone, leaving only the almost incandescent joy of making love with him. She had never said it aloud, but her body said it, and she always echoed it in her mind: *I love you.* She said the inner words again as he began moving, and she wondered if it would be for the last time.

Later, she woke from a light doze to hear the shower running. She knew she should get up and begin preparations for a meal, but she was caught in a strange inertia. She couldn't care about food when the rest of her life depended on what happened between them now. She couldn't put it off any longer.

Maybe tonight *wouldn't* be the last time. Maybe. Miracles had happened before.

She might hope for a miracle, but she was prepared for a less perfect reality. She would be moving out of this chic, comfortable apartment Saxon had provided for her. Her next living quarters wouldn't be color-coordinated, but so what? Matching carpets and curtains didn't matter. Saxon mattered, but she wouldn't be able to have him. She only hoped she would be able to keep from crying and begging; he would hate that kind of scene.

Being without him was going to be the most difficult thing she had ever faced. She loved him even more now than she had two years before, when she had agreed to be his mistress. It always squeezed her heart the way he would do something considerate, then go out of his way to make it appear as just a casual gesture that had happened to present itself, that he hadn't gone to any trouble to do something for her. And there was the concern he had shown over minor colds, the quiet way he had steadily built up an impressive stock portfolio in her name so she would be financially secure, and the way he always complimented whatever she cooked.

She had never seen anyone who needed to be loved more than Saxon, nor anyone who rejected any sign of love so fiercely.

He was almost fanatically controlled—and she adored it when his control shattered when they made love, though never before had he been as frenzied, as *needy,* as he had been tonight. Only when they were making love did she see the real Saxon, the raw passion he kept hidden the rest of the time. She cherished all of his expressions, but her most cherished image was the way he looked when they made love, his black hair damp with sweat, his eyes fierce and bright, all reserve burned away as his thrusts increased in both depth and speed.

She had no photographs of him. She would have to keep those mental images sharp and polished, so she could take them out and examine them whenever the loneliness became too intense. Later, she would painstakingly compare his beloved face with another that was equally precious, and search for the similarities that would both comfort and torment her.

She smoothed her hands over her stomach, which was still flat and revealed nothing yet of the child growing within.

She had had few symptoms to signal her pregnancy, though she was almost four months along. This last period was the first one she had skipped entirely; the first one after conception had been light, and the second one little more than heavy spotting. It was the spotting that had sent her to the doctor for a precautionary exam, which had revealed that she was in good physical condition and undoubtedly pregnant. She had had no morning sickness, only a few isolated bouts of queasiness that had held no significance except in retrospect. Her breasts were now becoming a bit tender, and she had started taking naps, but other than that she felt much as she had before. The biggest difference was in the almost overwhelming emotions she felt for this baby, Saxon's baby: delirious joy at its presence within her; fierce protectiveness; a powerful sense of physical possession; impatience to actually hold it in her arms; and an almost intolerable sense of loss, because she was terrified that she would lose the father as she gained the child.

Saxon had made it plain from the start that he would accept no strings, and a child wasn't merely a string, it was an unbreakable chain. He would find that intolerable. Just the knowledge of her pregnancy would be enough to drive him away.

She had tried to resent him, but she couldn't. She had gone into this with her eyes open; Saxon had never tried to hide anything from her, never made any promises, had in fact gone out of his way to make certain she knew he would never offer anything more than a physical relationship. He had done nothing other than what he'd said he would do. It wasn't his fault that their birth control had failed, nor was it his fault that losing him would break her heart.

The shower had stopped running. After a minute he walked naked into the bedroom, rubbing a towel over his wet hair. A small frown pulled his brows downward when he saw she was still in bed; he draped the towel around his neck and came over to sit beside her on the bed, sliding his hand under the sheet in search of her warm, pliant body. His hand settled on her belly. "Are you all right?" he asked with concern. "Are you sure I didn't hurt you?"

She put a hand over his. "I'm fine." More than

fine, lying there with his hand resting over the child he had given her.

He yawned, then shrugged to loosen the muscles of his shoulders. There was no sign now of his former tension; his expression was relaxed, his eyes lazy with satisfaction. "I'm hungry. Do you want to eat in or go out for dinner?"

"Let's eat in." She didn't want to spend their last night together in the middle of a crowded restaurant.

As he started to get up, she tightened her hand on his, keeping him in place. He gave her a look of mild surprise. She took a deep breath, knowing she had to get this over with now before she lost her nerve, yet when the words came out they weren't the ones she had planned. "I've been wondering...what would you do if I happened to get pregnant?"

Like a shutter closing, his face lost all expression and his eyes frosted over. His voice was very deep and deliberate when he said, "I told you in the beginning, I won't marry you, under any circumstances, so don't try getting pregnant to force my hand. If you're looking for marriage, I'm not the man, and maybe we should dissolve our arrangement."

The tension was back, every line of his big body taut as he sat naked on the side of the bed and waited for her answer, but she could see no sign of worry in his face. He had already made his decision, and now he was waiting to hear hers. There was such a

heavy weight crushing her chest that she could
hardly bear it, but his answer had been no more than
what she had expected.

But she found that she couldn't say the words that
would make him get up, dress and walk out. Not
right now. In the morning. She wanted to have this
last night with him, held close in his arms. She
wanted to tell him that she loved him just one more
time, in the only way he would allow.

Chapter 2

Saxon woke early the next morning and lay in the dim light of dawn, unable to go back to sleep because of the echo of tension left behind by the question Anna had asked the night before. For a few nightmarish moments he had seen his entire life caving in around him, until Anna had smiled her quiet smile and said gently, "No, I'd never try to force you to marry me. It was just a question."

She was still sleeping, her head pillowed on his left shoulder, his left arm wrapped around her, his right hand resting on her hip. From the very first he hadn't been able to sleep unless she was close to him. He had slept alone his entire adult life, but when Anna had become his mistress he had abruptly found, to his surprise, that sleeping alone was almost impossible.

It was getting worse. Business trips had never bothered him before; he had, in fact, thrived on them, but lately they had been irritating the hell out of him. This last trip had been the worst yet. The delays, glitches and aggravations hadn't been anything out of the ordinary, but what he had once taken for granted now grated almost unbearably. A late flight could send him into a rage; a mislaid blueprint was almost enough to get someone fired; a broken piece of equipment had him swearing savagely; and to top it off, he hadn't been able to sleep. The hotel noises and unfamiliar bed had been particularly annoying, though he probably wouldn't have noticed them at all if Anna had been there with him. That admission alone had been enough to make him break out in a sweat, but added to it was a gnawing need to get back home to Denver, to Anna. It wasn't until he had had her beneath him in bed, until he had felt the soft warmth of her body enfold him, that he had at last been able to relax.

He had walked through the door of the apartment and desire had hit him like a blow, low down and hard. Anna had looked up with her customary smile, her dark eyes as calm and serene as a shadowy pool, and his savage mood had faded, to be replaced by pure sexual need. Walking through that door had been like walking into a sanctuary to find a woman made specifically for him. She had poured him a drink and brushed close to him, and he had smelled the sweet scent of her skin that always clung to their sheets, the scent that had been maddeningly absent from the hotel linens. The ferocity of the desire that had taken hold of him still left him a little shaken this morning.

Anna. He had noticed that serenity, and the feminine scent of her, from the very first day when he had hired her as his secretary. He had wanted her from the beginning, but had controlled his sexual urges because he had neither wanted nor needed that sort of complication on the job. Gradually, though, the wanting had grown stron-ger, until it had become an unbearable need that gnawed at him day and night, and his control had begun crumbling.

Anna looked like honey, and he had been going mad wanting to taste her. She had silky, light brown hair, streaked with blond, and dark-honey eyes. Even her skin had a smooth, warm, honey tone to it. She would never be flashy, but she was so pleasant to look at that people continually turned her way. And those honey eyes had always been warm and calm and inviting, until finally he had been unable to resist the invitation. The frenzy of that first night still startled him, even in memory, because he had never lost control—until then. He had lost it with Anna, deep inside her hot, honeyed depths, and sometimes he felt that he had never gotten it back.

He had never let anyone get close to him, but after that first night he had known that he couldn't walk away from her as he had from the others. Acknowledging that simple fact had terrified him. The only way he had been able to handle it had been to completely separate her from the other parts of his life. She could be his mistress, but nothing else. He couldn't let her matter too much. He still had to constantly guard against letting her get too close; Anna could destroy him, and something deep inside him knew it. No one else had ever even threatened his defenses, and there were times when he wanted to walk out and never come back, never see her again, but he couldn't. He needed her too much, and he constantly fought to keep her from realizing it.

But their arrangement made it possible for him to sleep with her every night and lose himself over and over in her warm, pliant body. In bed he could kiss her and smooth his hands over her, wrap himself in her scent and touch. In bed he could feed his craving for honey, his savage need to touch her, to hold her close. In bed she clung to him with abandon, opening herself to him whenever he wanted, her hands sliding over him in bold, tender caresses that drove him wild. Once they were in bed together, it seemed as if she never stopped touching him, and despite himself, he reveled in it. Sometimes it was all he could do to keep from groaning in a strange, not completely physical ecstasy as she petted and stroked and cuddled.

Yet for all that they had virtually lived together for two years—the small distance that he insisted on retaining, so necessary for him, was in fact negligible in terms of time—he knew little more about her now than he had before. Anna didn't bombard anyone with the details of her past or present life, and he hadn't asked, because to do so would give her the same right to question him about his own past, which was something he seldom allowed himself to even think about. He knew how old she was, where she had been born, where she had gone to school, her social security number, her former jobs, because all that had been in her personnel record. He knew that she was conscientious, good with details and preferred a quiet life. She seldom drank alcohol, and lately seemed to have stopped drinking altogether. She read quite a bit, and her interests were wide and varied in both fiction and nonfiction. He knew that she preferred pastel colors and didn't like spicy foods.

But he didn't know if she had ever been in love, what had happened to her family—in her personnel file, ''None'' had been listed in the next-of-kin column—if she had been a cheerleader or ever gotten into trouble for childish pranks. He didn't know why she had moved to Denver, or what her dreams were.

He knew only the surface facts that were there for anyone to see, not her memories or hopes.

Sometimes he was afraid that, because he knew so little about her, she might someday slip away from him. How could he predict what she would do when he knew nothing of her thoughts and had only himself to blame? He had never asked, never encouraged her to talk to him of those parts of her life. For the past two years he had lived in quiet terror, dreading the day when he would lose her, but unable to do anything to stop it. He didn't know how to reach out to her, how to hold her, when even the thought of letting her know how vulnerable he was to her had the power to make him physically sick.

The hunger grew in him as he thought of her, felt her lying so soft against his side, and his manhood swelled in response. If they had no other form of contact, they at least had this, the almost overwhelming sexual need for each other. He had never before wanted anything from a woman except sex; it was bitterly ironic that now he was using sex to give him at least the semblance of closeness with her. His heartbeat kicked into a faster rate as he began stroking her, easing her awake and into passion so he could ease himself into her and forget, for a while, everything but the incredible pleasure of making love to her.

It was one of those sunny days when the brightness seemed almost overwhelming, the air was clear and warm for late April, a perfect day, a mockery of a day, because she felt as if her heart were dying inside of her. She cooked breakfast, and they ate it on the terrace, as they often did during good weather. She poured him another cup of coffee and sat down across from him, then folded her hands around her chilled glass of orange juice so they wouldn't shake.

"Saxon." She couldn't look at him, so she focused on the orange juice. She felt nauseated, but it was more a symptom of heavy dread than of her pregnancy.

He had been catching up on the local news, and now he looked up at her over the top of a newspaper. She felt his attention focus on her.

"I have to leave," she said in a low voice.

His face paled, and for a long minute he sat as if turned to stone, not even blinking. A slight breeze rattled the newspaper, and finally he moved, folding the pages slowly and painstakingly, as if every movement were painful. The time had come, and he didn't know if he could bear it, if he could even speak. He looked at Anna's lowered head, at the way the sun glinted on the pale, silky streaks, and knew that he had to speak. This time, at least, he wanted to know why.

So that was the question he asked, that one word, and it came out sounding rusty. "Why?"

Anna winced at the raw edge to his voice. "Something has happened. I didn't plan it. It—it just happened."

She had fallen in love with someone else, he thought, fighting to catch his breath over the knot of agony in his chest. He had always trusted her completely, had never even entertained the thought that she might be seeing other men during his absences, but obviously he'd been wrong.

"Are you leaving me for another man?" he asked harshly.

Her head jerked up, and she stared at him, stunned by the question. He looked back at her, his eyes fierce and greener than she had ever seen them before.

"No," she whispered. "Never that."

"Then what?" He shoved himself away from the table and stood, his big body taut with barely controlled rage.

She took a deep breath. "I'm pregnant."

Just for an instant his fierce expression didn't change; then all of a sudden his face turned to stone, blank and hard. "What did you say?"

"I'm pregnant. Almost four months. It's due around the end of September."

He turned his back on her and walked to the terrace wall to look out over the city. The line of his shoulders was rigid with anger. "By God, I never thought you'd do this," he said, his voice harshly controlled. "I've been suckered all the way, haven't

I? I should have known what to expect after the question you asked last night. Marriage would be more profitable than a paternity suit, wouldn't it? But you stand to make a good profit either way.''

Anna got up from the table and quietly walked back into the apartment. Saxon stood by the wall, his fists knotted as he tried to deal with both blind rage and the cold knot of betrayal, as well as the pain that waited, crouched and ready, to come to the fore at the least abatement of anger.

He was too tense to stand there long; when he couldn't bear it any longer, he followed her, determined to find out the depths of his own stupidity even though that would only deepen the pain. It was like the way a tongue would continually probe a sore tooth, in search of the pain. No matter how she tore him to shreds, he had to know, and then he would be invulnerable; no one would ever get to him again. He had once thought himself invulnerable, only to have Anna show him the chink in his emotional armor. But once he got over this, he would truly be untouchable.

Anna was calmly sitting at her desk, writing on a sheet of paper. He had expected her to be packing, at the very least, anything but sitting there scribbling away.

''What're you doing?''

She jerked a little at his harsh voice, but continued writing. Perhaps it was only that his eyes hadn't adjusted to the dimmer light, but she looked pale and drawn. He hoped savagely that she was feeling just a fraction of what he was going through right now.

"I said, what are you doing?"

She signed her name to the bottom of the page and dated it, then held it out to him. "Here," she said, using an enormous effort to keep her voice calm. "Now you won't have to worry about a paternity suit."

Saxon took the paper and turned it around to read it. He skimmed it once, then read it again with greater attention and growing disbelief.

It was short and to the point. *I swear, of my own free will, that Saxon Malone is not the father of the child I carry. He has no legal responsibility, either to me or my child.*

She stood up and moved past him. "I'll be packed and gone by tonight."

He stared down at the paper in his hand, almost dizzy with the conflicting emotions surging back and forth inside him. He couldn't believe what she had done, or how casually she had done it. With just a few words written on a sheet of paper she had prevented herself from receiving a large sum of money, because God knew he would have paid any amount, even bankrupted himself if necessary, to make certain that baby was taken care of, not like—

He started shaking, and sweat broke out on his face. Rage welled in him again. Clutching the paper in his hand, he strode into the bedroom just as she was tugging her suitcases out of the closet.

"That's a damn lie!" he shouted, and threw the crumpled paper at her.

Anna flinched but hung on to her calm demeanor. Privately she wondered how much more she could take before she broke down and began sobbing. "Of course it's a lie," she managed as she placed the suitcases on the bed.

"That baby is mine."

She gave him an odd look. "Did you have any doubt? I wasn't admitting to being unfaithful, I was trying to give you some peace of mind."

"Peace of mind!" It seemed as if all his control had been demolished. He was shouting at her again, when in the entire three years they had known each other he had never before even raised his voice to her. "How the hell am I supposed to have any peace of mind knowing that my kid...my kid—" He stopped, unable to finish the sentence.

She began emptying her dresser drawers into the open suitcases, neatly folding and placing each garment. "Knowing that your kid—what?" she prompted.

He shoved his hands into his pockets and knotted them into fists. "Are you even going to have it?" he asked raggedly.

She went stiff, then straightened to stare at him. "What do you mean by that?"

"I mean, have you already planned an abortion?"

There was no warmth or softness at all in her brown eyes now. "Why do you ask?" she questioned evenly.

"It's a reasonable question."

He really had no idea, she thought numbly. How could he even consider the idea that she might abort his child if he had any inkling at all about the way she felt? All of the love that she had expressed during those long, dark hours might as well have been kept hidden for all the notice he'd paid it. Maybe he had just accepted her passion as the skillful act of a kept woman, designed to keep a sugar daddy happy.

But she didn't say any of that. She just looked at him for a moment before stating abruptly, "No. I'm not having an abortion," then turning back to her packing.

He made an abrupt motion with his hand. "Then what? If you're going to have it, then what are you going to do with it?"

She listened to him with growing disbelief. Had she gone crazy, or had he? What did he think she was going to do? A variety of answers occurred to her, some obvious and some not so obvious. Did he expect her to list the numerous activities involved in caring for a baby, or was he asking what her plans were? Given Saxon's usual precision of speech, always saying exactly what he meant, she was even more bewildered.

"What do you mean, 'what am I going to do with it?' What mothers usually do, I suppose."

His face was grayish and covered with a sheen of sweat. "That's my baby," he said, striding forward to catch her shoulders in his hard hands. "I'll do whatever it takes to keep you from throwing it away like a piece of garbage!"

Chapter 3

Cold chills of horror trickled down her spine, rendering her momentarily incapable of speech. All she could do was endure his tight grip on her shoulders, wide eyes fastened on him and her mouth slightly parted in disbelief. She tried several times to speak, and when she finally managed it, her voice was a hoarse croak. "*Throw it away?* Dear God! That's *sick!* Why on earth would you ever say something like that?"

He was shaking. She could feel it now, in his hands; see it in the visible tremors of his big body. His distress had the effect of relieving her own as she suddenly realized that he was upset and in need of reassurance even more, perhaps, than she was, though she didn't know why. Instinct took over and ruled her actions as she placed her hands on his chest.

"I would never do anything to harm your baby," she said gently. "Never."

His trembling intensified. His green eyes were stark with some savage emotion that she couldn't read, but he took a deep breath and locked his jaw as he fought to regain control. She saw the battle, saw what it cost him to win it, but in just a moment his hands were steady and his face, if still colorless, was as blank as rock. With great care he released her shoulders and let his hands drop to his sides.

"You don't have to leave here," he said, as if that was what they had been discussing. "It's a good apartment. You could take over the lease...."

Anna whirled away from him to hide the sharp upthrust of pain, all the more hurtful because, just for a moment, she thought he had meant that things didn't have to change. But he wasn't offering to preserve the status quo; he still intended to sever the relationship. "Don't," she said, warding off the words with a hand held back toward him. "Just...don't."

"Don't what?" he challenged. "Don't try to make it comfortable for you?"

She inhaled raggedly and let her head drop as she, in turn, tried to marshal her own control, but all she could find was weariness and a need for the truth. If this was the end, why not tell him? Pride? That was a pitiful reason for hiding something that had changed her life. She took another deep breath. "Don't ask me to stay here without you," she said. "You're the reason I'm here. Without you, I have no reason to stay." She turned and faced him, lifting her head so she could see him as she said in a clear, deliberate voice, "I love you. If I hadn't, I never would have come here at all."

Shock rippled across his face, turning it even whiter. His lips moved but made no sound.

"I planned to leave because I thought that was what you would want," she continued steadily. "You made it more than plain from the beginning that you didn't want any ties, so I didn't expect anything else. Even if you wanted to continue our—our arrangement, I don't think it's possible. I can't be a mother and continue to be your undemanding mistress, too. Babies tend to have their own priorities. So, under the present circumstances, I have to leave. That doesn't mean I'll stop loving you." *Ever,* she added in her thoughts.

He shook his head, either in disbelief or denial, and moved jerkily to sit down on the bed, where he stared unseeingly at the open suitcases.

Concern welled in her as she watched him. She had expected him to react with anger or cold retreat, but he truly seemed in shock, as if something terrible had happened. She walked over to sit beside him, her gaze fastened on his face in an effort to catch every fleeting nuance of expression. Saxon was hard enough to read when he was relaxed; his face looked like marble now.

Anna gripped her fingers tightly together. "I never expected you to act like this," she murmured. "I thought...I guess I thought you just wouldn't care."

His head jerked up, and he gave her a look like a sword edge, sharp and slicing. "You thought I'd just walk away and never give another thought to either you or the baby?" His tone was harsh with accusation.

She didn't back down. "Yes, that's exactly what I thought. What else could I think? You've never given me any indication that I was anything more to you than a convenient sexual outlet."

His heart twisted painfully, and he had to look away. She thought she was only a convenience, when he measured his life by the time he spent with her. Not that he had ever let her know; she was right about that. He had gone out of his way to keep her from knowing. Was that why he was losing her now? He felt as if he had been shredded, but he was in too much pain to be able to tell which was hurting worse, the knowledge that he was losing her or that he had fathered a baby who was also lost to him.

"Do you have a place to go?" he asked numbly.

She sighed inaudibly, releasing the last frail grasp of hope. "No, not really, but it's okay. I've looked around a little, but I haven't wanted to commit on anything until I talked to you. I'll go to a hotel. It won't take me long to find another apartment. And you've made certain I won't be strapped financially. Thank you for that. And thank you for my baby." She managed a faint smile, but he wasn't looking at her and didn't see it.

He leaned forward and braced his elbows on his knees, massaging his forehead with one hand. Lines of weariness were cut into his face. "You don't have to go to a hotel," he muttered. "You can look for another place from here. There's no point in moving twice. And we have a lot of legal stuff to get sorted out."

"No we don't," she said. He slanted his head to the side to give her another of those incisive looks. "We don't," she insisted. "You've made certain of my financial security. I'm more than able to provide for my baby. If you think I'm going to be bleeding you dry, you can just think again!"

He straightened. "What if I want to support it? It's my kid, too. Or didn't you plan on ever letting me see it?"

She was frankly bewildered. "Do you mean you *want* to?" She had never expected that. What she had expected was a cold and final end to their relationship.

That look of shock crossed his features once again, as if he had just realized what he'd said. He gulped and got to his feet, striding restlessly around the room. He had so much the look of a trapped animal that she took pity on him and said softly, "Never mind."

Instead of reassuring him, her words seemed to disturb him even more. He ran his hands through his hair, then turned abruptly toward the door. "I can't—I have to think things through. Stay here as long as you need."

He was gone before she could call him back, before she truly realized he was leaving. The front door slammed even before she could get up from the bed. She stared at the empty space where he had stood, and recalled the haunted look in his eyes. She recognized that he was more deeply disturbed than she had ever considered possible, but had no clue as to why. Saxon had kept his past so completely private that she knew absolutely nothing about his childhood, not even who his parents were. If he had any family at all, she didn't know about them. But then, it didn't necessary follow that she would; after all, he still had his own apartment, and his mail still went there. Nor did she think it likely that he would have given out his mistress's telephone number so his family could contact him if he didn't answer his own phone.

She looked around at the apartment she had called home for two years. She didn't know if she would be able to stay here while she looked for someplace else, despite his generous offer. She had been telling him nothing less than the truth when she had said that she didn't want to stay here without him. The apartment was permeated with his presence, not physical reminders so much as the sharp memories that would be a long time fading. Her child had been conceived in the very bed she sat on. She thought about that for a moment; then her lips curved in a wryly gentle smile. Perhaps not; Saxon had never felt the need to limit their lovemaking to the bed, though they had usually sought it for comfort's sake. It was, she supposed, just as likely to have happened in the shower, or on the sofa, or even on the kitchen counter, one cold afternoon when he had arrived while she was cooking dinner and hadn't been inclined to wait until bedtime.

Those days of wondrous passion were over now, as she had known they would be. Even if Saxon hadn't reacted as she had anticipated, the end result was the same.

Saxon walked. He walked automatically, without aim or care. He was still reeling from the twin blows Anna had dealt him, incapable of ordering his thoughts or controlling his emotions. He had controlled every aspect of his life for so long, closing a door in his mind on the things that had happened years before, and he had thought the monster tamed, the nightmare robbed of horror. Yet all it had taken to destroy his deceptively fragile peace was the knowledge that Anna was pregnant. And she was leaving him. God, she was leaving him.

He felt like raising his fists to the sky and cursing whatever fate had done this to him, but the pain was too deep for that. He would have crouched on the sidewalk and howled like a demented animal if it would have relieved even a portion of the swelling agony in his chest and mind, but he knew it would not. The only surcease he would find would be where he had always found it: with Anna.

He couldn't even begin to think of the future. He had no future, no anchor. The image of endless days stretching before him refused to form; he simply couldn't face even one more day, let alone an eternal procession of them. A day without Anna? Why bother?

He'd never been able to tell her how much she meant to him. He could barely tolerate even admitting it to himself. Love, in his experience, was only an invitation to betrayal and rejection. If he allowed himself to love, then he was making himself vulnerable to a destruction of the mind and soul. And no one had loved him, not ever. It was a lesson he had learned from the earliest reaches of memory, and he had learned it well. His very survival had depended on the hard shell of indifference he had cultivated, so he had formed layer after layer of armor.

When had it changed from protection to prison?

Did the turtle ever long for freedom from its boxy shell, so it could run unhindered? Probably not, but he wasn't so lucky. Anna had said that she loved him, and even if it wasn't true, in saying it she had given him the opportunity to stay just a little while longer, if only he had dared to take it. He hadn't, because it would have meant shedding at least a few layers of his armor, and the prospect filled him with a terror founded in earliest childhood and strengthened through long years of abuse.

When he arrived in front of his apartment door he stood staring at it in bewilderment, not quite certain of his location. When he finally realized that he was, in fact, at his own apartment, that he had walked several miles to reach it, he fumbled in his pocket for the keys.

The apartment was silent and musty when he entered, without any sweet welcoming presence. Anna had never been here, and it showed. He could barely stand to spend any time here. It was dark and empty, like a grave, and he was incapable of bringing any light into it. The only light he'd ever known had been Anna's, and he had shared it for too short a time, then driven her away with his own unbridled lust. He'd never been able to keep his hands off her. He had made love to her far more often than he ever would have thought possible, his male flesh rising again and again for the incredible sweetness of sinking into her and joining his body to hers. He had made her pregnant, and because of it he had lost her.

What would he do without her? He couldn't function, couldn't find it in himself to give a damn about contracts, or whether the job got done or not. Even when he had spent days on a job, he had always done it knowing that she was waiting for him. By working so hard, even if it took him away from her, he was able to take care of her and make certain she never had to do without anything. Every time he had expanded the stock portfolio he had set up for her, he had felt an intense satisfaction. Maybe he had thought that his diligent efforts in that would keep her with him, that they would show her that she was better off with him than with anyone else, or out on her own.

He couldn't let himself think, even for a moment, that she might have stayed with him only because he *was* establishing her financial security. If he thought that about Anna, then he truly had nothing left to live for. No, he had always known that she had disliked that part of their arrangement.

There had been no reason at all for her to stay...unless she *did* love him.

For the first time, he let himself think about what she had said. At the time, it had been too much for him to take in, but now the words circled tentatively in his consciousness, like frail birds afraid to light.

She loved him.

He sat in the silent apartment for the rest of the day and into the night, too far withdrawn into himself to feel the need for light or noise, and sometime during the dark hours he crossed an internal barrier. He felt as if he were pinning his desperate hopes on the slimmest of chances, as if he were shooting for the longest odds, but he faced the cold gray fact that he could do nothing else.

If Anna loved him, he couldn't let her go like this.

Chapter 4

Anna had a bad night. She couldn't sleep; though she hadn't expected to sleep well, neither had she expected to lie awake for hours, staring at the dark ceiling and physically aching at the empty space beside her. Saxon had spent many nights away from her before, on his numerous business trips, and she had always managed to sleep. This, however, was different, an emptiness of the soul as well as of space. She had known it would be difficult, but she hadn't known it would leave this wrenching, gnawing pain inside. Despite her best efforts, she had cried until her head had started throbbing, and even then she hadn't been able to stop.

It was sheer exhaustion that finally ended the

tears, but not the pain. It was with her, unabating, through the long dark hours.

If this was what the future would be like, she didn't know if she could bear it, even with the baby. She had thought that his child, immeasurably precious, would be some consolation for his absence, and though that might be so in the future, it was a hollow comfort now. She couldn't hold her baby in her arms right now, and it would be five long months before she could.

She got up toward dawn without having slept at all, and made a pot of decaffeinated coffee. Today of all days she needed the kick of caffeine, but her pregnancy forbade it. She made the coffee anyway, hoping that the ritual would fool her brain into alertness, then sat at the kitchen table with a thick robe pulled around her for comfort while she sipped the hot liquid.

Rain trickled soundlessly down the glass terrace doors and jumped in minute splashes on the drenched stone. As fine as the day before had been, the fickle April weather had turned chilly and wet as a late cold front swept in. If Saxon had been there, they would have spent the morning in bed, snuggled in the warmth of the bed covers, lazily exploring the limits of pleasure.

She swallowed painfully, then bent her head to the table as grief welled up overwhelmingly again. Though her eyes felt grainy and raw from weeping, it seemed there were still tears, still an untapped capacity for pain.

She didn't hear the door open, but the sound of footsteps on the flagstone flooring made her jerk upright, hastily wiping her face with the heels of her hands. Saxon stood before her, his dark face bleak and drawn with weariness. He still had on the same clothes he'd worn the day before, she saw, though he had thrown on a leather bomber jacket as protection against the rain. He had evidently been walking in it, because his black hair was plastered down, and rivulets of moisture ran down his face.

"Don't cry," he said in a raw, unnatural tone.

She felt embarrassed that he had caught her weeping. She had always taken pains to hide any bouts of emotion from him, knowing that they would make him uncomfortable. Nor did she look her best, with her eyes swollen and wet, her hair still tousled from a restless night, and swaddled from neck to foot in a thick robe. A mistress should always be well-groomed, she thought wryly, and almost burst into tears again.

Without shifting his gaze from her, he took off his jacket and hung it over the back of a chair. "I didn't know if you had stayed," he said, the strain still evident in his voice. "I hoped you had, but—" Then, abruptly, he moved with that shocking speed of his, scooping her up in his arms and carrying her quickly into the bedroom.

After a small startled cry, Anna clung to his shoulders. He had moved like that the first time, as if all his passion had been swelling behind the dam of his control and the dam had finally given way. He had swept her off her feet and down to the floor in the office almost in the same motion, then had come down on top of her before her surprise could give way to gladness. She had reached for him with desire that rose quickly to match his, and it had been hours before he had released her.

She could feel the same sort of fierceness in his grip now as he placed her on the bed and bent over her, loosening the robe and spreading it wide. Beneath it she wore a thin silk nightgown, but evidently even that was too much. Silently she stared up at his intent face as he lifted her free of the robe, then tugged the nightgown over her head. Her breath quickened as she lay naked before him, and she felt her breasts tighten under his gaze, as hot as any touch. A warm, heavy pooling of sensation began low in her body.

He opened her thighs and knelt between them, visually feasting on her body as he fumbled with his belt and zipper, lowering his pants enough to free himself. Then his green gaze flashed upward to meet the drowning velvet brown of hers. ''If you don't want this, say so now.''

She could no more have denied him, and herself, than she could willingly have stopped breathing. She lifted her slender arms in invitation, and he leaned forward in acceptance, sheathing himself in both her body and her embrace with one movement. He groaned aloud, not just at the incredible pleasure, but at the cessation of pain. For now, with her slender body held securely beneath him, and himself held just as securely within her, there was no distance between them.

Anna twisted under the buffeting of a savagely intense sensual pleasure. The shock of his cold, damp clothing on her warm bare body made her feel more naked than she ever had before. The single point of contact of bare flesh, between her legs, made her feel more sexual, made her painfully aware of his masculinity as he moved over and inside her. It was too overwhelming to sustain, and she arched into climax too soon, far too soon, because she wanted it to last forever.

He stilled, holding himself deep inside her for her pleasure, holding her face and planting lingering kisses over it. "Don't cry," he murmured, and until then she hadn't known that there were tears seeping out of her eyes. "Don't cry. It doesn't have to end now."

She had cried it aloud, she realized, had voiced her despair at the swift peaking.

He brought all the skill and knowledge of two years of intimacy into their lovemaking, finding the rhythm that was fast enough to bring her to desire again, but slow enough to keep them from reaching satisfaction. There was a different satisfaction in the lingering strokes, in the continued linking of their bodies. Neither of them wanted it to end, because as long as they were together like this they wouldn't have to face the specter of separation. Withdrawal, right now, would mean more than the end of their lovemaking; it would be a parting that neither could bear.

His clothing became not a sensual pleasure, but an intolerable barrier. She tore at the buttons on his shirt, wanting the wet cloth out of the way, needing the pressure of his skin on hers. He rose enough to shrug his wide shoulders out of the garment and toss it aside; then he lowered his chest, and she whimpered in delight at the rasp of his hair on her sensitive nipples.

He cupped her breasts in both hands and pushed them together, bending his head to brush light kisses over the tightly drawn nipples. They were a bit darker, he noticed, and the pale globes were a little swollen, signs of his baby growing within her flat belly. He shuddered with unexpected excitement at the thought, at the knowledge that the same act he was performing now had resulted in that small life.

He had to grit his teeth in an effort to keep from climaxing right then. His baby! It seemed that knowledge wasn't quite the same thing as realization, and he had just been hit by the full realization that the baby was his, part of him, sharing his genes. Blood of his blood, bone of his bone, mingled inseparably with Anna, a living part of both of them. He felt a wave of physical possession like he'd never known before, never even dreamed existed. His baby!

And his woman. Honey-sweet Anna, smooth warm skin and calm, gentle dark eyes.

The crest had been put off too long to be denied any longer. It swept over them, first engulfing her, then him, her inner trembling too much for him to bear. They heaved together in a paroxysm of pleasure, crying out, dying the death of self and surfacing into the quiet aftermath.

They lay entwined, neither of them willing to be the first to move and break the bond of flesh. Anna slid her fingers into his damp hair, loving the feel of his skull beneath her fingers. "Why did you come back?" she whispered. "It was hard enough watching you leave the first time. Did you have to put me through it again?"

She felt him tense against her. Before, she would never have let him know her feelings; she would have smiled and retreated into her role of the perfect mistress, never making demands. But she had left that shield behind, baring herself with her declaration of love, and there was no going back. She wasn't going to deny that love again.

He rolled to his side, taking her with him, wrap-

ping his arm around her hip to keep her in place.
She shifted automatically, lifting her leg higher
around his waist for greater comfort. He moved
closer to deepen his tenuous penetration, and they
both breathed infinitesimal sighs of relief.

"Do you have to go?" he finally asked. "Why
can't you just stay?"

She rubbed her face against his shoulder, her dark
eyes sad. "Not without you. I couldn't bear it."

She felt the effort it took him to say, "What
if...what if I stay, too? What if we just go on as
before?"

She lifted her head to look at him, studying his
beloved features in the rain-dimmed light. She
wasn't unaware of what it had taken for him to make
such an offer; he had always been so diligent in
shunning even the appearance of caring, yet now he
was actually reaching out to her, asking for the ties
of emotion. He needed to be loved more than any
man she had ever seen, but she didn't know if he
could tolerate it. Love brought responsibilities, obligations. It was never free, but required a high payment in the form of compromise.

"Can you?" she asked, the sadness as evident in
her tone as in her eyes. "I don't doubt that you
would try, but could you stay? There's no going
back. Things have changed, and they'll never be the
same again."

"I know," he said, and the stark look in his eyes

hurt her, because she could see that he didn't really believe he could succeed.

She had never before pried into his past, just as she had never before told him that she loved him, but their insular little world had unraveled with frightening speed and turned things upside down. Sometimes, to make a gain, you had to take a risk.

''Why did you ask me if I would throw our baby away?''

The question hung in the air between them like a sword. She felt him flinch, saw his pupils contract with shock. He would have pulled away from her then, but she tightened her leg around him and gripped his shoulder with her hand; he stopped, though he could easily have moved had he wanted to pit his strength against hers. He stayed only because he couldn't bring himself to give up her touch. She bound him with her tenderness when strength couldn't have held him.

He closed his eyes in an instinctive effort to shut out the memory, but it didn't go away, couldn't go away with Anna's question unanswered. He had never talked about it before, never wanted to talk about it. It was a wound too deep and too raw to be eased by ''talking it out.'' He had lived with the knowledge his entire life, and he had done what he'd had to do to survive. He had closed that part of his life away. It was like tearing his guts out now to answer, but Anna deserved at least the truth.

"My mother threw me away," he finally said in a guttural tone; then his throat shut down and he couldn't say anything else. He shook his head helplessly, but his eyes were still closed, and he didn't see the look of utter horror, swiftly followed by soul-shattering compassion, on Anna's face. She watched him through a blur of tears, but she didn't dare break down and begin crying, or do anything else that would interrupt him. Instead she gently stroked his chest, offering tactile comfort rather than verbal; she sensed that words weren't adequate to the task, and in any case, if she tried to speak, she would lose her battle with her tears.

But as the silence stretched into minutes, she realized that he wasn't going to continue, perhaps couldn't continue without prompting. She swallowed and tried to regain her composure; it was an effort, but finally she was able to speak in a voice that, if not quite normal, was still soft and full of the love she felt.

"How did she throw you away? Were you abandoned, adopted...what?"

"Neither." He did twist away from her then, to lie on his back with his arm thrown up to cover his eyes. She mourned his loss, but gave him the distance he needed. Some things had to be faced alone, and perhaps this was one of them. "She threw me into the garbage when I was born. She didn't put me on the church steps or leave me at an orphanage so

I could make up little stories about how much my mother had really loved me, but she had been really sick or something and had had to give me away so I'd be taken care of. All the other kids could make up stories like that, and believe them, but my mother made damn sure I was never that stupid. She dumped me into a trash can when I was a few hours old. There's not much way you can mistake an action like that for motherly love.''

Anna curled into a little ball on her side, her fist shoved into her mouth to stifle the sobs that kept welling up, her streaming eyes fastened on his face. He was talking now, and though she had wanted to know, now she had to fight the urge to clap her hand over his mouth. No one should ever have to grow up knowing about such ugliness.

''She wasn't just trying to get rid of me,'' he continued in an emotionless voice. ''She tried to kill me. It was winter when she threw me away, and she didn't bother to wrap me in anything. I don't know exactly when my birthday is, either January third or fourth, because I was found at three-thirty in the morning, and I could have been born either late on the third or early on the fourth. I almost died of exposure anyway, and I spent over a year in the charity hospital with one problem after another. By the time I was placed in an orphanage, I was a toddler who had seen so many strangers come and go that I wouldn't have anything to do with people. I guess that's why I wasn't adopted. People want babies, infants still wrapped up in blankets, not a thin, sickly toddler who screams if they reach for him.''

He swallowed and took his arm down from his eyes, which stared unseeingly upward. ''I have no idea who or what my parents are. No trace of my mother was ever found. I was named after the city and county where I was found. Saxon City, Malone county. Hell of a tradition to carry on.

''After a few years I was placed in a series of foster homes, most of them not very good. I was kicked around like a stray puppy. Social services got so desperate to place me that they left me with this one family even though I was always covered with a variety of bruises whenever the caseworker came around. It wasn't until the guy kicked in a couple of my ribs that they jerked me out of there. I was ten, I guess. They finally found a fairly good foster home for me, a couple whose own son had died. I don't know, maybe they thought I'd be able to take their son's place, but it didn't work, for them or me. They were nice, but it was in their eyes every time they looked at me that I wasn't Kenny. It was a place to live, and that was all I wanted. I made it through school, walked out and never looked back.''

Chapter 5

What he had told her explained so much about the man Saxon had become and why it was so hard for him to accept any semblance of love. If the first eighteen years of his life had taught him anything, it was that he couldn't depend on what others called love but which he'd never known himself. As he had said, there was no fooling himself with pretty stories that his mother had loved him when her actions had made it plain that she not only hadn't cared, but she had deliberately left him to die. Nor had he received any real affection from the overworked staff of the charity hospital. Children learn early; by the time he had been placed in an orphanage, he had already known that he couldn't trust anyone to take care of him, so he had retreated into himself as the only surety in his life. He had depended on no one except himself for anything.

It was a lesson that had been reinforced by his childhood, shunted from one foster home to another, meeting with abuse in some of them and fitting in at none of them. Where did an outcast learn of love? The simple, heartbreaking answer was that he didn't. He had had to rise above more than simple poverty. He had needed to surmount a total lack of the most simple human caring. When she thought of what he had accomplished with his life, she was awed by his immense willpower. How hard had he had to work to put himself through college, to earn not only an engineering degree but to finish so high in his class that he'd had his choice of jobs, and from there go on to form his own company?

After the gut-wrenching tale of his childhood, they had both been emotionally incapable of probing any deeper. By mutual consent they had gotten up and gone through the motions of a normal day, though it was anything but. The past twenty-four hours had taken a toll on both of them, and they had retreated into long period of silence, punctuated only by commonplace matters such as what they would have for lunch.

He was there. He showed no indication of leaving. She took that as a sign of hope and did no packing herself. Right now, all she asked for was his presence.

It was late afternoon on that rain-drenched day when he said flatly, "You never really answered my question this morning. Can we go on as we did before?"

She glanced at him and saw that though stress was still visible on his face, he seemed to have come to terms with it. She wasn't too certain of her own reaction, but she would rather bear the strain herself than take the risk of putting him off now at a time when that might be enough to drive him away again.

She sat down across from him, trying to marshal her thoughts. Finally she said, "For myself, I would like nothing better. It nearly killed me to lose you, and I'm not too certain I can go through that again. But I can't just think of myself. We can't just think of our own arrangement. What about the baby? At first, nothing will matter to it but Mommy and Daddy, but assuming that we stay together for years, what happens when it starts school and finds out that other mommies and daddies are married? This is Denver, not Hollywood. And though no one frowns on a couple living together, the circumstances change when a baby is involved."

He looked down at his hands and said very carefully, "How is it different if you move out? Its parents still won't be married, but you'll be trying to raise it alone. Is that supposed to be better for it? I don't know what kind of a father I'd make, but I think I'd be better than nothing."

Her lips trembled, and she fiercely bit down on them. Dear God, was she making him *beg* to be included in his child's life? She had never intended that, especially in light of what he'd told her that morning. "I think you'd be a wonderful father," she said. "I've never intended to prevent you from seeing your child. It's our living arrangement I'm not sure of."

"I am. I want you, and you...you want me." He still couldn't say that she loved him. "We don't have to do anything right now. Like you said, it'll be years before it's old enough to compare us with other parents. You still have a pregnancy to get through, and God knows I won't sleep at night if I don't know you're okay. At least stay until the baby's born. I can take care of you, go with you to those childbirth classes, be with you during delivery." Though his tone was confident, his eyes were pleading, and that was what broke down her resolve. If she pushed him away now, he might never recover.

"There's nothing I'd like better," she said huskily, and saw the lightning flash of relief in his eyes before he masked it.

"I'll move my clothes in tomorrow."

She could only blink at him in surprise. She had expected him to return to the status quo, sleeping almost every night with her but returning to his own apartment every morning to change clothes before going to work. The thought of his clothes hanging next to hers in the spacious closet made her feel both excited and a little alarmed, which was ridiculous, because she had never wanted anything as much as she had wanted a full, complete life with him. But things were changing so swiftly, and her life was already in upheaval with her pregnancy. Control of her body was slipping further from her grasp with every passing day, as the baby grew and demanded more of her. Though her early symptoms had been scant, she could now see definite changes.

She had been fighting one of those changes all day, and it was all suddenly too much. Tears welled in her eyes as she looked at him, and began to roll down her face. Instantly he was beside her, putting his arms around her and tucking her head against his shoulder. "What's wrong?" he demanded, sounding almost frantic. "Don't you want me to move in? I thought I could take care of you better."

"It isn't that," she sobbed. "Yes, it is. I'm happy, damn it! I've always wanted you to move in with me, or ask me to move in with you. But you didn't do it for my sake, you did it because of the baby!"

Saxon tilted her face up and used his thumbs to wipe away her tears. His black brows were drawn together in a scowl. "Of course I'm doing it for you," he said impatiently. "I don't know the baby. Hell, I can't even see much evidence of it yet! I don't want you to be alone any more than necessary." The scowl intensified. "Have you been to a doctor?"

She sniffed and wiped her eyes. "Yes, I didn't realize I was pregnant until I saw the doctor. I went because my last period was just spotting, and the one before that was really light. I've hardly had any symptoms at all."

"Is that normal?"

"As normal as anything else is. The doctor told me everything looked fine, that some women spotted for the first few months and some didn't, that some women had morning sickness and some didn't. All I've really noticed is that I get tired and sleepy and that I want to cry a lot."

He looked relieved. "You mean you're crying because of the baby?"

"No, I'm crying because of you!"

"Well, don't." He pulled her close and pressed a kiss to her forehead. "I don't like it when you cry."

There was no way he could know how it felt to be coddled and cuddled like that, how she had yearned for it. Love had been in short supply in her life, too, though she had never known the direct brutality Saxon had suffered. Her most cherished dreams had always been about having a home with him, just an ordinary home, with the sweet security of routine and the sure knowledge that he was coming home to her every day. In her dreams he had always held her and shown her how much he cared, while in reality he had offered her physical intimacy and an emotional desert. This sudden turnaround was so much like a dream come true that she was afraid to believe in it. Even so, she wasn't going to do anything to end it prematurely. For as long as he stayed, she intended to savor every moment.

True to his word, he moved in the next day. He didn't say anything to her about it, but a couple of phone calls, one from someone interested in leasing his other apartment and another from a utility company double-checking the address for the forwarding of his bill, made it obvious that he was completely giving up his official residence. That, more than anything, told her how serious he was about preserving their relationship.

She watched him closely for signs of edginess, because their relationship had changed in far more fundamental ways than simply that he no longer had dual residences. She had told him that she loved him, words that couldn't be erased or forgotten; by his reaction to their short estrangement, he had revealed a lot more about how much he cared than he ever had before. Though they had been physically inti-mate for two years, this sort of closeness was totally new to him, and she could tell that sometimes he didn't know how to act. It was almost as if he were in a foreign country where he didn't speak the language, cautiously groping his way about, unable to read the road signs.

He was increasingly curious about the baby and insisted on going with her to her next doctor's appointment, which was scheduled for only a few days after he'd moved in. When he discovered that an ultrasound photo later in her pregnancy might tell them the baby's sex, he immediately wanted to know when they would be able to do it, and how often the doctors were mistaken. Since it was the first interest he had shown in the baby's sex, she wondered if he was imagining having a son. He hadn't indicated a preference either way, and she had no decided preference, either, so they had somehow always referred to the baby as "it" rather than "he" or "she."

How would a son affect him? He would see more of himself in a boy, and it would be, in a way, a chance for him to correct the horror of his own childhood by making certain his own son never knew anything but love. In her mind's eye she saw him patiently showing a grubby, determined little boy how to swing a bat or field a pop fly. There would probably be years of attending a variety of ball games and watching with fierce pride every move the boy made. Every hit would be the best hit ever made, every catch the most stupendous, because the boy making it would be *theirs*.

Despite the dampening whispers of her common sense, she couldn't stop dreaming of a future with

Saxon. One miracle had already happened: he hadn't disappeared when he'd learned of her pregnancy. She would continue hoping for another miracle.

Lying in bed that night, she nestled her head on his chest and listened to the strong, steady boom-*boom* of his heart. Her hand strayed down to her abdomen; the baby was hearing her own heart steadily pumping in the same rhythm, soothing and reassuring it just as Saxon's heartbeat soothed her. It was a wonderfully satisfying sound.

"You seemed really interested in the ultrasound," she said sleepily.

"Mmm," he grunted by way of a reply. Her head moved as she glanced up at him, though all she could see was his chin, and that not very well in the darkened room.

"Are you anxious to know what the baby is?"

He shifted restlessly. "I'd like to know, yeah. What about you? Do you have your heart set on a little girl?"

"Not really," she said, and yawned. "I just want a healthy baby, boy or girl, though it would be convenient to know ahead of time so we can have a name picked out and a nursery decorated without having to use greens or yellows."

"A nursery," he said in a faintly surprised tone. "I hadn't thought that far ahead. All I can picture is this little person about the size of a skinned rabbit, all wrapped up in a blanket. It'll stay where we put it and won't take up much space. Why does something that small need an entire room for itself?"

She grinned in the darkness. "Because otherwise the entire apartment would be cluttered with all the paraphernalia necessary for taking care of a baby. And where did you think it would sleep?"

The question startled him; then he laughed, the rare sound booming under her ear. "With us, I guess. On whichever arm you weren't using. I would say it could sleep on my chest, but I understand they aren't housebroken."

She snickered, and he laughed again. More content than she could ever remember being in her life, she snuggled even closer. "I imagine you want a boy. All day today I kept having daydreams about you teaching him how to play baseball."

Saxon stiffened, his body going rigid all along her side. "Not especially," he finally said in a strained voice. "I'd really rather have a girl."

Surprise kept her silent, particularly because she didn't know what about the question had upset him. He didn't say anything for a while, and she began to drift off to sleep, but all drowsiness left her when he said quietly, "Maybe if it's a girl you'll love it more."

Chapter 6

"What about your family?" he asked carefully the next morning, as if wary of treading on unstable ground. In his experience, family was something other people had and, from what he'd seen at his foster homes, it wasn't desirable. But he wanted to know more about Anna, wanted to find out all he could about her in case some day he came home to find her gone. "Have you told them that you're having a baby, or anything about me?"

"I don't have any family," she replied as she poured skim milk over her cereal. Her manner was casual, but his interest sharpened immediately.

"No family? Were you an orphan?" He had seen a lot of orphans, sad and terrified children who had lost their entire world and didn't know what to do. Maybe his situation, dire as it had been, was preferable to theirs. At least he hadn't lost someone he loved. His mother hadn't died; she had simply dumped him in the trash. Probably both she and his father were still alive somewhere, though he sincerely doubted they were together. He was more than likely the result of a short affair, at best, and more probably a one-night stand.

"Yes, but I was never in an orphanage. My mother died when I was nine, and my dad said he couldn't take proper care of me, so he sent me to live with his half sister. To tell the truth, he simply didn't want the responsibility. From what my aunt said, he'd always been irresponsible, never holding down a job for long, spending his money in bars and chasing after other women. He died in a car accident when I was fourteen."

"What about your aunt?" he asked, remembering the "None" she had listed beside the next-of-kin information. "Do you still see her?"

"No. She died about a year before I went to work for you, but I doubt I'd ever have seen her again anyway. It wasn't a fond relationship. She and Uncle Sid had seven kids of their own. I was just an unwelcome extra mouth to feed, especially since she had never gotten along with Dad anyway. Aunt Cora looked as if she had posed for the painting 'American Gothic,' all prune-faced and disapproving, soured on life. There was never enough money to go around, and it was only natural that she provided for her own children first.''

Anger swelled in him as he pictured her, a thin, lost little girl with big honey eyes, standing off to the side as he had often stood, never quite a part of a family unit. That had been the better part of his childhood, but it infuriated him that Anna had been subjected to such treatment. ''What about your cousins? Don't you ever see them, or hear from them?''

''No, we were never close. We got along as well as most children who have been thrown together, but we never had much in common. They've all moved off the farm, anyway, and I don't know where they are. I suppose I could trace them if I wanted, but there doesn't seem any point in it.''

Somehow he had never pictured Anna as being alone in the world, or of having a background in common with him. It shook him to realize that, in a different way, she had been just as deprived of nurturing as he had. She had never suffered the physical abuse, and perhaps that was why she was still able to reach out, to express her love. Even before he could remember, he had learned not to expect, or hope, or offer anything of himself, because that would leave him open to hurt. He was glad Anna hadn't known a life like that.

Even so, it couldn't have been easy for her to tell him that she loved him. Had she been braced for rejection? That was what he'd done, panicked and thrown her love back in her face. He had been terrified the next morning that she wouldn't be able to stand the sight of him after the way he'd run out on her. But she had taken him back, and thank God, she not only loved him, but she seemed to love his baby. Sometimes it seemed impossible.

"What about the foster family you stayed with?" she asked. "Do you ever call them, or visit?"

"No. I haven't seen them since the day after my high-school graduation, when I packed and left, but they didn't expect me to keep in touch. I told them goodbye and thanked them, and I guess that was good enough."

"What were their names?"

"Emmeline and Harold Bradley. They were good people. They tried, especially Harold, but there was no way they could turn me into their son. It was always there, in their eyes. I wasn't Kenny. Emmeline always seemed to resent it that her son had died but I was still alive. Neither of them ever touched me if they could prevent it. They took care of me, provided me with a place to stay, clothes, food, but there wasn't any affection there. They were relieved when I left."

"Aren't you curious if they're still alive, or if they've moved?"

"There's no point in it. There's nothing for me there, and they wouldn't be overjoyed to see me."

"Where did they live?"

"About eighty miles from here, in Fort Morgan."

"But that's so close! My cousins lived in Maryland, so it's at least reasonable that we haven't kept in touch."

He shrugged. "I left the state when I went to college, so it wasn't exactly convenient for me to visit. I worked two jobs to pay my tuition, and that didn't leave a lot of free time."

"But you came back to Colorado and settled in Denver."

"There's more demand for engineers in a large city."

"There are a lot of cities in this country. The point is, you're so close, but you never called them to tell them how college turned out, or that you were back in the state."

Temper edged into his voice. "No, I didn't, and I don't intend to. For God's sake, Anna, it's been fifteen years since I got out of college. They sure as hell haven't kept a candle in the window for me all this time. They knew I wouldn't be back."

She dropped the subject, but she didn't forget it. Harold and Emmeline Bradley. She committed their names to memory. Despite what Saxon thought, they had spent years raising him and were likely to be more than a little interested in what had become of him.

He left for work in silence, and returned that af-

ternoon in the same brooding mood. She left him
alone, but his silence made her quietly panic. Had
her questions bothered him so much that he was considering terminating their arrangement? But he had
started it by asking about her family, so he had only
himself to blame. In the few days since she had told
him of the baby she had become accustomed to
thinking of him as more approachable, more *hers,*
but suddenly she was very much aware of the wall
that still surrounded him. She had knocked a few
chinks out of it, but it was far from demolished.

Saxon hadn't liked all that talk about his foster
family, but it had started him thinking. Unless he and
Anna took steps to prevent it, this baby wouldn't
have much of a family, either. He couldn't picture
them having other children under their present circumstances, and to his surprise, he liked the idea of
more children. He wanted them to be a family, not
just live-in lovers who happened to have a baby.

He hadn't had pretty fantasies about his mother,
but he had often wondered, with a child's bewildered
pain, what it would be like to have a real family, to
belong somewhere and have someone who loved
him. It was a fantasy that hadn't lasted long under
the merciless weight of reality, but he still remembered how he had imagined it, the feeling of security
that was at the center of it and held everything together. He hadn't been able to picture parents, beyond tall shadowy figures that stood between him

and danger. He never wanted his baby to have those kinds of fantasies; he wanted it to have the reality of a stable home.

Less than a week ago, just the idea of what he was now considering would have been enough to make him break out in a panicky sweat, but he had since learned that there were worse things. Losing Anna was worse. He hoped he never in his life had to live through another day and night like he'd endured then, because he didn't think his sanity could take it. In comparison, what he was thinking now was a snap.

Thinking it was one thing, actually putting it into words was another. He watched Anna with troubled eyes, though he knew it was useless trying to predict her answer. Behind her customary serenity she was deep and complicated, seeing more than he wanted her to see, understanding more than was comfortable. With so much of her thought processes hidden from him, he wasn't at all certain how she would react, or why. If she loved him there should be no hesitation, but that wasn't necessarily the case. She was capable of sacrificing her own happiness—assuming he could make her happy—for what she thought best for the baby.

It was strange what an impact the baby had had on their lives months prior to its birth, but he didn't regret the changes. It was frightening; he had the sense of living on the edge, where any false move

could send him over, but at the same time the increased openness and intimacy he shared with Anna
were, without a doubt, worth every minute of worry.
He didn't think he could go back to the previous
loneliness he had taken for granted, even embraced.

Still, it was a decision that racked him with
nerves. In the end, he couldn't say the words that
would be an offer of himself, a statement of his feelings and vulnerability; instead he threw them out
couched as a suggestion. "I think we should get
married."

There was nothing he could have said that would
have astounded her more. Her legs went weak, and
she sat down heavily. "Marriage!" she said with a
mixture of disbelief and total surprise.

He wasn't pleased that the solution hadn't occurred to her. "Yes, marriage. It makes sense. We're
already living together, and we're having a baby.
Marriage seems the logical next step."

Anna shook her head, not in refusal but in a futile
effort to clear her head. Somehow she had never expected to receive a marriage proposal couched as
"the logical next step." She hadn't expected a marriage proposal, period, though she had wanted one
very badly. But she had wanted him to propose for
different reasons, because he loved her and couldn't
live without her. She suspected that was the case,
but she would never know for sure if he never told
her.

It wasn't an easy decision, and she didn't rush into speech. His face was impassive as he waited for her answer, his green eyes darkened and watchful. Her answer meant a lot to him, she realized. He wanted her to say yes. She wanted to say yes. The question was whether she was willing to take the chance that he did love her and marry him on blind faith. A cautious woman wouldn't want to make a hasty decision that would affect not only the two of them, but their child as well. A broken marriage inevitably left its scars on all concerned.

She had taken a leap of blind faith in quitting her job to become his mistress, and she didn't regret it. The two years of loving him had been the best of her life, and she could never wish them undone. Pregnancy altered everything, she thought with a faint curving of her lips. She couldn't just think of herself now; she had to think of the baby. What was logical wasn't necessarily the best choice, even though her heart clamored for a quick acceptance.

She looked at him, her dark eyes grave. "I love you, you know," she said.

Once such a statement would have made his face go blank in a refusal to hear. Now he steadily returned her gaze. "I know." The knowledge didn't make him panic; instead he treasured it, savored it, as the most precious gift of his life.

"I want to say yes, more than anything I've ever wanted, but I'm afraid to. I know it was your idea for us to stay together, and you've been wonderful, but I'm not certain that you'll still feel the same after the baby's born. As the old saying goes, then it becomes a whole new ball game. I don't want you to feel trapped or unhappy.''

He shook his head as if to forestall the answer he sensed was coming. ''There's no way to predict the future. I know why you worry about the way I'll react, and to tell you the truth, I'm a little scared myself, but I'm excited, too. I want this baby. I want you. Let's get married and make it official.'' He smiled wryly. ''The baby could have Malone for a last name. The second generation of a brand-new family.''

Anna took a deep breath and denied herself what she had wanted more than anything else. ''I can't give you an answer now,'' she whispered, and saw his face tighten. ''It just doesn't feel right. I want to say yes, Saxon, I want that more than anything, but I'm not certain it would be the right thing to do.''

''It is,'' he said roughly.

''Then if it is, it will still be the right thing a month from now, or two months from now. Too much has happened too fast—the baby…you. I don't want to make the wrong decision, and I think I'm operating more on my emotions now than on brainpower.''

The force of his willpower shone out of his eyes, intensely green and focused. ''I can't make you say yes,'' he said in a slow, deep voice. "But I can keep asking. I can make love to you and take care of you until you won't be able to imagine life without me.''

Her lips trembled. "I can't imagine that now.''

"I don't give up, Anna. When I go after something, I don't stop until I've gotten it. I want you, and I'm going to have you.''

She knew exactly what he meant. When he decided something, he focused on it with a fierce tunnel vision that didn't let him rest until he had achieved his objective. It was a little daunting to think of herself as the object of that kind of determination.

He smiled then, a smile that was more than a little predatory. "You can take that to the bank, baby.''

Chapter 7

Marriage. The thought of it hovered in her consciousness during the day and crept into her dreams at night. Several times every day she started to throw caution to the winds and tell him yes, but there was a part of her that simply wasn't ready to take such an immense step. She had been willing before to settle for being his mistress, but now she was unable to settle for being his wife; she wanted him to love her, too, and admit it to both her and himself. She might be certain that he did love her, but until he could come to terms with his feelings, she couldn't rely on that. He could say "I want you," but not "I love you."

She couldn't blame him for having difficulty with

the emotion. Sometimes when she was alone she cried for him, at first a discarded infant, then a lonely, frightened toddler, and finally an abused youngster with no one he could turn to for help. No one could have endured such a childhood without emotional scarring, without losing the ability both to give and accept love. When she looked at it clearly, she saw that he had reached out to her far more than could reasonably be expected.

She didn't really expect more, but she wanted it.

She couldn't get the Bradleys out of her mind. From what he had said, he had spent six years with them, from the time he was twelve until he was eighteen. Six years was a long time for them to keep him and not feel something for him. Was it possible that they had offered him more than duty, but at the time he hadn't been able to see it for what it was? And how had they felt at not hearing from him ever again?

Surely they had worried, if they had any hint of human warmth about them. They had raised him from a boy to a young man, given him the only stable home life he had ever known until Anna had become his mistress and made a sanctuary for him in the apartment. It was always possible that it had been exactly as he remembered it, that losing their son had prevented them from feeling anything for him beyond duty and a sense of pity. Pity! He would have hated that. If he had sensed that they pitied him, no wonder he hadn't gone back.

But though she fretted about it for several days, she knew that she wasn't accomplishing anything with her worrying. If she wanted to know for certain, she would have to drive to Fort Morgan and try to find the Bradleys. It might be a useless trip, since nineteen years had passed; they could have moved, or even died.

Once she made the decision to go, she felt better, even though she knew Saxon would be adamantly against the idea. However, she didn't intend to let his opposition stop her.

That didn't mean she intended to be sneaky about it. After dinner that night she said, "I'm going to Fort Morgan tomorrow."

He tensed, and his eyes narrowed. "Why?"

"To try to find the Bradleys."

He folded the newspaper away with an angry snap. "There's no point in it. I told you how it was. Why are you worried about it, anyway? That was nineteen years ago. It's nothing to do with us now. You didn't even know me then."

"Curiosity, partly," she answered with blunt honesty. "And what if you're wrong about the way they felt? You were young. You could have misread them. And if you were wrong, then they've spent nineteen years feeling as if they lost two sons instead of just one."

"No," he said, and from the command in his voice she knew he wasn't refuting her suggestion but issuing an order.

She lifted her brows at him, mild surprise in her eyes. "I wasn't asking permission. I was letting you know where I'd be so you wouldn't worry if you called and I wasn't here."

"I said no."

"You certainly did," she agreed. "But I'm not your mistress anymore—"

"It sure as hell felt like you were last night," he interrupted, his eyes turning greener as anger intensified the color.

She didn't intend to argue with him. Instead she smiled, and her soft face glowed as she sent him a warm look. "That was making love." And it had been wonderful. Sex between them had always been hot and urgent, but since he had moved in with her it had taken on an added dimension, a shattering tenderness that hadn't been there before. Their lovemaking was more prolonged; it was as if, before, he had always been aware that he was going to have to get up and leave, and the knowledge had driven him. Now he was relaxed and leisurely in a way he hadn't been before, with increased pleasure as a result.

There was a flicker of tension across his face at the word "love," but it was quickly gone, with no lingering echoes.

"I'm not your mistress," she repeated. "That arrangement is over with. I'm the woman who loves you, who lives with you, who's having your baby.''

He looked around at the apartment. ''You may not think you're my mistress anymore,'' he said with soft anger, ''but things look pretty much the same to me.''

''Because you support me? That's your choice, not mine. I'll find a job, if it will make you feel better. I've never enjoyed being a kept woman, anyway.''

''No!'' He didn't like that idea at all. It had always been in the back of his mind that, if he kept her totally dependent on him, she would be less likely to leave. At the same time he had invested in stocks in her name to make certain she would be financially secure. The paradox had always made him uneasy, but he wanted her to be taken care of in case something happened to him. After all, he traveled a lot and spent a lot of time on construction sites, not the safest of places. He had also made a will a year ago, leaving everything to her. He'd never told her.

''I don't want you driving that far by yourself,'' he finally said, but he was grasping at straws, and he knew it.

''It's less than a two-hour drive, the weather forecast is for clear and sunny conditions tomorrow. But if you want to go with me, I can wait until the weekend,'' she offered.

His expression closed up at the idea. He had never been back, never wanted to go back. The Bradleys hadn't mistreated him; they had been the best of all the foster homes he'd been in. But that part of his life was over. He had shut the door on it when he'd left, and he'd spent the following years working like a slave to make himself into someone who would never again be helpless.

"They may have moved," she said, offering comfort. "I just want to know."

He made a weary gesture. "Then pick up the telephone and call information. Talk to them, if they're still there. But don't involve me in it. I don't want to talk to them. I don't want to see them. I don't want anything to do with this."

She wasn't surprised at his total rejection of the past; it was hardly the type of memory he would embrace. And she hadn't expected him to go with her.

"I don't want to talk to them over the telephone," she said. "I want to drive up there, see the house. I may not approach them at all. It depends on what I find when I get there."

She held her breath, because there was one appeal he could make that she wouldn't be able to deny. If he said, "Please don't go, for my sake," then she wouldn't go. If he actually asked for anything for himself, there was no way she could turn him down. He had been rejected so much in his life that she wouldn't add to it. But because of those prior rejections, she knew he wouldn't ask in those terms. He would never put things in the context of being a personal consideration for him. He would order, he would make objections, but he wouldn't simply ask and say, "Please don't."

He refused to talk about it anymore and got up restlessly to stand at the terrace doors and look out. Anna calmly returned to her own section of the paper, but her heart was beating fast as she realized this was the first normal domestic quarrel they had ever had. To her delight, they had disagreed, and nothing major had happened. He hadn't left, nor did he seem to expect her to leave. It was wonderful. He was already able to trust her enough that he wasn't afraid a disagreement could end their relationship.

She had worried that he would overreact to arguments, since they were part and parcel of every relationship. Normal couples had disagreements; probably even saints had disagreements. Two years ago, Saxon wouldn't have been able to tolerate such a personal discussion.

He was really trying, even though it was extraordinarily difficult for him to open up. Circumstances had forced him into revealing his past, but he hadn't tried to reestablish those protective mental walls of his. He seemed to accept that once the emotional boundaries had been crossed, he couldn't make them inviolate again.

She didn't know what she could accomplish by finding the Bradleys again. Perhaps nothing. She just wanted to see them, to get a feel for herself of what that portion of Saxon's formative years had been like. If they seemed interested, she wanted to reassure them that their foster son was alive and well, that he was successful and would soon be a father himself.

With his back still to her, Saxon asked, "Are you afraid to marry me because of my past? Is that why you want to find the Bradleys, so you can ask them questions about me?"

"No!" she said, horrified. "I'm not *afraid* to marry you."

"My parents could be anything—murderers, drug users. My mother may be a prostitute. The odds are pretty good she was. There may be a history of mental illness in my background. *I'd* be afraid to marry me. But the Bradleys won't be able to tell you anything, because no one knows who my parents were."

"I'm not concerned with your parents," she said levelly. "I know you. You're rock solid. You're honest, kind, hardworking and sexy."

"So why won't you marry me, if I'm such a good catch?"

Good question, she thought. Maybe she was being foolish in waiting. "I don't want to rush into something that might not be right for either of us."

"I don't want my baby to be born illegitimate."

"Oh, Saxon." She gave a sad laugh. "I promise you I'll make a decision long before the baby is born."

"But you can't promise me you'll say yes."

"No more than you can promise me our marriage would work."

He gave her a brief, angry look over his shoulder. "You said you love me."

"And I do. But can you say that *you* love *me?*" she asked.

He didn't answer. Anna watched him, her eyes sad and tender. Her question could be taken in two ways. He did love her, she thought, but was incapable of actually *saying* it. Maybe he felt that as long as he didn't say the words aloud, he hadn't made the emotional commitment.

Finally he said, "Is that what it'll take for you to marry me?"

"No. It isn't a test that you have to pass."

"Isn't it?"

"No," she insisted.

"You say you won't marry me because you don't know if I can handle it, but I'm willing to try. You're the one who's resisting making a commitment."

She stared at him in frustration. He was too good at arguing, agilely taking her previous arguments and using them against her. She was glad that he felt sure enough of her to do it, but she could see what she'd be up against in the future if they did get married.

It would take a lot of determination to win an argument against him.

She pointed her finger at him, even though his back was still turned and he couldn't see her. "I'm not resisting making a commitment, I'm resisting making it *now*. I think I have a right to be a little cautious."

"Not if you trust me."

That turned back was making her suspicious. She gave him a considering look, then suddenly realized he had turned his back so she wouldn't be able to read his expression. Her eyes narrowed as she realized what he was doing. He wasn't as upset or even as indignant as he sounded; he was simply using the tactic as a means of maneuvering her into agreeing to marry him. It was all part and parcel of his determination to have his way.

She got up and went over to him, wrapping her arms around his lean waist and leaning her head against his back. "It won't work," she said softly. "I'm on to you."

To her surprise, she felt his chest expand with a low laugh; then he turned within the circle of her arms and looped his own around her. "Maybe you know me too well," he muttered, but his tone was accepting.

"Or maybe you need acting lessons."

He chuckled again and rested his cheek against

the top of her head. But all humor was absent from
his tone a minute later when he said, ''Go see the
Bradleys, if you have to. There's nothing there to
find out.''

Chapter 8

Fort Morgan was a small town of about ten thousand people. Anna drove around for a little while to get her bearings, then stopped at a phone booth to look up the Bradleys' address. What she would do if they weren't in the book, she didn't know. It could mean they had moved or died, or it might just mean that their number wasn't listed.

She could have asked Saxon, but she hadn't wanted to ask him for information to help her to do something of which he didn't approve. Besides, it had been nineteen years, and there was no guarantee the Bradleys would still live in the same house, even if they had remained in Fort Morgan.

The phone book wasn't very big. She flipped

through it to the *B*s, then ran her finger down the column. "Bailey...Banks...Black...Boatwright... Bradley. Harold Bradley." She wrote down the address and phone number, then debated whether she should call them to get directions. She decided not to, because she wanted to catch them unawares, as it were. People could mask their true reactions if they were given warning.

So she drove to a gas station, filled up and asked directions of the attendant. Ten minutes later she drove slowly down a residential street, checking house numbers, and finally stopped at the curb in front of a neat but unpretentious house. It looked as if it had been built a good forty or fifty years before, with an old-fashioned roofed porch across the front. The white paint showed signs of wear but wasn't at the point where one could definitely say the house was in need of repainting. An assortment of potted plants was sunning on the porch, but there weren't any ornamentals in the small yard, which gave it a bare look. A one-car, unconnected garage sat back and to the side of the house.

She got out of the car, oddly reluctant now that she was here, but she walked up the cracked sidewalk and climbed the three steps to the porch. A porch glider, with rust spots showing where the thick white paint had chipped, was placed in front of the windows. Anna wondered if the Bradleys sat out there during the summer and watched the neighbors go about their business.

There wasn't a doorbell. She knocked on the frame of the screen door and waited. A gray-and-white cat leaped up onto the porch and meowed curiously at her.

After a minute, she knocked again. This time she heard hurried footsteps, and her pulse speeded up in anticipation. With it came a wave of nausea that had her swallowing in desperation. Of all the times to have one of her rare bouts of morning sickness! She only hoped she wouldn't disgrace herself.

The door opened, and she found herself face-to-face with a tall, thin, stern-faced woman, only the thin screen separating them. The woman didn't open the screen door. Instead she said, "Yes?" in a deep, rusty-sounding voice.

Anna was dismayed by the lack of friendliness and started to ask for directions as an excuse for being there, planning to leave without ever mentioning Saxon. But the tall woman just stood there with her hand on the latch, patiently waiting for Anna to state her business before she opened the door, and something about that strength of will struck a cord.

"Mrs. Bradley?"

"Yes, I'm Mrs. Bradley."

"My name is Anna Sharp. I'm looking for the Bradleys who used to be foster parents to Saxon Malone. Is this the right family?"

The woman's regard sharpened. "It is." She still didn't unlatch the door.

Anna's hopes sank. If Saxon hadn't been exposed to any sort of love even here, where he had grown up, he might never be able to give or accept it. What sort of marriage could she have under those conditions? What would it do to her own child to have a father who always kept at a distance?

But she had come this far, so she might as well carry on. She was aware, too, of the compelling quality of the woman's steely gaze. "I know Saxon," she began, and with an abrupt movement the woman flipped the latch up and swung the screen door outward.

"You know him?" she demanded fiercely. "You know where he is?"

Anna moved back a step. "Yes, I do."

Mrs. Bradley indicated the interior of the house with a jerk of her head. "Come inside."

Anna did, cautiously, obeying an invitation that had sounded more like a command. The door opened directly into the living room; a quick look around told her that the furniture was old and threadbare in spots, but the small room was spotless.

"Sit," said Mrs. Bradley.

She sat. Mrs. Bradley carefully relatched the screen door, then wiped her hands on the apron she wore. Anna watched the motion of those strong, work-worn hands, then realized that it was more of a nervous wringing than it was a deliberate movement.

She looked up at her reluctant hostess's face and was startled to see the strong, spare features twisted in a spasm of emotion. Mrs. Bradley tried to school herself, but abruptly a lone tear rolled down her gaunt cheek. She sat down heavily in a rocker and bunched the apron in her hands. "How is my boy?" she asked in a broken voice. "Is he all right?"

They sat at the kitchen table, with Mrs. Bradley drinking coffee while Anna contented herself with a glass of water. Mrs. Bradley was composed now, though she occasionally dabbed at her eyes with the edge of the apron.

"Tell me about him," Emmeline Bradley said. Her faded blue eyes were alight with a mixture of joy and eagerness, and also a hint of pain.

"He's an engineer," Anna said, and saw pride join the other emotions. "He owns his own company, and he's very successful."

"I always knew he would be. Smart! Lordy, that boy was smart. Me and Harold, we always told each other, he's got a good head on his shoulders. He always got A's in school. He was dead serious about his schooling."

"He put himself through college and graduated near the top of his class. He could have gone to work with any of the big engineering firms, but he wanted to have his own business. I was his secretary for a while.''

''Fancy that, his own secretary. But when he made up his mind to do something, he done it, even when he was just a boy.''

''He's still like that,'' Anna said, and laughed. ''He says exactly what he means and means exactly what he says. You always know where you stand with Saxon.''

''He didn't talk much when he was here, but we understood. The child had been through so much, it was a wonder he'd talk at all. We tried not to crowd him, or force ourselves on him. It about broke our hearts sometimes, the way he would jump to do every little thing we mentioned, then kinda hold himself off and watch to see if we thought he'd done it right. I guess he thought we were going to throw him out if he didn't do everything perfect, or maybe even kick him around the way they'd done in some of those other homes.''

Tears welled in Anna's eyes, because she could see him all too plainly, young and thin and still helpless, his green eyes watchful, empty of hope.

''Don't cry,'' Emmeline said briskly, then had to dab at her own eyes. ''He was twelve when we got him, bone-thin and gangly. He hadn't started getting his height yet, and he was still limping where the woman who had him before us knocked him off the porch with a broom handle. He twisted his ankle pretty bad. He had some long, thin bruises across his back, like the broom handle had caught him there, too. I guess it was a regular thing. And there was a burn mark on his arm. Mind you, he never said anything about it, but the caseworker told us a man ground out his cigarette on him.

"He never acted scared of us, but for a long time he'd get real stiff if we got too close to him, like he was getting ready to either fight or run. He seemed more comfortable if we stayed at a distance, so we did, even though I wanted to hug him close and tell him no one was ever going to hurt him again. But he was kinda like a dog that's been beat. He'd lost his trust of people."

Anna's throat was tight when she spoke. "He's still distant, to some extent. He isn't comfortable with emotion, though he's getting better."

"You know him real well? You said you used to be his secretary. Don't you still work for him?"

"No, I haven't worked for him for two years." A faint blush stained her cheeks. "We're having a baby, and he's asked me to marry him."

The color of Emmeline's eyes was faded, but her vision was still sharp. She gave Anna a piercing once-over. "In my day we did things in reverse order, but times change. There's no shame in loving someone. A baby, huh? When's it due? I reckon this is as close to a grandchild as I'll get."

"September. We live in Denver, so we aren't that far away. It'll be easy to visit."

A sad look crept over Emmeline's lined face. "We always figured Saxon didn't want to have nothing to do with us again. He said goodbye when he graduated from high school, and we could tell he meant it. Can't blame him, really. By the time we got him, his growing-up years had marked him so deep we knew he wouldn't want to think about any foster home. The caseworker told us all about him. The woman who gave birth to that boy has a lot to answer for, what she did to him and the living hell she caused his life to be. I swear, if anyone had ever found out who she was, I'd have hunted her down and done violence to her."

"I've had the same thought myself," Anna said grimly, and for a moment her velvet brown eyes didn't look so soft.

"My Harold died several years back," Emmeline said, and nodded in acknowledgment of Anna's murmur of sympathy. "I wish he could be here now, to hear how well Saxon's turned out, but I guess he knows anyway."

Her rough, simple faith was more touching than any elaborate protestation could have been. Anna found herself smiling, because there was something joyous in Emmeline's surety.

"Saxon said you lost your own son," she said, hoping she wasn't bringing up a source of grief that was still fresh. Losing a child was something a parent should never have to experience.

Emmeline nodded, a faraway expression coming over her face. "Kenny," she said. "Lordy, it's been thirty years now since he took sick that last time. He was sickly from birth. It was his heart, and back then they couldn't do the things they can now. The doctors told us from the time he was a baby that we wouldn't get to keep him all that long, but somehow knowing don't always help you prepare for it. He died when he was ten, poor little mite, and he looked about the size of a six-year-old."

After a minute the dreamy expression left her face, and she smiled. "Saxon, now, you could tell right off, even as thin and bruised up as he was, he was a strong one. He started growing the next year after we got him. Maybe it was having regular meals that did it. Lord knows I poked all the food down him I could. But he shot up like a bean pole, growing a foot in about six months. Seemed like every time we got him some jeans, he outgrew them the next week. He was taller than Harold in no time, all legs and arms. Then he started to fill out, and that was a sight to behold. All of a sudden we had more young gals walking up and down the street than I'd ever imagined lived within a square mile of this house, giggling to each other and watching the door and windows, trying to get a glimpse of him."

Anna laughed out loud. "How did he take being the center of attention like that?"

"He never let on like he noticed. Like I said, he was real serious about his schooling. And he was still leery about letting folks get close to him, so I guess dating would have been uncomfortable for him. But those girls just kept walking past, and can't say as I blame them. He made most boys his age look like pipsqueaks. He was shaving by the time he was fifteen, and he had a real beard, not a few scraggly hairs like most boys. His chest and shoulders had gotten broad, and he was muscled up real nice. Fine figure of a boy."

Anna hesitated, then decided to touch on the subject of Kenny again. Emmeline tended to get carried away talking about Saxon, perhaps because she had been denied the privilege for so many years. Now that she had finally met somebody who knew him, all the memories were bubbling out.

"Saxon told me that he always felt you resented him because he wasn't Kenny."

Emmeline gave her a surprised look. "Resented him? It wasn't his fault Kenny died. Let me tell you, you don't ever get over it when your child dies, but Kenny had been dead for several years before we got Saxon. We'd always planned to either adopt or take in foster kids, anyway, after Kenny left us. Kenny's memory laid a little easier after Saxon came to live with us. It was like he was happy we had someone else to care about, and having Saxon kept us from brooding. How could we resent him, when he'd been through such hell? Kenny didn't have good health, but he always knew we loved him, and even though he died so young, in some ways he was luckier than Saxon.''

''He needs to be loved so much,'' Anna said, her throat tightening again. ''But it's so hard for him to reach out to anyone, or let anyone reach out to him.''

Emmeline nodded. ''I guess we should have tried harder, after he'd had time to realize we weren't going to hurt him, but by then we were kinda used to keeping our distance from him. He seemed more comfortable that way, and we didn't push him. Looking back, I can see what we should've done, but at the time we did what it seemed like he wanted.'' She sat for a minute in silence, rocking back and forth a little in the wooden kitchen chair. Then she said, ''Resent him? Never for a minute. Land sakes, we loved him from the beginning.''

Chapter 9

Saxon's face tightened when she told him Harold was dead, and the brilliant color of his eyes dimmed. She had expected him to refuse to listen to anything about the Bradleys, but he hadn't. If he was curious, though, he was hiding it well, because he hadn't asked any questions, either. The news of Harold's death jolted him into showing interest, though reluctantly. "Emmeline is still living in the same old house by herself?"

She told him the address, and he nodded. "It's the same house."

"She seems to be in good health," Anna said. "She cried when I told her I knew you." She took a deep breath. "You should go see her."

"No," he said shortly, dismissing the idea with a frown.

"Why not?"

She could feel him withdrawing, see his face closing up. She reached out and took his hand, remembering what Emmeline had said about letting him pull away when they should have pulled him closer. "I won't let you shut me out," she said. "I love you, and we're in this together."

His eyes were unreadable, but she had his attention. "If I had a problem, would you want to help me, or would you leave me to deal with it on my own?" she pressed.

There was a flicker of expression, gone too fast for her to decipher. "I'd take care of it for you," he said, and his hand tightened on hers. "But I don't have a problem."

"Well, I think you do."

"And you're determined to help me with it whether I think it exists or not, is that it?"

"That's it. That's the way relationships work. People butt in on other people's business because they care."

Once he would have thought it was an intolerable encroachment on his privacy, but though her determination was irritating him, at the same time it made him feel oddly secure. She was right; this was the way relationships worked. He'd seen it, though this was the first time he'd experienced it. Somehow their "arrangement" had become a "relationship," full of complications, demands and obligations, but he wouldn't have chosen to go back. For the first time in his life he felt accepted as he really was; Anna knew all there was to know about him, all the hideous details of his birth and childhood. She knew the worst, yet she hadn't left.

On a sudden impulse he lifted her astride his lap so he could look full into her face while they talked. It was an intensely personal position for talking, both physically and mentally, but it felt right. "It wasn't a good time of my life," he said in an effort to explain. "I don't want to remember it, or revisit it."

"The way you remember it is distorted by everything that had gone before. You think of them as cold and resentful of you because you weren't their son, but that isn't at all the way they felt."

"Anna," he said patiently, "I was there."

She framed his face with her hands. "You were a frightened boy. Don't you think it's possible you were so used to rejection that you expected it, so that's what you saw?"

"So you're an amateur psychiatrist now?"

"Reasoning doesn't require a degree." She leaned forward and stole a quick kiss. "She talked for hours, telling me all about you."

"And now you think you're an expert."

"I *am* an expert on you," she snapped. "I've

studied you for years, from the minute I went to work for you.''

"You're pretty when you're mad," he said, abruptly enjoying this conversation. He realized with surprise that he was teasing her, and that it was fun. He could make her angry, but she would still love him anyway. Commitment had its advantages.

"Then I'm about to get a lot prettier," she warned.

"I can handle it."

"You think so, big guy?"

"Yes, ma'am." He cupped his hands on her hips and moved her suggestively. "I'm pretty sure I can."

For a moment her eyelids drooped heavily in response; then she opened her eyes wide and glared at him. "Don't try to distract me."

"I wasn't trying."

No, he was accomplishing, without effort. She was far from finished with her efforts to convince him, though, so she started to get up. His hands tightened on her hips and kept her in place. "Stay right where you are," he ordered.

"We can't talk in this position. You'll get your mind on sex, and then where will we be?"

"Probably right here on this couch. Not for the first time, either."

"Saxon, would you please be serious about this?" she wailed, then stopped in astonishment at what she

had just said. She couldn't believe she had just had
to plead with him to be serious. He was the most
sober of men, seldom laughing or even smiling. She
had probably seen him smile more in the past week
or so than in the rest of the three years she had
known him.

"I *am* serious," he said. "About this position, and
about Emmeline. I don't want to go back. I don't
want to remember."

"She loves you. She called you 'her boy,' and she
said that our baby would be her grandchild."

He frowned a little, his attention caught. "She
said that?"

"You should talk to her. Your memory is one-
sided. They understood that you were wary of adults
getting close to you, after the abuse you'd received,
and that's why they didn't try to touch you. They
thought they were making it easier on you."

A stark look came into his eyes as memories sur-
faced.

"Did you want them to hug you?" she asked.
"Would you have let them?"

"No," he said slowly. "I couldn't have stood it.
Even when I started having sex, in college, I didn't
want the girl to put her arms around me. It wasn't
until—" He broke off, his eyes unfocused. It wasn't
until Anna that he had wanted the feel of arms
around him, that he had wanted her to hold him
close. With all the other women, he had held their

hands above their heads, or he had been up on his knees out of their reach. But that had been sex; with Anna, from the very beginning, it had been making love, only it had taken him two long years to realize it.

He would never have allowed Emmeline or Harold to hug him, and they had known it.

Had his perceptions, and therefore his memories, been so distorted by his previous experiences? If what he had seen had been reflections in the carnival mirror of his mind, then nothing was as it had seemed. The beatings and general abuse he had suffered at the other foster homes had trained him to expect rejection, and he had been too young to be analytical.

"Can you really get on with your life unless you know for sure?" she asked, leaning closer to him. Those honey-dark eyes were pools he could drown in, and suddenly he pulled her tight against his chest.

"I'm trying to get on with my life," he muttered against her hair. "I'm trying to build a life, with you. Let the past go. God knows I've spent enough years trying to do that, and now that it's working, why dig it up again?"

"Because you can't let go of it! You can't forget your past. It's part of what made you the man you are. And Emmeline loves you. This isn't all for your sake. Part of it is for hers. She's alone in the world now. She didn't whine about it, or complain because you'd been gone for nearly twenty years and had never been back to see her. She just wanted to know if you were all right, and she was so proud to hear how well you've done.''

Saxon closed his eyes, fighting to keep the images from forming in his mind, but it was a useless battle. Emmeline had always been the stronger personality; Harold had been softer, gentler. He could still see her face, strong-boned, plain, as spare as a desert landscape. Never malevolent, but stern and upright. Her standards of cleanliness had been of the highest; for the first time in his life, he had always had good, clean clothes, clothes he hadn't been ashamed to go to school in.

He didn't want to think that she had spent twenty years wondering about him, worrying. No one had ever worried about him before, so the possibility simply hadn't occurred to him. All he had thought about was making a clean break with his past, making something of himself and never looking back.

Anna thought you had to look back, to see where you had been, as if the landscape changed once you had passed it. And maybe it did. Maybe it would look different now.

From habit he thrust emotion away from him, and the logic of the thing was suddenly clear to him. He didn't want to go back. He wanted Anna to marry him. Anna wanted him to go back. The three ideas fell into place, and all at once he knew what he would do.

"I'll go back," he said softly, and her head jerked up, her doe-eyes big and soft and questioning. "On one condition."

They faced each other in silence for a moment. He remembered the beginning of their relationship, when she had said she would be his mistress on one condition, and he had refused it, forcing her to take him on his terms. She was remembering, too, and he wondered if she would refuse on principle. No, not Anna. She was infinitely forgiving, and wise enough to know that the one instance had nothing to do with the other. He also accepted that he wouldn't always win, but that was okay, as long as Anna was the victor. As long as she won, he won, too.

"So let's hear it," she said, though she already knew. "What's the condition?"

"That you agree to marry me."

"You'd reduce our marriage to a condition that has to be met?"

"I'll do whatever it takes, use whatever argument I have to. I can't lose you, Anna. You know that."

"You aren't losing me."

"I want it signed and sealed, on record in the county courthouse. I want you to be my wife, and I want to be your husband. I want to be a father to our kids." He gave her a crooked smile. "This is kind of like a way for me to make up for my own lousy childhood, to give my kids something better and have a real childhood through them.''

Of all the things he could have said, that one got to her fast and hard. She hid her face against his neck so he wouldn't see the tears welling up in her eyes and swallowed several times so she would be able to speak normally. ''All right,'' she said. ''You have yourself a wife.''

They couldn't go to Fort Morgan immediately, because of his business commitments. Looking at the calendar, Anna smiled and made plans for them to go the following Sunday, and called Emmeline to let her know. It wasn't in Emmeline's character for her to bubble over with enthusiasm, but Anna could hear the pure joy in her voice.

The day finally came. As they made the drive, Saxon could feel himself tensing. He had been in foster homes all over the state, but he had lived in Fort Morgan the longest, so he had more memories of it. He could picture every room in that old house, every piece of furniture, every photograph and book. He could see Emmeline in the kitchen, dark hair pulled tightly back in a no-nonsense bun, a spotless apron protecting her plain housedress, while mouth-watering smells from the stove filled the entire house. He remembered that she had made an apple pie that was almost sinful, rich with butter and cinnamon. He would have gorged himself on that pie if he hadn't always been wary of anything he liked being taken away, so he had always restricted himself to one slice and forced himself not to show any enthusiasm. He remembered that Emmeline had baked a lot of apple pies.

He drove to the house without any difficulty, its location permanently etched in his mind. When he parked at the curb, his chest tightened until he felt almost suffocated. It was like being caught in a time warp, stepping back almost twenty years and finding nothing had changed. There *were* changes, of course; the porch roof was sagging a little, and the cars parked in the street were twenty years newer. But the house was still white, and the undecorated lawn was still as neat as a hatbox. And Emmeline, stepping out on the porch, was still tall and thin, and her gaunt face was still set in naturally stern lines.

He opened the car door and got out. Without waiting for him to come around, Anna had climbed out on her side, but she made no move to walk forward and join him.

Suddenly he couldn't move. Not another step. With only the small expanse of lawn separating them, he looked at the woman he hadn't seen in two decades. She was the only mother he'd ever known. His chest hurt, and he could barely breathe. He hadn't known it would be like this, that he would suddenly feel like that terrified twelve-year boy again, brought here for the first time, hoping it would be better than the others, expecting more of the same abuse. Emmeline had come out on the porch then, too, and he had looked up at that stern face and felt only the old rejection and fear. He had wanted acceptance, wanted it so much that his heart had been pounding in his chest and he had been afraid he would disgrace himself by wetting his pants, but he hadn't let himself show it, because not having it at all was easier than facing another rejection. So he had closed himself off, protecting himself in the only way he knew.

Emmeline moved toward the steps. She wasn't wearing an apron; she had dressed up in one of her Sunday dresses, but she was wiping her hands on the skirt out of habit. She stopped and stared at the tall, powerful man who was still standing at the curb. It was Saxon, without a doubt. He had turned into a breathtaking man, but she had always known he would, with that olive-toned skin, black hair and eyes like the clearest emeralds. She could see his eyes now, and the expression in them was the same as it had been twenty-five years ago when the caseworker had brought him to them, scared and desperate, and needing to be loved so much it had wrung her heart. He wouldn't come any closer, she knew. He wouldn't have back then, either, except for the caseworker's grip on his arm. Emmeline had remained on the porch rather than frighten him by rushing at him. And maybe it had been a mistake, waiting for him to be brought to her. Saxon needed for people to reach out to him, because he didn't know how to make the first move.

Slowly her face relaxed into a smile. Then Emmeline, that stern, reserved woman, walked down the steps to meet her son, her mouth trembling and tears running down her cheeks, her arms outstretched. And she never stopped smiling.

Something broke inside him with an audible snap, and he broke, too. He hadn't cried since he'd been an infant, but Emmeline was the only anchor he had ever had in his life, until he'd met Anna. With two long strides he met her in the middle of the sidewalk, caught her in his arms, and Saxon Malone cried. Emmeline put her arms around him and hugged him as tight as she could, as if she would never let go, and she kept saying, ''My boy! My boy!'' In the middle of his tears he reached out to Anna, and she flew around the car and into his arms. He held them both tight in his embrace and rocked them together, the two women he loved.

It was the twelfth of May. Mother's Day.

Epilogue

Anna woke slowly from what seemed like the deepest sleep she'd ever had and opened her eyes. The first sight she saw kept her from moving for a long, long time, as she reveled in the piercing sweetness of it. Saxon was sitting beside her hospital bed, just as he had been beside her all during labor and delivery. She had seen his face taut with worry and torment over her pain, filled with jubilation when she finally gave birth, his green eyes brilliant with tears as he stared wordlessly at his tiny, squalling offspring.

He held the sleeping baby in his arms now, all his attention focused on the little creature. With infinite care he examined the tiny, perfect hands and minuscule fingernails, almost holding his breath as the little fingers folded over his big one in a surprisingly tight reflexive grip, even in sleep. He traced a finger over the almost invisible eyebrows, down the downy soft cheek, to the pink bud of a mouth. Their son fit almost perfectly in his big hands, though he had weighed in at a respectable seven pounds.

She eased around onto her side, smiling at Saxon when he snapped his attention to her. "Isn't he gorgeous?" she whispered.

"He's the most perfect thing I've ever seen." Awe was in his tone. "Emmeline has gone down to the cafeteria to get something to eat. I practically had to fight her to get him away from her."

"Well, he is her only grandchild. For now."

He looked incredulous, remembering her labor, but then he looked at the baby in his arms and understood how she could consider the result as being well worth the effort. Then he smiled at his wife, a slow smile that melted her bones. "As long as the next one is a girl."

"We'll try our best."

"We still haven't decided on a name for him," he said.

"You can pick out his first name. I've already decided on his middle name."

"What is it?"

"Saxon, of course," she said. "The second Saxon

Malone. We're starting a new family tradition, remember?''

He reached out and took her hand, then eased himself onto the side of her bed, and together they ad-
mired their son.

*   *   *   *   *

Dear Reader,

I am the mother of two boys, Matthew and Alexander (whose names I borrowed for the Paxton twins in *Baby by Design.*) Both are grown now, but as I look back on the days when they were just little guys, I have this vivid image of grubby hands, peanut-butter-smeared faces and nonstop noise. In those days our backyard was invariably filled with hoydens of both sexes who were invariably up to some new devilment.

Two vivid impressions stand out in my mental scrapbook of precious memories. The first involved Alex when he was about three and a friend of his, Scotty, a burly little slugger who was more than happy to be Alex's sidekick in mischief.

It was summer, and the California clay that made up our backyard was hard as rock, and thus, perfect for throwing. Which these two little imps proceeded to do with great enthusiasm and glee—right into our swimming pool. By the time "Mom" looked up from the flower bed she was weeding, the sparkling pool she had just spent an hour cleaning had turned to thick, red mud.

The second memory involved these same two pistols, as well. They were playing cowboy, each coveting this disreputable black felt hat. A fight ensued, a real free-for-all brawl, with small fists flying and stubborn chins jutting. In this case, Mom was the one who ended up grabbing the combatants by the overall straps, but in *Family by Fate,* I let the soon-to-be dad Max Savage do the honors. I have to admit it's one of my all-time favorite scenes, just as Max is one of my most favorite heroes. I hope you agree.

All the best,

Paula Detmer Riggs

Family by Fate
Paula Detmer Riggs

For Floss.
I treasure your friendship.

Prologue

"Fifth Avenue Securities, Francoise Vargas here."

As the sound of her mother's voice came over the line, Elizabeth Vargas felt the tears puddle behind her eyes, but her voice was calm. "Mom, it's—"

"Liza! Thank God, I've been so worried! You promised to call no later than noon your time, and your daddy has called three times to ask me if I'd heard from you."

"I'm sorry, Mom. After I saw Dr. Jarrod, I drove to this little park overlooking the Columbia and meditated until I was calm enough to think rationally."

An affectionate chuckle shivered over the line. "You are definitely your father's daughter, dear heart.'' Her mother took a breath. ''So am I to be a grandmother at the impossibly young age of forty-nine?''

Liza glanced down. Beneath the vividly striped sweater and tailored slacks was nestled a tiny new life. In spite of all their precautions, she and Max had made a baby. Her throat tightened, and she had to clear it before she could speak. ''Yes, I'm definitely pregnant. He or she is due on August twenty-fourth.''

''Oh, darling, I am so pleased. Your biological clock was starting to click very loudly.''

Liza rolled her eyes, even though Francoise couldn't see her. ''Mom, I'm only twenty-eight.'' Something banged against the other side of her living room wall and she winced. The de Marcos were fighting again.

''I have to move,'' she muttered, rubbing the spot on her right temple that was beginning to throb. ''Dr. Jarrod told me about this house that's for sale next to his on Mill Works Ridge. It has three bedrooms and a nice big yard.'' Her mouth softened into a dreamy smile as she pictured a toddler running toward her across a velvet lawn—a sturdy broad-shouldered little boy with his father's irresistible smile, perhaps. Or a petite little girl with storm-gray eyes and curly black hair.

''A house? But dear, won't that require a great deal of upkeep?''

"Yes, but now that I'm going to have a family, I'll need more room." A family, she repeated to herself in a little glow of happiness. "I need to find a new job, of course. I can't very well pick up and jet off to Europe for months at a time with a baby in tow."

She'd worked hard to be respected in the highly competitive field of art restoration, but that was behind her now. Though she still hadn't made up her mind, she was thinking seriously of opening a daycare facility.

"Darling, what about the baby's father? Have you been able to reach him yet?"

Liza let her head fall back against the pillows. Though it had only been ten weeks and two days since she'd seen the man she loved, it seemed like a lifetime. "Not yet. I left a message." She'd called more times than she'd left a message, just to hear that deep, rich baritone on his machine. "He's probably out of town. He warned me he was hard to reach."

Her mother cleared her throat. "So you haven't told him he's to be a father?"

"No. It seems like such a special moment, telling the man you love he's about to be a father. I want to see his eyes light up." She went soft and warm inside. Max had beautiful gray eyes, with the most wonderful laugh lines and thick curly golden lashes.

"Do think about having the wedding here, darling. All I need is a week's notice."

Liza smiled. "I can't commit until I talk it over with Max."

"Of course. It's your wedding, after all. Still, I think I'll give Armand a call. He catered the office Christmas party and served the most wonderful pâté."

Liza thought about the canned ham and stale crackers she'd served Max after they'd made love the first time, and stifled a laugh. "I'll let you know, I promise. In the meantime, tell Daddy I'm fine, and I'll call on Sunday."

"We'll count on it. And much love, darling. To you and my adorable grandchild."

After hanging up, Liza went into the kitchen and poured herself a glass of milk, then carried it back to the sofa where she curled into the cushions. She and Max had drunk powdered milk flavored with cocoa, the best the ski patrol hut had had to offer. It had tasted like imported champagne, but then they'd been high on adrenaline and the joy of being alive.

They'd met on a skiing trip to Mount Bachelor, her first—and only—time on skis. More interested in the glorious, heart-thrilling views than proving her athletic prowess, she'd gotten separated from her friends and ended up on a slope that had been way too difficult.

Like an arthritic crab in a designer ski parka and

rented skis, she'd been slowly making her way toward the fuzzy, oblong blob at the bottom of the mountain that she'd taken to be the lodge when a sound like an approaching freight train had split the air. The next thing she knew a huge man had come swooping toward her from nowhere to scoop her over his shoulder, skis and all. A heartbeat later she'd been lying on her back in the snow behind a huge boulder while the massive stranger covered her with his body. She'd scarcely gotten out a bellow of protest when an enormous river of snow had gone rumbling by, the froth at the fringe settling over them.

Giddy with relief and joy at being alive, she'd thrown her arms around her white knight and kissed him. Something changed inside her at that moment. Something soul-deep and important. Later she realized she'd slipped into love with a man before she'd even known his name. Somehow she'd just…known, the way her sculptor father knew what kind of glorious shape was hidden in a blob of clay the instant he touched it.

His name was Max Savage, he'd told her as he'd helped her out of the snow and brushed her off. Six-two, with a linebacker's body and the tawny looks of a prowling lion, he'd told her he was a cop from Portland on vacation.

Cut off by the avalanche, it had been sheer luck that they'd stumbled on the ski patrol cabin. Barely nine by nine, it had rough cedar walls, an efficient wood stove, crude shelves stocked with emergency rations and a narrow bed with warm blankets.

They'd awakened to a total whiteout. A blizzard, Max had told her before adding that they were stuck there until the snow stopped. It had seemed the most natural thing in the world to make love. Max had had amazing stamina—and the most delicious imagination.

When he told her he'd fallen in love with her after knowing her only three days, she believed him. Not because she was a featherheaded ditz, as one would-be lover had so kindly put it after she'd turned him down, but because the instincts that had protected her all her life told her that he was an honorable and decent man.

Marry me, he'd urged when they'd reached the lodge. *Now, as soon as we can find a minister.* But she'd been scheduled to fly to London in two days to restore a mildew-damaged painting the Tate Museum had just purchased. Her bags were already packed. So they'd exchanged phone numbers and she'd promised to call the moment she returned. In fact, she'd called twice from London, only to get his machine. As soon as she landed, she'd called again.

That had been six days ago, and since then, she raced like a madwoman to the phone every time it rang. Every time she'd been disappointed, she'd beaten up on herself for not getting his address. And now...

"A baby," she whispered, touching her tummy. It had always been more rounded than flat. In a few months she was going to look like a beach ball—and she couldn't wait.

After setting down her glass, she picked up the phone again, punching out the number she'd come to know by heart. Her heart thudding, she waited for the sound of his voice. This time she would leave a more detailed message, telling him to call the minute he got back in town, no matter how late the hour.

She heard a click and held her breath, waiting for the familiar sound of his voice. The recording started, but the voice was female—and terribly familiar. "The number you have reached has been disconnected. There is no new number."

Chapter 1

Four months later

The sun had broken through the heavy morning overcast while Liza had been inside Portland General Hospital's maternity wing registering for her delivery. The air felt wonderfully warm on her skin as she walked toward her car in the visitors' lot. Squinting a little in the sudden brightness, she pulled her just-in-case hat from her bag and plopped it on her head.

A matronly woman walking toward her slowed to offer a smile. "False alarm?" she asked, gazing pointedly at Liza's protruding tummy.

"Trial run," Liza said as she returned the smile.

"Don't worry, you'll be fine," the woman said before walking on.

Of course she would. Hadn't she been telling herself that very thing for the last six and a half months? Not that she was marking off the days or anything, she told herself as she turned down the aisle where she'd left her Miata.

Her heart sank when she saw her little toy car sandwiched between a monster truck and one of those annoying sport utility vehicles. Two minutes and her entire repertoire of swear words later, she conceded defeat. The car door would only open a piddling little twelve inches. Maybe an anorexic supermodel could squeeze behind the wheel, but a woman with a baby on board hadn't a prayer.

As she turned to retrace her steps in search of a security guard to help her, a midnight blue Saturn with a new car sticker in the back window suddenly backed out of a space and slowly headed her way. Giving in to a sudden impulse, she stepped to the middle of the aisle and held up her hand, forcing the driver to stop short.

The large man behind the wheel was wearing a ball cap and dark shades. Pasting on a polite smile, she opened her mouth to beg a favor, but the words were suddenly dammed. From someplace inside she heard herself repeating his name.

For an instant Max Savage couldn't breathe.

Pregnant. God help him, Liza was pregnant. Hard

on the thought came another that took his breath. It had to be his child. Thinking about it now, he realized her last message on his machine asking him to call had been edged with an urgency he hadn't let himself hear.

"My God, Max, I can't believe it's really you." Even trembling with shock, her throaty voice had the power to enchant him.

Twelve years as a cop had taught Max to watch both his front and his back. The last five as an undercover nark had taught him to slip easily into the role of a vicious street punk. Now, as his heart thudded in his throat and his chest tried to squeeze the air from his lungs, he slipped into yet another character. The one in which he came off as a callous, self-centered son of a bitch. The kind of man Liza would hate.

"Hello, Liza. This is a...surprise."

"I called, left messages." She frowned, then rushed on in a fevered kind of eagerness. "Or...or maybe you didn't get them? I know my machine sometimes eats messages."

"I got them."

"I...see." He saw her struggling to hide her disappointment, and bled. "Is that why you changed your number? So you wouldn't be bothered by calls from an ex-lover?"

Somehow he found the strength to shrug. "It seemed less...complicated, yeah."

"Okay, Max, I get the picture." Her voice was cool, her expression composed, but her gaze didn't quite mesh with his. "I called to tell you about the baby. Your baby, Max." Her hand cupped her belly protectively, her expression suddenly as soft as snowfall. He bled deep into an already raw wound.

"Guess we weren't as careful as we thought."

"That's it? That's all you have to say?"

"What else do you want me to say, Liza? That I'm sorry I knocked you up? Okay, consider it said."

Her face paled. "In other words, all those things you said at Mount Bachelor about falling in love and wanting to marry me were just lies?"

He felt his edge slip. Conning scum had become second nature. Conning the only woman he'd ever loved was torture. He leaned back, his hands deliberately easy on the wheel.

"Tell me what you think is a fair amount to cover your delivery and absolve me of any further responsibility. If it seems reasonable, I'll write you a check."

The stunned hurt that stuttered into her dark eyes had his gut twisting. *Trust me, angel, it's for your own good,* he wanted to blurt. Almost as much as he wanted to open the damn car door and haul her inside.

"If you wanted to hurt me, you've succeeded," she said in that Lauren Bacall voice of hers that still haunted his dreams.

"Just making sure you understand the truth according to Savage, is all."

She drew a careful breath. There was a dignity about her that shamed him. "In that case, I imagine you'd have no objection to relinquishing parental rights."

Something tore inside him. "None whatsoever," he said in a bored tone.

"Fine." The disappointment in her eyes flat-out broke his heart. "If you'll give me your address, I'll send you the papers as soon as they're drawn up. In return, I'd also like your medical history and that of your family." Head down, shoulders stiff, she rested her bilious green bag on her tummy and rummaged through it.

He drew a breath and filled his mind with her for the last time. The soft glow of her skin, the vibrant energy that seemed to crackle the air, the swirl of her dark silky hair against her proud shoulders. It seemed longer. Silk sliding over his skin. He realized he was staring and pulled back.

"Damn, I know I put my notebook in here this morning," she muttered, sneaking a peeved glance his way. "Uh, you don't happen to have a scrap of paper on you, do you?"

He froze the impulse to grin. "Care of Portland Police Bureau," he said coldly.

The look she shot him could have curdled milk.

"I called their personnel department when I couldn't reach you by phone. Three different departments, in fact, and three very bored, impatient officials swore they'd never heard of you."

He gave her a pitying look. "Department policy. Personnel *never* gives out information to civilians."

"Civilians who pay your salary, which means we ought to have a right to know who we've hired," she muttered, shoving a handful of baby-care pamphlets back into her bag.

Damn, but she was cute when she was indignant. Her mouth had just enough of a pout to tempt a man beyond reason. Most men, anyway. Bitterness uncoiled in his gut, reminding him of the path his life had taken. He had to get out of here now, before he did something really stupid, like spoil the only unselfish thing he'd ever done in his life.

"Sorry to cut this short, babe, but I've got things to do." Straightening, he started the car and put it into gear.

"Wait!" she cried as a look of alarm ran over her face. "I almost forgot why I stopped you. Some idiot parked too close to my car and I can't get baby and me into the driver's seat."

He choked back a laugh. "Guess that might be a problem, at that."

"But not for you, so if you wouldn't mind backing her out of the space—"

"Sorry, sweet cakes," he said, hating himself and the whole frigging world. "You'll have to find yourself another good Samaritan type. I'm already late, and the lady is too hot to piss off."

He made sure she was well away from the car, then burned rubber, taking the turn to the exit so fast he fishtailed toward the safety fence. Driving automatically on streets he'd memorized when he'd been in uniform, he headed west, toward a place he knew. The road led to a secluded cul-de-sac overlooking a deep ravine. To his great relief the area was deserted. Feeling as though he were choking to death, he pulled into the shade of a huge maple and killed the engine.

He stared straight ahead, his eyes focused on a wash of green, but it was Liza he saw. Big wounded eyes looking out of a face that had lost its glow.

God help him, he'd hurt her so much. She was carrying his child, and he'd coldly, deliberately humiliated her. It didn't matter that he had no other option. Or that he was only doing it for her own good.

"Sweet Liza, I'm so damn sorry," he whispered into the empty silence. *You'll find someone else,* he wanted to tell her. *Someone who can love you the way you deserve to be loved. Someone who'll love your baby as his own.*

A hard lump scoured his throat at the thought of never holding his child. Of never waking in the night to curl around Liza in the dark when the stark images of his past kept him from sleeping. Of never breathing the clean scent of her skin when he hugged her, never sharing the laughter that seemed to bubble out of her.

Every man had his breaking point. Max knew a lot of guys in stir who figured he'd never reach his. Six months ago he figured the same thing. Now he knew better. Letting his shoulders slump, he crossed his arms over the wheel, buried his face and cried.

Chapter 2

Liza loved her little Victorian cottage on Mill
Works Ridge. By the end of the first month in her
new house, she felt as though she'd been adopted
into a large, rambunctious family. The four ladies
who called themselves the Mommy Brigade—Prudy
Randolph, Stacy MacAuley, Raine Paxton and
Maddy Jarrod—were her sisters, teasing her out of
her recurring bouts of prenatal terror, listening to her
when she was blue, commiserating when her once
svelte figure swelled to monster proportions. The
daddies were her big brothers, taking care of her
more strenuous chores, building her an enclosed
porch where her day-care kids could play when it
rained, making sure her car was serviced.

The moms had been thrilled to find out Liza planned to open a day care in her new home. All four worked outside the home. Stacy taught kindergarten. Maddy had just started as a guidance counselor for one of the high schools. Raine ran her own bookstore downtown. Last month trauma nurse Prudy had introduced Liza to two other nurses who'd been eager to enroll their preschoolers. With ten little ones enrolled, even on a part-time basis, Liza had been off to a running start.

In deference to the heat, the door to the Randolphs' house was open, and a child's happy laughter wafted through the screen door as Liza rang the bell. "Prue, it's me, Liza," she shouted through the screen door even before the sound of the chimes had faded.

"Come on in," Prudy yelled, her voice slightly muffled—and definitely harried. "Oh, rats, I forgot. I hooked the screen door when I came inside. Hang on, Liza, I'll be right with you."

A split second later she heard a burst of happy music start somewhere in the house, followed by the familiar slap-slap of Prudy's favorite thong sandals on the utility room tile.

"Sorry to take so long," Prudy said as she unhooked the screen. "Chloe's at a birthday party for a friend, and I figured it was the perfect opportunity to trim Lily's hair. Lily, being Lily, hates sitting still that long, so I bribed her with a new video which should give us some peace and...oh, my goodness, sweetie, you look terrible.''

Liza grimaced. ''That's not exactly the word I would have chosen. More like stunned witless, which as we know is a condition that often strikes otherwise intelligent adults who converse primarily with toddlers on a regular basis.''

Laughing in spite of the concern in her hazel eyes, Prudy opened the door and stepped back to allow Liza to waddle past. ''Has anyone ever told you that you're a lousy liar?''

Choking off a laugh, Liza realized she was sick to death of being brave and independent and spunky. Especially spunky. ''You're right, Prue. I'm about as far from fine as a body can be.''

''In that case, sit down and put up your feet. I can offer you lemonade, milk or grape juice.''

''Lemonade, please,'' Liza decided, comfortable enough in Prudy's home to fetch the glasses from the cupboard.

''So are you going to tell me what's got you so shook, or do I have to wheedle it out of you?'' Prudy asked as she took a pitcher from the fridge's top shelf.

''Oh, Lord, not the wheedling. Anything but the wheedling.''

Prudy laughed, splashing the lemonade she was pouring onto the counter. Liza grabbed the towel from the rod and mopped. "I don't suppose you have any brownies?"

"Sorry, Case found my stash last night. The best I can do are snicker doodles. They're in the cookie jar."

"Desperation is so pathetically humbling," Liza muttered as she dug into the ceramic Pooh-Bear for a generous handful. "Where is the Row's resident tough guy, anyway?"

"Downtown. This is his weekend to work. He's promised to bring me and the girls pizza from that new place next to the station house."

Prudy returned the lemonade to the fridge while Liza carried the cookies to the bleached pine table and sat down. Prudy brought the glasses. "Cheers," she said, handing Liza hers before sitting.

Liza took a thirsty drink, then took a deep breath. "Just as I was leaving the hospital I ran into the baby's father in the parking lot."

Prudy's eyes widened. "Ran into him how?"

After taking another bracing sip, Liza explained about her Miata and stopping Max's car to beg a favor. "After he made it crystal clear he had zero interest in me or the baby, he just drove off, leaving me standing there with my mouth hanging open and his son kicking in my belly."

"Too bad he didn't run into a post," Prudy muttered darkly.

"Actually he almost did. It was obvious he wanted to get away from me as fast as possible."

"About parental rights, the Paxtons used a local attorney when they adopted Morgana. I'm sure Raine will be happy to give you his name."

"Thanks. I'll stop by and ask her on my way home." Liza shifted in an attempt to ease the dull throbbing in her back.

"How about coming back tonight for pizza? Case always brings more than we can eat."

"Can I let you know later? My folks are traveling, and they promised to call sometime today."

"Sure, absolutely." Prudy reached over to squeeze her arm. "I'm sorry things didn't work out. But I hope you know we're here for you, all of us. Boomer will have four doting aunts and four adoring uncles, not to mention a whole corral of cousins."

Liza nodded. "I've been very blessed, I know that. I also know that we really can't have it all, although I have to admit it's sometimes hard to remember that when I see...all of you."

"I know, sweetie. But remember this. Maddy had just been rejected by her husband when she came here to have her baby. Now she's so happy she could light up the room with the glow in her eyes, and Luke's just as bad. Case says it's damn embarrassing to be around them."

Liza laughed. "The man does dote on her."

"Trust me, the right man will come along for you, too. If that's what you want."

Was it? For six months she'd wanted Max. At night, she'd dreamed of him. During the day she imagined him walking in the door at the end of the day, his beautiful gray eyes shining with desire and happiness because she and their son were waiting for him. When she woke in a sweat, terrified something was wrong with the baby, she'd hugged her pillow and pretended it was his arms holding her.

Some dreams die hard, she realized with a silent keen of sorrow. But they did die. "No matter what it takes, I intend to forget Max Savage before this baby is born," she vowed fiercely. "And you can take that to the bank."

Instead of the laugh she expected, Prudy was gaping at her, a look Liza couldn't label on her face. "Let me get this straight," she said slowly and distinctly. "This jerk we're going to hate forever is named Max Savage?"

Liza nodded. "Why do you look so surprised? I'm sure I've mentioned his name before."

"Not to me, you haven't. You just told me how you met, and that the relationship ended badly. We all pretty much had the feeling you didn't want to talk about it, so we never pressed."

"I know, and I'm grateful."

Prudy picked up her glass, then set it down. "This

Max Savage doesn't happen to be a Portland cop, does he?''

She felt a jolt of alarm. "Prue, please tell me Max isn't Case's best friend."

"No, nothing like that," Prudy hastened to assure her. "But I doubt there are two Max Savages on the force, so—" Prudy stopped abruptly, her gaze narrowing. "Something's wrong here. Why don't you already know this? It was in all the papers."

"*What* was in the papers?"

Prudy took a deep breath, let it out with terrible slowness. "It was right after Thanksgiving. Max was working undercover. Something went wrong, and he took two bullets in the back. I was on duty when they brought him in. The trauma surgeon called a Code Blue on him twice."

"Oh, my God." Liza wondered how she could feel overheated one minute, icy cold the next. "I...I'd already left for England then," Liza said, her lips barely moving. "I didn't get home until the third of January."

Prudy drew a deep breath, then went on very gently. "His spinal column was traumatized, leaving him paralyzed from the hips down. When he left the hospital, he was in a wheelchair. As far as I know, he's still in it."

Flat on his back, his breath coming in gasps, Max stared grimly at the barbell he'd just manhandled into the brackets. The extra ten-pound weights he'd added might have been a mistake, he conceded as he lifted the end of the towel he'd slung around his neck to wipe the sweat from his hot face.

Damn near every muscle in his chest and arms throbbed. Even his abs were screaming. It would be worse when he started crutch walking, they'd warned him. With his long legs, the braces he would have to wear would weigh ten or twelve pounds apiece, maybe more.

The injury and lengthy recovery had sapped his strength big time. Even with daily therapy, it had taken months to regain half of what he'd had before. It hadn't taken more than a day or two outside the rehab center to realize that the stuff they'd taught him about activities of daily living was pathetically inadequate. No matter what the bright-eyed, terminally cheerful therapists preached, life as a paraplegic was one frigging hassle.

As strong as he was becoming, getting himself off the weight bench and into a hot shower was almost more than he wanted to tackle. Setting his jaw to keep from groaning, he pressed one hand against his aching stomach and sat up. He was reaching for his chair when the doorbell jangled.

On the other side of the door Liza's heart was beating so fast she could scarcely breathe. It had taken her two trips around the block and all her affirmations to work up the courage to pull into the huge complex's parking lot.

After Case had given her the address—along with a fierce bear hug for luck—she'd taken two days to prepare herself. It would be rough, she knew. According to the information Case had managed to pick up from Max's co-workers, he'd cut himself off from everyone, even his family in Seattle.

"He's hurting bad, Liza," Case had warned. "And a wounded animal is dangerous."

"So is a mama-to-be," she whispered to the squirming puppy in her arms.

An instant later the door opened to reveal a large, sweaty, scowling man in old gray sweats. She'd prepared herself for a wheelchair. His was dark blue and sleek. One of those lightweight models she'd read about. Easy to get in and out of—but still a chair. A visible reminder of disability.

The large feet on the footrests were encased in thick athletic socks, the soles pristine white. He'd obviously been exercising, and the thick hair the color of wheat in the sun was damp, the ends curling and clinging to his forehead. Above the stretched neck of the sweatshirt, the strong, rough-cut face she loved was lined with weariness. Like his sex appeal, the scowl on his hard lips was truly lethal.

"Don't you dare shut the door," she said when his face darkened with anger.

"Let it go, Liza," he said in a voice that sounded

weary in spite of the hard-bitten edge. "There's nothing here for you."

"Ah, but I have something for you." Before she lost her nerve, she stooped to put the fat little Australian shepherd on the threshold. Legs already churning, the pup shot past Max, streaked left and disappeared from view.

"Hey!" Max bellowed, turning his chair to look behind him. "Damn it, Liza, that…it just piddled on my floor." He shot her a look that was part shock, part outraged male, and she burst out laughing.

"It's a she. I've been calling her Tilly, but feel free to change her name. She's a gift."

"Not a chance!"

Liza summoned a bright smile. "Fine. You take her back to the pound, then. I'm pretty sure they give puppies a good week to be adopted before they…you know." She drew the flat of her hand across her throat.

He glared at her. His gray eyes narrowed, and his jaw was hard. "If this is some kind of game—"

"No game. A gift from Boomer and me." She caressed her tummy with a hand that wasn't quite steady, for all her positive self-talk. His gaze followed her hand, the shiver of his sinfully thick lashes the only sign of emotion she could detect. "I'm having your son, by the way. At least it sure looks that way on the ultrasound. I don't know about his skiing ability yet, of course. But he's already perfected his soccer kick and is now working on his tumbling routine for the 2020 Olympics.''

His face changed, and for an instant sadness so profound it hurt seeped into his eyes. Her courage wavered, but the memory of what was at stake steadied her. "Sorry I can't stay to chat," she went on blithely, smiling again. "Boomer and I have errands to run." Before he could react, she leaned down to kiss him hard on the mouth. His breath hissed in, and his huge, stiff shoulders jerked involuntarily.

"Have a good life, Max," she said as she straightened. "Oh, and one more thing, your son and I don't give two hoots in hell whether you can walk or not. We just flat out love you."

She turned and hurried as fast as she could down the walk to the parking lot. Behind her she heard the sound of a harsh curse, followed by the loud bang of a door being brutally slammed.

"That's it?" Stacy MacAuley said, her green eyes registering incredulity beneath the brim of her baseball cap. "You just walked away?"

Liza handed baby Oliver Jarrod the teething ring he'd just dropped onto the patio table, then leaned forward to take a mock bite of his chubby little foot. Ollie squealed and kicked against the padded edge of the baby seat.

"Well, waddled would be the more appropriate term," she said, leaning back against the chair cushion. "But yes, I went to my car, calmly drove out of the parking lot, very calmly found the nearest service station and very, very calmly threw up in the rest room."

Tonight, while the men told lies and smoked cigars in the Paxtons' kitchen, the ladies and assorted offspring had gathered at Liza's. While the kids watched a video in the den, the ladies were gorging on junk food in the screened-in deck.

"So you figured a puppy would charm him out of his depression?" Stacy asked as she dipped a chip into Raine's world-famous clam and pepper dip.

"Partially. I also figured it would give me an excuse to stop by again. You know, to check on Tilly and maybe bring her a toy."

Stacy lifted an eyebrow. "And then?"

"Then I wing it," Liza admitted, nibbling on a tortilla chip.

"Seduction is always a good option." Raine contributed the comment with a devious grin.

Liza groaned, a vision of Max's naked—and magnificently aroused—body filling her mind. "I wonder if cold showers really work," she muttered, her entire body suddenly on fire.

Maddy laughed. "In a word, no."

When the laughter subsided, Prudy cleared her throat, then said almost hesitantly, "It's possible Max has lost more than the use of his legs." She met Liza's gaze with solemn eyes. "Have you thought about what it would be like to be married to a man who can't make love to you?''

Liza felt the energy surrounding them turn tense. "I've thought about it, and I've...cried at the thought of what it must be like for a man who was so supremely physical to be suddenly restricted. I'm selfish enough to want to feel him inside me, but if it's not possible, so be it. I'll take what he can give me and make it enough.''

"You love him that much?" Maddy asked gently.

Liza nodded. "He's just so...male, so...well, powerful is the word that comes to mind. And yet, he has this incredible sweetness that just poured out of him that first night in the hut when I woke up screaming, thinking I was being smothered by snow.'' She felt the tears well, and blinked hard.

"Damn him, I don't care if he can't make love to me or dance with me or carry me off the ski slopes. I need him to hold me when I'm scared and tell me it'll be okay.'' Her voice broke, and she grabbed a tissue from the box she kept handy for the kids. The portable phone Liza kept on one of the bookcases in case of an emergency rang.

Prudy was closest and got up to retrieve it for Liza, who nodded her thanks, then cleared her throat and squared her shoulders. Expecting her father to be on the other end, she put a smile on her voice before answering, "Hi, this is Liza.''

"Yeah, well, this is the man who's going to wring

that pretty little neck of yours unless you get your fanny over here ASAP and remove this pathetic excuse for a dog from my house.'' Before she could reply, Max slammed down the phone in her ear.

Chapter 3

It was nearly eight-thirty when she pulled into the parking lot of the large, neat apartment complex. Max's car was parked in one of three handicapped spots.

After pulling into a visitor's slot and shutting off the engine, she sat quietly for a moment, letting her jumpy nerves settle. The man who'd railed at her in the hospital parking lot was hurting and scared and feeling helpless, she reminded herself. But at his core, he was still the man who had risked his life to save a stranger from a horrible, smothering death.

"All he needs is understanding and patience, Boomer," she murmured as she maneuvered out from under the wheel and levered herself to her feet.

The sun was just slipping behind a tall pine at the edge of an open area between buildings when she took a deep breath and rang the bell.

"It's open," Max called from inside, his voice anything but friendly.

He was seated in his chair across the room, his arms crossed over his deep, wide chest, watching her as she entered, a quiet, controlled, remote stranger with an air of restless vitality surrounding him, as though he resented sitting still for even a minute or two.

He seemed even bigger than she remembered. Ominously big, in fact. His eyes were narrowly focused, unfriendly, without a hint of the teasing glint she'd missed so much. In fact, from the way he was staring at her, she half expected him to tell her she had a right to an attorney and all that other cop stuff. *Not good,* she thought as she took her time closing the door behind her.

On the other hand, he had recently shaved, his hair was glossy clean and neatly brushed, and he was dressed in a chest-hugging rugby shirt that looked new and tailored khaki chinos with a knife crease. On his feet were brown leather moccasins, the kind she'd always found sexy. For sheer sexual impact, she gave Max Savage a twenty on a scale of ten—and that was being conservative.

"My fanny and I are here, as ordered, sir," she said with her best cheerleader smile.

His expression said he wasn't impressed. "Your 'gift' is in the bathroom." As though on cue, the pup began to whine, then yip. Liza hid a pang of disappointment as she glanced around.

Though small, the living room was eclectically attractive in a spare, chrome-and-leather sort of way. On the soft pearly walls hung prints of excellent quality, thoughtfully arranged by someone who had a sense of proportion and scale. A lovely mix of color and subject, she thought. Restful, yet not boring. A lifetime surrounded by art and artists had taught her that a person's choice of art was a mirror of the soul. Max's definitely had touches of romance and complexity, with a deep grain of sensuality.

"At least she has good lungs," she said as the pup's protests increased in volume.

"Trust me, she can do that for hours." It wasn't exactly a smile because the dimple she knew lurked in one hard cheek remained hidden, but it wasn't exactly a scowl, either. Her instinct told her that he wasn't quite as unmoved as he appeared.

"She wants to be with you," Liza offered, dropping her bag on a comfortable-looking brown leather recliner before walking toward him.

"Yeah, well, I don't want to be with her. Little mongrel is a royal pain." He jerked his head toward the fireplace. Newspapers were spread nearly wall-to-wall. Potty training in progress. There was also a well-chewed running shoe lying half under the couch—along with a soft toy, the kind she'd almost picked up for the pup at the pet store. Next to it was a bunch of what looked liked a random assortment of chewed brown leather.

She realized that the pup was no longer whining. Lying low, no doubt, she thought. The little sweetie.

Conscious that Max was watching her, she moved closer to prod what looked like the stitched point of a leather collar with the toe of her sandal. "Don't tell me," she mused after a moment's study. "Your favorite leather jacket."

He inclined his head, and his mouth flattened. "A present from my grandfather, who wore it on twenty-five missions over Germany," he said, his words distinctly spoken. "It is, as you might imagine, irreplaceable."

Liza's heart sank. She had her own small store of precious keepsakes, too, in an old Lily Dache hatbox in the top of her closet. Like the silver-backed brush her grandmother had used when she'd braided Liza's hair, and the rosary from her namesake, her father's older sister. She would be heartbroken if she lost any one of them.

"I'm really sorry, Max. But Tilly didn't mean any harm. I mean, she is still a baby."

Max saw the wash of tears in her eyes and felt like scum. Okay, so he'd loved that old jacket, but Liza was right. It wasn't the pup's fault Max had never had a dog as a kid. How was he supposed to know dogs teethe just like human babies? Hell, he had a whole closet of things he'd never use again that she could have chewed, like the new pair of baseball cleats he'd bought the day before he'd been hit. Instead, she'd eaten his jacket, then chewed his toes bloody while he'd been asleep. With half his body dead, he hadn't even felt those sharp little teeth breaking skin.

Bitterness crashed over him, a familiar companion these days. When it was on him, he wasn't fit company for anyone, especially a woman with love in her eyes. As much as he wished it was so, the Max Savage Liza loved no longer existed. Because she was loyal and stubborn and kindhearted, she just couldn't see that yet.

"Look, I didn't mean to take it out on you." He found himself saying the words anyway. "It's been a rough day."

"I'll buy you another jacket. I know it won't be the same, but you can put your own memories in it and then pass it down to Boomer to pass onto his son someday."

"I don't want a jacket, Liza. That's not the point." He plowed his hand through his hair. He'd been so sure she would hate him after the things he'd said. Deliberately, he glanced at his legs. For the rest of his life he would be chained to this chair—or at best limited to dragging braced legs everywhere he went. An object of pity. Someone able-bodied guys who used to be his friends avoided because they didn't want to be reminded that it could just as easily be one of them sitting in a chair for the rest of his life. A cripple who was barely potty-trained these days.

Think about that, Savage, when you're tempted to grab what she's offering and squeeze tight. Think about the times you peed your pants in the hospital because you couldn't get to the can fast enough. The familiar humiliation bit hard. Instead of flinching, he welcomed it. Fed it, until he was sick with it. "I know you meant well, Liza, but a pup takes more time than I have to give it."

"Her," she corrected before stooping to pick up the fuzzy doll the guy at the pet store had sworn puppies needed to be happy—along with a hundred bucks worth of other stuff the damned mongrel ignored.

"She's a good dog, Max," she said as she got to her feet with a wobbly awkwardness that tore at his heart. "She's just playful, but—"

"No, Liza. A dog needs someone who can take her for long walks and play Frisbee with her. Someone *able-bodied* to make sure she doesn't get herself hurt running into the street." He hesitated, then added pointedly, "The same things a kid needs."

"So?"

He felt his patience thinning. The woman was as stubborn as she was adorable. "So I am not that person,'' he enunciated slowly. ''I will never be that person.''

''Of course you are. Just because you can't walk doesn't mean you're any less of a father. Or a man.''

He snorted, then curled a lip and snarled. ''Tell me another one, babe. That one's been used so often it's frayed around the edges.'' His alter ego on the streets, Mac the Knife, couldn't have done it better.

Stubborn, Liza thought. And proud. Double-edged swords. ''Okay, how about this,'' she said, advancing on him with her big belly leading the way. Safe inside, Boomer gave her a little punch of encouragement.

''In spite of all evidence to the contrary, I am not a woman who falls into bed with a man on a whim. I fell in love with you about, oh, fifteen seconds after I looked into those beautiful eyes of yours. And you know why? Because I saw a man who was honorable and decent and kind. And if we had simply slept in each other's arms instead of making love, I would still have left that cabin loving you.''

He closed his eyes and let his shoulders slump for a beat before squaring them. When he looked at her, the fury was gone. The remoteness that replaced it was far worse. ''It's no good, Liza. God knows I don't want to hurt you, but I have.''

''I understand—''

''No, you don't. No one who can get up and walk

across a room without giving it a second thought can understand.''

''All right, I'll concede that. But I can empathize.''

His mouth twisted. ''Empathize this, then. I *hate* the way I have to live, the never-ending restrictions and limitations and frigging hassles.'' Eyes blazing with fury, he thumped a hard fist onto his lifeless thigh. ''Every morning when I wake up, I tell myself I'll feel more today. Today is the day I'll move my toe or feel pain. Something.''

''If not today, then tomorrow,'' she said urgently.

''What if I don't?''

''Then we'll grieve for what you've lost, and then go on to make a great life.''

The word he snorted was straight from the gutter. ''That only happens in fairy tales, Liza. In real life, Prince Charming ends up hating the beautiful princess because she makes him want things he can't have.''

''What about all the things you can have, like a woman who loves you and a son who'll love you because you're strong and brave and funny? A family, Max. Our family, just the way we planned.'' Desperate, she dropped to her knees and placed both hands on his where they were clenched tight around the chair wheels. ''Max, please listen to me. What we had in that cabin was magical and rare. We didn't only make love, we…we touched each other's souls.

In that instant we became a part of each other. What hurts you hurts me. What makes you sad makes me sad. By the same token I can give you my optimism and my belief in you when yours flags.''

His head jerked, but his eyes remained shuttered, his thoughts hidden. ''Don't,'' he ordered in a harsh voice that seemed ripped from him.

''Let me be here for you. Be with me when our baby comes into the world. Build a life with me.''

He shook his head, his jaw tight. ''You say you want that now, but what about a year from now? A year with a man who can't give you more children, who can't even make love to you.''

''I'd rather have a man who would love me with his hands and his mouth and his heart than one who simply pounds me into the mattress.''

He jerked his head again, his gaze riveted on hers. He saw the force of some powerful emotion all but overwhelming her. ''No, Liza, no.''

''Yes, Max! Don't you see? Together we're stronger than we are separately. In fact, we're... invincible.''

His chest heaved. He jerked one hand from beneath hers and lifted it to cup her face. Her heart tore when she realized the big callused hand that had loved her so tenderly wasn't quite steady. ''You don't know how much I wish I really were the man you think I am,'' he said in a tortured voice. ''But I'm not. Maybe I never was.''

She covered his hand with hers, loving the feel of the hard roped sinew against her palm. "You're afraid, and I understand, but—"

"Damn it, Liza, I'm paralyzed," he grated, withdrawing his hand. "I can barely take care of myself, let alone a wife and baby."

"We'll take care of each other."

His face closed up, and his eyes narrowed. Once again he was that remote, angry stranger in the parking lot. "I'd appreciate it if you'd take Tilly and leave before we both say things we'll regret."

Liza felt the energy drain from her body, leaving her limp and empty. Much as she hated to give up, the intuition that had served her so well told her not to push him any further than she already had.

"If that's what you want," she said quietly, preparing to stand. Overbalanced, she nearly toppled into his lap before he caught her. "Sorry, I'm a little wobbly these days," she said with a shaky laugh, her hands on his knees.

His face changed. "Damn you," he grated, his voice raw. And then, somehow, she was on his lap, his arms imprisoning her.

"Oh Max," she managed to say before his mouth came down hard on hers.

Chapter 4

Liza felt a moment of exhilaration, a jolt of heat. And then she was kissing him back, her mouth hungry, wild for him. He groaned, his body shuddering as his arms turned to steel, forcing her closer. Joy burst inside her as powerful as any drug. She didn't need the words, not when she could feel the love pouring from him, as hot as the sun and just as healing.

"I've wanted you," he said between kisses, his need a living thing.

"Me, too," she whispered, her hands buried in that thick soft mane of wheat-colored hair. "I ache for you."

He made an inarticulate sound before taking her

mouth again, his tongue plunging deep. *Touch me,* she begged silently, and then, as if in answer to her unspoken plea, he slid his hand up her leg, the callused palm wonderfully abrasive against her bare skin. The muscles of her thigh bunched as he slipped his fingers beneath the lace of her panties. Her mind clouded, then shimmered as he slipped a finger inside her. He knew her body, knew her needs, and he'd remembered. His hand touched, caressed, so gentle, loving her. Just like that, she came apart, shuddering against him, her head thrown back as a cry was wrenched from her throat.

"Max, oh, Max," she whispered when her breath returned to her body. Happy tears of relief and anticipation filled her eyes as she buried her face in his shoulder and let them fall. He stiffened, then gradually relaxed, his big hand stroking her back with long, soothing caresses that helped bring her back into her body.

It felt so good to be close to him again. To feel the thud of his heart against her breast. To inhale the clean scent of his skin. To know the comfort of his touch. Everything was going to be okay. Together they would raise this baby and ease each other over the rough bumps she knew waited ahead. She smiled, then stretched out a leg that was beginning to cramp.

"Would you mind if we finished this in your bed?" she murmured. "Boomer and I have been up since six."

The lingering wisps of drowsy contentment in her voice ripped though half-healed scar tissue, leaving Max bleeding out his life.

Get it done, he told himself. "I sleep alone these days, Liza, and I like it that way."

Emotions raced over her face almost too fast to read. Surprise, hurt and finally a wary puzzlement. She moistened her lips then took a careful breath. "In other words you're throwing me out?"

"I'm asking you to leave, yes. I'd prefer not to use force."

Slowly, she untangled herself and got to her feet. Her dress was wrinkled, and her hair was a wild tangle where his hands had torn through the curls. The swell of her belly both mocked and drew him. He'd never seen a more beautiful woman. He knew he never would.

She brushed back her hair, her eyes bright as she looked at him. "Before I go tell me one thing. Why did you make love to me?"

He deadened his emotions. "Call it an experiment." He tossed the words off with a shrug.

She frowned. "To see if you could still turn me on?"

"No, to see if I could still function as a man." He glanced at his lap before giving her a mocking smile. "Obviously, I can't."

"So this was just...clinical?"

"That's about it, yeah." His voice was cold, his

eyes colder. Mac the Knife's last con. Digging deep for the stillness he needed, he kept his gaze steady on hers, the man who loved her buried behind the ice. His heart slammed against his ribs, but his cop's hands were steady enough to plant six quick rounds into a bull's-eye half a block away.

"In other words, you don't want the baby and me in your life." Her voice was quiet, but there was pride in the angle of her chin and challenge in her gaze. The woman had steel under the silk. No matter how long he lived, he would always ache whenever he thought of the life he might have had with her at his side and in his bed.

"I don't want you, no."

Slowly, so slowly it seemed to play out forever, the disbelief in her brown velvet eyes dissolved into a vivid splash of pain. "If I leave now, I won't be back," she said, her voice thick.

He accepted that with the iced-over bitterness that had been his constant companion since the day he'd forced the doctor to lay out the odds for a full recovery. "Since you've managed to scare up my home address, you might as well have your attorney send those release papers here." He felt a stab of pain in his lower back and eased into a more comfortable position. "I'd appreciate it if you simply forgot we ever knew each other."

She choked out a laugh, her hand going to her belly. "You selfish jerk," she whispered. "I won't let myself hate you, because negative emotion is bad for the baby, but I really, really want to.'' Looking every inch a Gypsy queen, she turned on her heel and walked down the hall.

Tilly was scratching at the door as she pushed it open enough to ease inside. The room was spacious, with a larger than average walk-in shower stall behind a clear glass door and a sink modified to accommodate a man in a wheelchair. Everything was sparkling white, including the towels. The only spot of color was a cushy brown rug in one corner, next to which were two bowls, one empty, one filled with water.

Spying a friendly face, the pup went into a yipping frenzy, her sharp little claws digging into Liza's bare legs as she tried to climb into her arms. A red bandana was loosely knotted around her throat instead of a collar, and her coat was shiny and sleek, as though she'd been recently brushed.

''Hi, baby,'' Liza murmured, sinking down on the closed lid of the john and lifting the little Aussie awkwardly into what remained of her lap. The pup felt heavier, as though she'd gained weight in the week since Liza had bought her. ''Have you been lonely, darling?''

The pup licked her chin, then tried to wiggle herself into a corkscrew. ''You smell like apples,'' Liza murmured, lifting her chin to avoid that little pink slurping tongue. As she did, her gaze lit on a waist-high shelf built into the shower stall. There, next to a shaving mirror and a razor, was a bottle of apple-scented shampoo.

"For a man who wants you out of his life, he's certainly been treating you like royalty," she murmured, her voice breaking. She let the tears flow, sliding down her cheeks to drop on the pup's head. When she was finally drained, she wiped her eyes with toilet paper, then hoisted Tilly awkwardly to her shoulder and left the bathroom.

The living room was empty. Next to her bag sat a shopping bag piled with doggie toys and a half-empty bag of puppy kibble. Somehow she managed to slip both over her shoulder without dropping the wiggling puppy, who kept looking around.

"Goodbye, Max," she whispered. "I wish you happiness." After one last look around, she opened the door and left.

"Sounds like the little guy is sleeping," Luke Jarrod said, removing the end of the stethoscope from Liza's tummy.

"That's because he was up all night perfecting his back flip," she said as Luke drew down her top and helped her sit up. "He has his days and nights mixed."

"Ollie did that for the first four months after we brought him home. If we hadn't had Tricia with us, I'm not sure Maddy and I would have made it."

Liza smiled. At seventeen, Maddy had given birth to Luke's daughter, then been forced to give her up for adoption. Twenty-two years later, after they'd fallen in love again, they'd been reunited with their child—and met their three-year-old grandson, who was deaf. It hadn't been easy for any of them, but they were all determined to become a family.

"How is your daughter?" she asked as he turned to make a note in the chart on the counter next to the sink.

"She has her good days and her bad days. Mace is enrolled in a special program for the deaf at Lewis and Clark, which helps." Looking more like the young bronc buster he'd once been than a grandpa, Luke turned and smiled. "Have you signed up for the Lamaze class yet?"

"Not yet." Liza swung her legs over the side of the examining table. "I put it off because…well, just because."

"Because you wanted Dad to be the coach?"

She glanced at her sandals. "Yes, but I'm over that now."

Luke closed the file and tucked his pen into the breast pocket of his starched jacket. "He came to see me last week. Made an appointment and insisted on paying the going rate for an office call. Had my usually unflappable Dorie stuttering something about testosterone overload."

"But…how did he know you were my doctor?"

Behind the horn-rim frames, his eyes crinkled. "He's a cop, so I reckon he used his cop skills."

Liza hadn't quite managed to numb her feelings, but she was working on it. "What did he want?" she demanded, her voice sharp enough to cut paper.

"Mainly to find out if you and the baby are healthy. Have to admit he'd done his homework on childbirth. Grilled me pretty good."

She felt a traitorous flurry of excitement. *Careful,* she reminded herself, reining in thoughts that wanted to race. "He actually asked about the baby?"

"Yep. Even called him Boomer. Coulda sworn he looked real proud, too."

"I doubt it. The papers my attorney sent him came back yesterday, signed in triplicate and notarized in all the right places."

"Maybe he changed his mind." He glanced at one of several family photos on his desk. It was an old one, taken when he and Maddy were teenagers, flushed with excitement of young love. "Sometimes a guy just flat-out panics at the thought of being a father and...tries to outrun his responsibility. If he's smart—and maybe lucky—he doesn't run so far he can't go home again."

Liza refused to let her hopes be raised. It was too painful when they crashed. "What did you tell him?"

"That as your doctor, I couldn't divulge anything specific about your medical condition, but as your friend I was worried about you. Said you hadn't been your usual spitfire self these past two weeks, and did he have any idea why that might be?" His mouth slanted. "I won't tell you his exact words, but he made it real clear he intended to hold me responsible if anything happened to you. Had me sweating bullets by the time he was finished with me." He leaned against the counter and crossed his arms over his chest. "Man is formidable."

"He's also stubborn and impossible."

"He wants to pay for the part of your delivery not covered by insurance. My fee, the hospital, a nurse for the first month—the works."

"I don't want his financial help. In fact, I won't accept it."

"Knowing you, I figure he's got that real clear in his head." Luke's words were flavored with a laconic amusement as he helped her from the examining table.

"He's just trying to salve his conscience."

"Maybe." His voice was suddenly dead serious. "Or maybe he's just trying to take care of you the best way he can right now."

"He threw me out of his apartment, Luke." Anger rose, a trusted friend that kept the worst of the pain at bay.

"Could be he's hurting so much he doesn't want to burden you."

"So he broke my heart instead?" She dug her

sunglasses from her tote and stabbed them on her nose before slinging the tote over her shoulder.

Luke cocked his head and studied her. "Don't take this wrong, sweet Liza, but I'm purely glad my Maddy has a more forgiving nature, or I'm damn sure I'd be looking about as ragged as Max about now."

"If he's looking ragged, it's his own fault."

Luke's gaze sliced toward the photo on his desk one more time. "Take it from a guy who knows, Liza. Hell is still hell, no matter who puts you there."

Stick a gold earring in one of Randall Torrance's droopy earlobes and he was an exact replica for the guy in the commercials, the one hawking some kind of cleaning junk. Since Max had gotten sprung from rehab almost four months ago, the big bald-headed bruiser had been his personal pain in the ass.

Best record in the whole physical therapy department for getting paras back on their feet, his doctor had assured him when he'd demanded the best. Every Monday, Wednesday and Friday 6:00 a.m. sharp Randall showed up with his portable massage table, sissy oils and a taunting grin that Max had threatened a thousand times to shove into his backbone.

"Eighty-two, eighty-three…come on, Savage, put

some muscle into it. Only wimps and old ladies quit before a hundred.''

"Screw you," Max gasped as he flopped on the bench and closed his eyes. His stomach muscles felt like wet strips of rawhide frying in the sun, and he had the mother of all headaches—a real skull-pounder.

"Been boozing again, have we, ace?''

"None of your frigging business.''

Max heard the telltale sounds of the massage table being unfolded and bit off a groan. Randall didn't just massage his muscles. He pummeled them until every hidden knot surrendered and Max was ready to commit mayhem.

"Told you when we started this that booze was what we medical types call contraindicated," the big guy muttered as he snapped the table legs into place. "Which to you thick-skulled laymen types means you can't concentrate on workin' out when your body's sweating out poison.''

"I can handle it.''

"Yeah? A month ago you could do a hundred of those sit-ups and still have juice left. You tell me it's not booze, then what the hell is it?''

It was a question Max didn't want to answer. Hell, he didn't even want to think about the past month. Purgatory would have been more fun. Especially after the cowboy doc with the steely eyes had all but accused him of making Liza so miserable it was endangering her health. And then the jerk had refused to tell him exactly what was wrong. Instead he'd given him a pamphlet on the mother's emotional outlook and how it could affect the baby. He'd gotten queasy just reading about all the things that could go wrong because of stress. He hadn't had a decent night's sleep since.

"Sure do miss that pup you had running around here a while back," Randall said, snapping open a towel. "First time since you and me started this gig I ever heard you laugh out loud, when you and her were playing keep-away with that smelly old sock of yours. Gave me a real encouraging feeling."

Max slitted his eyes to slant Randall a warning look. "You want to chat, go find a shrink," he muttered. "They get paid to listen."

Randall snorted. "Way you've been lately you could do with some quality time on the couch."

Max gave him the old one-finger salute, and Randall laughed. "Just for that you can get yourself up on this table without help from yours truly." He shot Max a "gotcha" grin before taking himself off to wash his hands.

Max clenched his jaw, sucked in a breath against the pain in his sore belly he knew was coming and sat up. Transferring to his chair was routine. One of the new skills they'd drilled into him. But other things, like pushing a grocery cart while manipulating his chair or hoisting himself those extra twelve

inches to the padded table with only the strength in
his arms, took ingenuity and persistence and so much
energy he was generally whipped by the time the sun
went down.

"You waiting for permission, ace?" Randall
asked when he reappeared.

"Shut up." Gritting his teeth, Max braced both
palms on the table and lunged. He hit the table with
his nose, and his legs dangled, but he'd made it.

"Good vault," Randall said as he straightened
Max's legs. "Not quite Olympics quality yet, but
you're getting there."

Max closed his eyes and waited for Randall's torture to begin. For the first time since he'd started
therapy, he wanted the pain to fill him the way it
had when he'd been shot. To torture his nerves into
screaming so loud he couldn't hear her telling him
she loved him.

An hour later he was drenched in sweat, and his
body was limp with exhaustion. The last thing he
heard as he slipped into a welcoming oblivion was
Liza's voice telling him she wouldn't be back.

Chapter 5

Located on what used to be the fringes of the city, Mill Works Ridge had in recent years become a hot area for young professionals, especially those who worked at Portland General, which was an easy ten-minute commute away. It was nicknamed Pill Hill by real estate types, and sector cops who worked the area considered it cushy duty because of the lower than average crime rate.

Max had been in the area only once—when he'd been a rookie getting the feel of the city. It had reminded him of the neighborhood where he'd grown up in Seattle. A nice, quiet, stable community of single-family homes in the mid-to-upper price range. A good place to raise kids.

Liza's house was the second from the corner on the second block, sandwiched between a two-story place on the south and a bungalow with bright green trim on the north. A tall white picket fence surrounded what he took to be the backyard.

Max felt his gut tighten as he propelled himself along a rough brick walk toward the gate in the fence. So far so good, he thought, feeling a little cocky that he'd gotten himself this far with minimal humiliation. Scooting crablike on his ass up the two steps from street level had been the worst of it. Lifting the chair had been awkward, but he was getting the hang of it. Facing Liza again—that was going to be the tough part.

The gate was latched from the inside. No sweat for a guy who stood six-two. Now, however, it was just another obstacle. Too sturdy to crash through, though he was tempted. Too high for him to get his arm over. His punishment for being so cocky, he decided, glaring at the frigging thing. He should have known. God never cut a sinner any slack.

Gritting his teeth, he leaned down to move one foot, then the other to the walkway. After locking the chair's brake, he leaned forward, grabbed a picket in each hand and pulled himself to a half-standing position. His head spun, but he managed to hang on long enough with one hand to get his arm over to release the latch. The gate moved a few inches, and he nearly landed on his keister before twisting his body far enough to drop into the chair.

The sound of children's laughter mingled with furious barking as he rolled himself into the backyard. As he shut the gate, he scanned the area. The yard was bigger than it had looked from the front, with a row of bright azaleas softening the inside line of the fence. Under the shade of a huge maple, a dozen yards ahead, two little girls, one with dark braids, the other with a fiery topknot that bobbed with each animated movement of her head, were playing in a large sandbox.

There was no sign of Liza, although her flowered hat sat on a glass-topped umbrella table near the screened-in porch. Two more little girls, definite cuties about five or six, sat at a small wooden picnic table on the large brick patio modeling something out of clay. A toddler in a pint-size ball cap and a tiny muscle shirt was riding a bright red trike back and forth along a cement walk leading to a back gate while Tilly ran alongside, yipping at the wheels and barking wildly.

At the edge of the patio, twin boys about the same age as the little girls were playing with a soccer ball. As Max wheeled himself closer, the little boy wearing the red shirt hauled off and booted the ball into his brother's chin. Max winced as the kid staggered, then let out a yowl and went for his brother.

A split second later the door to a screened-in

porch slammed open and Liza came bustling out, a baby dressed in diapers and a miniature T-shirt riding one hip. She looked harried and hot and so darn cute in her little white shorts and flip-flops it took his breath. Hers was still functioning as she let out a shout. "Matthew and Alexander Paxton, stop that fighting this instant!"

Neither kid paid any attention. Instead, the one in the blue shirt flipped his brother to his back, then straddled him. At least he wasn't quite pounding his brother's head into the dirt, Max saw with some relief as he shot the chair forward far enough to get a grip on the seat of the kid's pants.

The kid was still swinging as Max hoisted him in the air. "Sorry, kid, you're busted," he said, setting him down on his pint-size sneakers. Just in case, he kept a tight grip on the kid's waistband.

"He started it!" the youngster shouted, his face turning pink.

"Did not!" replied the one in red, scrambling to his feet, fists ready. "You hit me wif the ball."

"Hey, guys, I saw the whole thing," Max interjected in his best traffic-cop tone. "It was an accident. Nobody's fault."

Two identical pairs of startled blue eyes stared at him with an equal mix of curiosity and belligerence. "Who are you?" the one in red demanded.

Max hid a smile. The kid had moxie. "Max. Who are you?"

"Alex. He's Matt."

Matt tugged at the hold Max had on his shorts, his brows drawn together over a blunt little nose. Max would lay odds the kid wouldn't make it much past puberty before that nose had a crook or two in it. "You promise not to swing on your brother if I let you go?"

Matt nodded, then glanced past Max's shoulder. "Hi, Liza, Max is here," he said with a bright-eyed grin before he and his brother ran off to resume their soccer game.

Steeling himself, Max turned his chair to face her. During the melee, she'd made her way down the two steps to the patio and stood watching him while the plump, barefoot baby on her hip eyed him with huge, innocent eyes the color of milk chocolate.

"Detective Savage," she said with well-bred politeness, more for the children's benefit than his, he suspected.

Max reminded himself that he was a veteran peace officer with two medals for valor in his service jacket. Hell, he'd faced more bad dudes than he could remember. Guys with knives, guys who carried Uzis in their pockets as if they were cigarettes. No way was Max Savage intimidated by a five-foot-something female carrying a baby. Right?

Right, he told himself, trying on a smile. "Nice place you got here. Very...homey." He flicked a glance at the sturdy wooden jungle gym surrounded by a cushy bed of sand. Tiny footprints had churned the sand into little waves. "Great place for kids."

"That *is* the idea."

She narrowed her gaze and compressed her lips until the softness he'd been enjoying disappeared. It didn't take a trained investigator to figure out he wasn't going to get back in her good graces without groveling. Payback was a bitch, all right.

"You're ticked off, and I don't blame you." He swallowed hard, then said the words he'd come to say. "I behaved like a jerk."

She lifted one finely arched brow. "And your point is?"

He didn't know whether to hug her or throttle her. "I'd like to make it up to you."

She shifted the baby to the other hip, then smoothed his wispy blond hair with a gentle hand. He cooed something, then popped his thumb in his mouth and sucked. "Luke told me you offered to pay for my delivery."

Luke? It took him a beat to realize the fast jolt of primitive emotion surging through his head was jealousy. It made him vulnerable, and he set his jaw against it. "I have the money, Liza, if that's what's worrying you."

"This isn't about money, it's about guilt." Though she kept her expression calm, her gaze pinned him in his chair. "Or more precisely, absolution. A basically decent man purging his conscience of a black mark.''

He stiffened. Blood surged to his face and seared his skin. The temper that had earned him a pot full of grief before he'd learned to control it struggled to explode. He took a breath and forced it back. ''I'll accept the decent part, though I'd prefer it without the qualifier. The rest you can stuff, Ms. Vargas.''

He thought he saw her mouth quirk before it flattened. ''Whatever your intention, you're off the hook.''

It was worse than he figured—and he'd had some rough moments going over possible scenarios in his head. To buy time, he leaned back and gave the place another once-over. The twins had stopped kicking the ball and were playing with Tilly, who was nipping at their ears. The kid on the trike had picked something off the sidewalk, and as Max watched he popped it into his mouth and began to chew. From where Max sat it had looked like a wad of discarded bubble gum, but it might have been a bug. Max averted his gaze and hoped to God it wasn't a bug.

''Uh, don't take this wrong, okay, but it looks like you could use someone to act as playground monitor.''

Her long lashes flickered. There was a little frown wrinkle between her eyes, the same one he'd seen when she'd been flat on her back in the snow, the thunder of the avalanche still ringing in their ears, her mouth open in a little O of shock. He'd had an instant desire to kiss her then. He had that same need now. After fifteen sleepless nights and miserable days, he'd stopped pretending he didn't care deeply about her. Or that he wouldn't give half of what was left of his life to be whole for her again.

"Two weeks ago you couldn't wait to get rid of me," she said in a voice that scared him because it was so flat.

"I could give you a bunch of excuses, some of 'em pathetic enough to wring that soft heart of yours, but bottom line, I couldn't handle all the things I was feeling." He drew a hard breath and forced his gaze to remain steady on hers. "A cop who works undercover learns to stuff his feelings deep. No excuse, just fact."

Her gaze flickered. "And what are you feeling now?"

Panic hit him right square below the belt. "Shame," he admitted, his jaw tight. "Worry." He let his gaze linger on her tummy. "Pride."

She closed her eyes, her mouth suddenly achingly vulnerable. "Max, I can't go through another scene. Tell me exactly what you want from me."

"Two things. First, for you to forgive me."

She studied him, then smiled. "All right."

He realized he'd been holding his breath and let it out slowly. "Number two, I'd really like to help out. Just until the baby's born and you're back on your feet."

"And then?"

Max steeled himself to keep his gaze on hers. "After the baby's born, I'd like to contribute to his support." He put enough firmness in his tone to make the point nonnegotiable. The disappointment in her eyes sliced deep.

"By sending a check every month?"

He nodded. "And setting up a college fund."

She frowned, took a breath. "And when your son graduates," she asked softly. "Will you be there to congratulate him?"

A part of him ached, the part that had always known he would turn a corner someday and plow into the right woman. The woman who would fit into that spot in his heart reserved for family and home and...forever. The day the docs had told him his chances of walking again were between "lousy" and "forget it", he'd sealed off that part of him for good.

"I know what you want to hear, Liza, and I could do a damned good job of lying to you. But I... respect you too much to run a con on you again."

Something changed in her eyes. A light he hadn't recognized suddenly went out, he realized, his chest suddenly tight. *Please understand,* he wanted to beg. Except he was done begging. The pathetic pleading he'd done with God in the dark hours of the night hadn't gotten feeling in his legs, had it? Or given him his ability to make love.

She shifted the baby again. After a few hiccuping whimpers, the little one puckered up his face and let out a real wail. Liza jiggled him, and he found his thumb again.

"I've started putting you out of my life, Max. I admit it's been...difficult, but it's necessary. I can't...I won't open myself up again no matter how much..." She faltered, took a breath, and her stomach...shifted.

Panic shot through him, and he wheeled closer. "God, sweetheart, are you...is he, uh, trying to get out?" As soon as he realized how lame he sounded, he scowled. "Tumbling practice, right?" he muttered, his face turning hot.

Her look softened. "I think he's ticked off because he's running out of room."

The panic eased, leaving him a little shaken. The books didn't mention how far the uterus could stretch without popping. And Liza had such little bones. "Does it hurt?" he couldn't help asking.

She smiled. "No, it feels comforting—except when he does it at 2:00 a.m."

Max had a quick image of her tucked into bed wearing a sexy little wisp of nothing much. When he realized it was *his* bed he was imagining, and *his* arms holding her close while his hand caressed her tummy, he ached. "I guess that'd be a problem, at that." He managed to speak, his voice a little rusty.

"Want to feel?" she said, moving closer.

Though he knew he shouldn't, he couldn't refuse. Just once, he told himself as he pressed a palm to her tummy. At first he felt nothing. And then whap! The kid gave him a good one.

"What do you know?" he said before his throat clamped shut. The feeling that moved through him was beyond his ability to describe. Part exhilaration, part awe—and a longing so strong it scared him. When he realized he was only a muscle twitch away from pulling her into his lap and never letting go, he pulled back. All the way back.

"Look, this was a dumb idea." He grated the words out, wheeling backward to give him room to turn. "Forget I bothered you. You've obviously got things handled and—"

He was cut short by another earsplitting bellow, this time from a toddler. Max whipped his head around to find the kid trying to push one of the twins—Alex, Max decided—off the red trike.

"Mine, mine, mine!" the toddler shouted. Or at least that was what Max thought he said.

"Alex, get off of B.J.'s trike!" Liza ordered.

Alex offered her a belligerent look. "He wasn't riding it."

"That's enough, Alexander. I warned you the next time you tormented B.J. you'd get a time-out, and now you're getting just that.'' Before Max could do more than blink, she plopped the baby on his lap. "Here, take care of Ollie while I tend to this."

Automatically, he grabbed the kid, then felt like an idiot. "Oh, no, you don't!" Max flinched as the kid clipped him a good one right on the jaw, then let out an earsplitting yowl.

Liza burst out laughing. "Way to go, Oliver! I couldn't have done better myself."

"Liza—"

"Suck it up, Savage," she said with grin. "You asked for a job. Well, now you've got one."

Chapter 6

Liza had finished settling the older children for their regular after-lunch nap and was returning to the living room to get Ollie when she heard him gurgling a laugh. When she'd left, Ollie and Max had been playing with the baby's oversize plastic blocks on the soft rug covering her beloved cherry floors. Now Max was sitting with his back propped against the sofa, one knee flexed. Still laughing, Ollie was curled into the crook of Max's brawny arm, his rapt brown eyes fixed on Max's face, listening while Max spun him a story about Lobo Jack Coon and his gang of bad-ass bikers.

Your daddy is a rogue, she told Boomer silently, stroking his restless little foot. Only Max would weave a child's story around a drug raid, she thought, then spin it out as sweetly as any lullaby. When Max got to the part about the best way to deflect a knife thrust, the baby's tiny eyelashes fluttered closed. By the time Max's voice had dropped to a hypnotic rumble, Ollie was snuggled against his big hard chest, looking blissfully content as he sucked earnestly on his thumb. It was a charming picture, the sweetest of moments. A strong man in love with a little boy who looked at him with total trust.

Oh, Max, can't you see how it could be? How can you look into those beautiful trusting eyes and not see the man you really are?

Liza's vision blurred, and she forced herself to look away until the tears were gone and a smile was in place. Max glanced up as she left the shadows of the hall and padded across the bare floor. "That's the most outrageous bedtime story I've ever heard," she whispered as she bent to lift the sleepy little boy into her arms.

"Worked, though," Max whispered, and the hard mouth that had been so controlled for so long relaxed into a half-smile, revealing the shallow crease that added a touch of the devil to features that were too bold and irregular to be considered handsome.

"Did you really slice off Lobo Jack's ear?" she asked, tucking Ollie against her hip.

He challenged her with a laconic look. "What do you think?"

Drawing her brows together, she studied the planes and shadows of a face that could be both harsh and tender. "I think I don't want to know," she said finally.

"Good choice."

She let his steely gaze hold hers for a moment longer before grinning. "You do lethal really well, Savage, but I've seen you playing dolls with the girls, remember? I know just how soft that heart of yours really is." She patted his head, letting her hand linger for a moment before carrying Ollie to his crib in her bedroom.

Max was stretched out on the floor when she returned, his eyes closed, his mouth grim. On the days when he had early morning therapy he talked less and moved slower, as though his muscles were protesting. A time or two she'd caught a quick flash of pain tightening his bronzed features when he moved. After the first time, when he'd nearly taken her head off for suggesting he take the day off, she'd kept her compassion to herself. Instead, she'd been the one to admit to a desperate need for a rest when the children were safely tucked up for an hour. After studying her face with those suspicious cop's eyes that had her backbone shivering, he'd allowed himself to do the same.

Stubborn, proud and difficult, she thought, smiling

as the adjectives piled up. He was also funny, sweet and incredibly brave—when he wasn't testing her patience. How was a woman supposed to fall out of love with a guy when he kept sneaking under her guard? she muttered under her breath as she went into the kitchen to pour herself a glass of milk. She had just taken the carton from the fridge when the phone rang. She lunged, afraid it would wake Max. Her voice was breathless as she answered.

There was a momentary pause before an abrupt male voice commanded, "This is Fletcher. Get me Savage."

Outraged, Liza stiffened. "He's—" She broke off when she placed the name. Max's superior officer. Somehow it didn't seem politic to tell the abrupt man on the other end that his leanest, meanest undercover type was taking a nap. "One moment, please. I'll get him."

Max hadn't moved. As soon as he heard her footsteps, he opened his eyes. "Telephone," she said, bending to hand him the portable. He waited until she had left the room before speaking into the receiver.

In the kitchen Liza poured her milk, drank it and rinsed the glass, then poured Max a cup of coffee and carried it into the living room. Conversation over, he was sitting with one arm resting on a bent knee, his face hard and closed, staring at one of her father's watercolors hanging on the wall opposite.

"I thought you'd like some coffee," she said quietly.

His lashes flickered, and he grated something she took to be thanks. She'd intended to hand him the mug, but one look at his face had her setting it on a nearby end table instead. She waited, but when he continued to stare at the turbulent seascape, she took a chance and settled herself next to him. "I used to date a boy named Fletcher once. He wore thick glasses and played the piccolo. I loved him for his mind—and his '57 T-bird."

She thought his mouth might have quirked. "Wrong Fletcher."

She grinned. "I kinda figured it was."

He kept his gaze on the seascape, but she had a feeling he wasn't seeing it. She felt a frisson of foreboding and braced herself. "Captain called to give me a heads-up on the brass's decision," he said finally, his voice as flat and cold as a blade. "As of the first of next month, I'm out. Officially retired."

She heard the despair buried beneath the hard-bitten words and ached. "There's nothing you can do?"

His jaw hardened, then relaxed marginally. "Already did it. The union rep fought all the way to the top. Decision's final."

Oh, my dear, I know it hurts, she thought, longing to hold him. "If I say I'm as sorry as I can be, will you bite my head off?'' she asked in the gently teasing tone he'd tolerated at other tense times.

His mouth moved. ''Probably.''

''I had a hunch you'd say that.'' She slipped off her sandals, then stretched out her legs and leaned against the sofa, her shoulder close enough to his to feel the tension radiating from him.

''That's my favorite picture of Daddy's.'' Her father had painted the sea right at dawn, with the sun bursting over the horizon and the waves reaching toward the retreating night. The scene was timeless and powerful and mystical. ''The few critics he allowed to see it said it was his best. It was also his last, which makes it even more valuable. The Museum of Modern Art offered him six figures for it.''

His lashes flickered. ''Nice nest egg.''

''My heirs might think so, but I'll never part with it.'' She smiled as she let herself remember. ''It's the view from our summer place on Martha's Vineyard. He painted it the year I turned thirteen. Two weeks after we returned home, a propane heater in his studio blew up, blinding him in both eyes.''

He flinched, but the look he gave her was hooded. ''That must have been rough.''

''It was, for all of us. It got better after Mama bought him a tub of clay and bullied him into trying his hand at sculpting. Turned out he was an even better sculptor than watercolorist. I saw one of his pieces at the Tate when I was there.''

His mouth slanted. "What a surprise, another inspirational story to buck up the cripple when he's down." His deliberate cruelty went in so smoothly it took her a stunned moment to realize he'd meant to stab deep.

"I admire my father more than any other man I've ever known," she said quietly. "He's not a big man or physically powerful. He's never faced a man like Lobo Jack, but he has more grit, more determination and heart than you'll ever have."

His face closed up, and his eyes became dangerous. "I'm sure you're right," he said quietly before reaching for his chair.

Drawing up her legs until they were snug against her belly, she leaned forward and closed her eyes. When she opened them, he was gone.

The flowers arrived while Liza, Raine and Maddy were watching the twins and Maddy's grandson, Mace, take turns sliding belly-first into the wading pool at the bottom of the jungle gym.

A dozen shimmering white orchids with deep purple throats.

"Wow," Raine said in an awed tone. "Have you ever seen anything more gorgeous? Like shimmering silk."

Liza smiled as she lifted them free of their tissue-paper nest. "They must be from my dad. He sounded worried when I talked to him last night."

"There's a card." Maddy leaned forward to pluck the tiny white envelope from the elegant silver and gold florist's box.

Still smiling, Liza laid the flowers gently on the table before taking the card. "Daddy wants me to come home to have the baby, but I..." Her voice stuttered to a stop, her jaw gaping as she stared at the backhanded scrawl. Somehow she knew, even before she read the words, that Max had written them.

I'm sorry, he'd written without bothering with a greeting or even her name. But it was the words that followed that had her heart speeding. *Can we start over?*

The kids were already in full gallop when Max arrived shortly before ten on Monday. The sky was clear, and the sun was hot on his skin. But inside he was icy with the kind of gut-sick frustration he'd come to associate with a bust gone wrong.

"Hey Max, look at me!" Alex yelled from one of the uppermost branches of the apple tree at the north edge of the patio. "I'm George of the Jungle."

"Uh-uh, *I'm* George of the Jungle!" Matt shouted, scrambling upward like an agile little monkey.

Max muttered a ripe curse as he wheeled across the grass toward the tree. Climbing any of the trees, even the small ones, was strictly forbidden, one of Liza's inflexible rules.

"Matt, Alex, get down from there now!" he ordered in the tone he'd once used to freeze bad guys in their tracks. It didn't faze the twins, who were engaged in a shoving match a good six feet above his head.

"Alex, stop—" But it was too late. With one roundhouse swing, Alex sent his brother toppling headfirst off the branch. Max braced himself, catching Matt against his chest. One knobby knee whacked him hard in the ribs, knocking the breath from his lungs for a couple of painful seconds before he managed to wheeze in air. Matt's arms went around his neck, and he held tight. One look at his white little face told Max the tongue-lashing he'd planned to lay on extra heavy would be pretty much overkill. At least for the time being.

"Down, Alex," he ordered, directing a stern look overhead. "Now." He watched for a moment to make sure the boy didn't falter. Satisfied that the kid was part monkey, he turned his attention to the silent hellion bunched into a ball of scared little boy on his lap.

"You okay?" he asked, ducking his head so that he could catch Matt's eye.

The boy gave a quick nod, then sucked in a breath, his gaze riveted on something behind Max's back.

"Uh-oh, Aunt Liza's mad," he muttered, burying his face against Max's shoulder.

"I sincerely hope not," Max muttered, turning his chair.

For a lady who was only seven weeks from delivery she was moving pretty fast. Close enough so that he could see her eyes, he realized she was also terrified, but controlling it. The kids in her care would never see the raw fear trembling behind the calm surface of her dark dreamer's eyes. It was the same with cops, he realized. The people they served rarely saw the carnage that existed behind the filthy walls and dark shadows of the mean streets.

"He's fine, just shaken," he said as her gaze met his. It hit him then, a fast shiver of surprise. She was wearing an orchid in her hair.

"You are both going to lose ice-cream privileges today and tomorrow," she told the twins sternly, fisting her hands on her hips. Sunlight shimmered in her hair and burnished her skin to a patina of palest gold. It occurred to him that he'd never been more aware of a woman, or more intrigued by the contradictions he kept discovering.

"Who wants dumb old ice cream anyway?" Alex declared before racing toward the sandbox.

"Yeah, who wants ice cream anyway?" Matt echoed, scrambling to follow.

Max watched him go, wondering what to do next. The orchid was a good sign. Still... He cleared his throat. "Hell of a way to start the week," he said, risking a look at her.

"I was looking out the kitchen window. It happened so fast. If you hadn't been there, he could have been seriously hurt." She took a shaky breath and hugged herself. "I never would have forgiven myself."

He reached up to take one of her hands. Her skin was icy, and he pressed it between his palms to warm her. That, at least, he could manage. "Liza, it wasn't your fault." He put enough of an edge in his voice to drive home the point. "You can't be everywhere at once."

She glanced at the leafy canopy. "Maybe I should have them all cut down," she murmured before meeting his gaze.

It was the same every time he saw her, that fast little jolt of sexual heat, followed by a slower burning desire to be close to her. Now, this minute, he wanted to strip her out of her clothes and explore every sleek, soul-stirring inch of her. And then he wanted to wrap her in his arms and grow old with her, watching their son grow strong and sturdy and brave, like his mom. When he felt his throat close, he realized he was staring and dropped his gaze.

"Thank you for the orchids," she said quietly. "And the apology."

He took a breath and glanced up, his gut twisting into a hard knot. "I was a cop for twelve years. It's all I ever wanted to be. Without the badge, I don't know who I am." He risked a smile. "Not that that's an excuse for behaving like...uh, a self-pitying wimp."

Amusement lighted her eyes, and he felt like shouting. "You'd just had bad news, so I'll spot you that one."

He laughed. "I appreciate that." He took a chance and pulled her into his lap. She gave a little sigh and put her arm around his shoulder. He was so tense his muscles felt like granite. "I meant what I said, Liza. I'd like to start over."

Her brow furrowed. "Start over from where?"

"My first preference would be the split second before you stopped my car in the hospital parking lot. If anyone else unloaded on you like that, I'd kill 'em."

It was the rough edge to his voice that got to her. She suspected Max wasn't a man who apologized easily, and yet he was asking her to forgive him for being less than perfect. Suddenly she was ashamed of herself.

"I would probably forgive you if you kissed me," she murmured, smoothing his windblown hair from his temple.

His eyes clouded, and she braced herself to accept his refusal. "I've taken worse punishment, and survived," he murmured before touching his mouth to hers.

She melted, twisting to get closer. He groaned and then his tongue was sliding over her lower lip. She felt herself softening, yearning. Her breasts swelled, ached, and she rubbed against him. Caught in his arms, she felt a shudder pass through him. With another strangled groan, he pulled back, easing his grip on her. Reeling a little, still dazed, she drew a shaky breath. "Any time you care to apologize again, do feel free," she said, her voice a little sultry.

"I'll keep that in mind." He smiled, then froze. "Whoa, I think I've just been kicked." His gaze found hers, his eyes suddenly vulnerable. "Little guy packs a wallop."

"You should be around at night. I think he's taken up judo."

His jaw tightened, and his arms relaxed. He glanced toward the house. "B.J.'s chewing on Tilly's rawhide bone again," he said pointedly. "Should I handle it, or do you want to do the honors this time?"

"Your turn, I think," she said with a sigh that had nothing to do with B.J.'s fondness for dog bones. Averting his gaze, he helped her to stand, then turned and wheeled toward the patio. Two steps forward and one step back, she thought as she crossed to the sandbox to check on the Randolph sisters.

Chapter 7

"Are you and Aunt Liza gonna get married like Uncle Luke and Aunt Maddy?" Shelby MacAuley asked as Max heaved himself up the steps to the sunroom. It was lunchtime, and Liza was inside fixing sandwiches. Because rain had been threatening for the past hour, she'd decided to eat inside.

"None of your business, squirt," he told her with a grin.

"Mommy said not to ask rude questions," Tory chided her sister as she waited to push Max's chair up after him.

"I like weddings, especially the cake," Shelby declared stubbornly as she stepped back to let Max scoot over the threshold.

"People don't get married just so they can have cake," Tory said with all the disdain of a soon-to-be first grader.

Max hid a smile as he grasped the frame of the chair and prepared to pull himself up. Tory hovered behind him, her small hands on the handles. After watching him get in and out of the chair a few times, she'd started holding the chair steady. It had made him edgy as hell—until Liza explained that helping out was Tory's way of showing affection. Just as she helped Liza by fetching and carrying, often without being asked. After that he let the little sweetheart do whatever she wanted.

"You ready, snooks?" He tossed the question over his shoulder.

She giggled. "Ready."

He tightened his grip and heaved. The chair flew backward, and he fell hard, banging his elbow and wrenching one shoulder. It hurt like hell and he turned the air blue. Liza came running, a half dozen youngsters hard on her heels, all talking at once. Tory started to cry.

"I'm s-sorry, Max. I f-forgot the brake." Tears ran down her cheeks, and she bit her lip so hard Max was afraid she'd break the skin.

"Hey, snooks, it's no big deal," he said, making an effort to keep the pain out of his voice.

"B-but you fell real hard and it's my f-fault." The

misery swimming in her eyes was almost more than he could handle.

"Nah, I'm just clumsy. Here, I'll show you." It cost him to move, but he managed to pull up his shirt and show her the saucer-size bruise on his side. "Got that when I fell out of bed yesterday morning. Landed on one of the weights I'd been lifting."

"Does it hurt?" Tory asked, bending for a closer look.

"A little, especially when I sneeze."

"I fell outta bed once." Chloe chimed up, pushing forward to inspect the vivid blue and purple splotch. "It didn't hurt, though. Daddy said that was 'cause I fell on my head and that's the hardest part of me."

"Daddy's right," Liza said before slipping an arm around Tory's shoulders. "Honey, Max meant it when he said it wasn't your fault." She smiled before glancing his way. "Isn't that right, Max?"

"You bet."

Tory sniffed, her mouth turned down in a forlorn little curve. "Would a hug make it better?"

"Can't think of anything I need more."

Looking a little sheepish, Tory stepped forward to wind her arms around his neck and squeeze hard. "All better now?" she asked anxiously when she drew back.

"Good as it gets, snooks. Thanks."

"You're welcome," she said in a solemn voice

before her smile burst again. "I won't forget the brake again, I promise."

"Okay, you guys," Liza ordered, clapping her hands. "Into the family room, all of you. Lunch is ready. Are you really okay?" Liza asked in a low tone when they were alone.

"Fine," he replied, feeling like a frigging exhibit in the zoo. "You tend to the kids. I'll tend to myself."

Using his chair as a support, she crouched, her hand automatically brushing his hair the way he'd seen her do with Alex Paxton this morning when he'd skinned a knee. Close to his limit, he caught her wrist, stilling her hand.

"Max, if you need help—"

"What I *need* is for you to leave me the..." He bit down hard on the foul obscenity, then took a ragged breath. "Liza, this is hard enough as it is," he admitted through a tight jaw. "Don't make it worse by bleeding pity all over me."

Hurt staggered into her eyes for only an instant before her chin came up and her mouth firmed. "Sorry, I thought I was dealing with an adult." She shot the words at him before stalking out.

"Well, hell," he muttered, reaching for his chair.

"Isn't Max hungry?" Alex asked before giving in to a huge yawn.

"If he is, he'll eat," Liza told him as she drew

the blinds in the spare bedroom where the little ones were settling onto the colorful floor mats for a nap.

"He missed the chocolate pudding," Lily said as she drew up her knees and snuggled with her much patched blanket. Because she couldn't sleep without it, Prudy had cut it in two so that Liza could keep one piece at her place.

"Max really, really likes chocolate pudding," Morgana Paxton murmured, her sleepy eyes anxious as she watched Liza walk toward the door.

"I know, punkin." Liza left the door open an inch or so, then stood listening. Other than a few coughs, a couple of whispered words and a deep sigh or two, the munchkins seemed content to drift off without the usual fuss.

Small favors, she thought as she returned to the kitchen to dispose of the lunch dishes. Five minutes and a satisfactory number of slammed cupboard doors later, she felt calm again.

Humming to herself, she took out the bag of puppy chow, then frowned. Tilly was usually nipping at her toes by now, begging for her lunch. Come to think of it, she couldn't remember the pup coming in with the kids earlier. No doubt the little dickens was asleep under the patio table, she told herself as she hurried through the utility room and opened the door to the deck.

Max was on the floor where she'd left him, his back propped against one of the fat, squishy beanbag chairs the kids loved. Tilly was lying next to him, her nose propped on one of his thighs. At the sound of the door opening, both looked at her. Tilly thumped her tail, her little tan eyebrows wiggling in greeting. Max glared, his face strained, his jaw tight.

"Napping, are we?" she asked, lifting her eyebrows.

"Real cute, Liza. I hear there's a new comedy club opening downtown. They need comediennes like you." Tilly nuzzled his hand, which somehow found the spot in back of the floppy ears that melted her puppy bones.

Liza let her breath out slowly. *Careful,* she cautioned herself. *Even the hardest steel has a breaking point.* "So, are you planning to stay there until you starve to death?" she inquired with deliberate unconcern. "Or just until hell freezes over?"

He snorted a laugh, and some of the harsh tension eased out of his face. "Don't tell Tory, okay? But I twisted the hell out of my shoulder when I fell. I can't put any weight on my arm."

"Maybe I could lift—"

"Forget it!" Max had been through some dark times since he'd opened his eyes in the ICU and realized he hurt damn near everywhere but his legs. But this, he decided as he saw the worry escalate in her eyes, was right up there with the worst of times.

"There has to be a way," she mused before pursing her lips in a half frown, half pout. "Wait! To-day's Friday, right?"

"Yeah, so?"

"So Luke takes every Friday afternoon off. He and Maddy were going on a picnic, but it's raining." Before he could protest—which he decided was just as well, given his present mood—she was out the door and hustling across the grass to the gate dividing her property from the Jarrods.

Max leaned back and closed his eyes. He had a feeling he was going to really, really hate the next few minutes.

"Can't say you're as heavy as the broncs I used to bust, but you got the same mad-as-hell look in your eye," Jarrod drawled as he slung Max's good arm around his shoulder and lifted him into his chair.

Max grunted his thanks before reaching down to position his feet. His head reeled at the sudden pain shooting through his shoulder, but he made himself get it done. Jaw tight, he eased into a sitting position, then leaned back. He counted it as a small mercy that Liza had gone to change out of her wet clothes and hadn't witnessed the worst of his humiliation.

"I'm no orthopod, but I think it's a fair bet that shoulder's gonna get worse before it gets better. Probably help if you can alternate hot and cold for the first twenty-four hours. Take some pain meds if you have any."

"I'll manage."

"Figured you would. While you're managing, though, it'd be best if you could keep that shoulder as immobile as you can. A sling would help, too. Take the weight off the stressed muscles."

Max glanced at the chair. "Yeah, well, that's kinda tough to do under the circumstances."

"Last year I was on the circuit, I took a bad spill. Spent nine weeks in the hospital, a year in a chair. First week I looked like a drunk driver before I figured it out."

Max was so used to deflecting sympathy it took him a couple of seconds to realize Jarrod had simply accepted him as he was without seeing what he wasn't. Grateful, and more than a little relieved, he held out his good hand. "I appreciate the help. I owe you one."

"I'll keep that in mind," Jarrod said as they shook. At the door he paused to give Max a thoughtful look, the kind Max had seen too many times in the last seven and a half months. More often than not bad news followed. It made him wary of all medics. Jarrod, in particular, had him shoring up his guard. To get the information he'd needed about Liza, he'd had to show Jarrod a part of himself he kept hidden from damn near everyone else in his life. The part that Liza had seen so clearly. It made him feel vulnerable.

"I'd consider it a real big favor if you could get

Liza to work less and rest more.'' Jarrod held up a hand that looked too powerful to belong to a medical type. "And no, she's not in trouble...yet."

Max felt his gut tighten. "*Yet* being what exactly?"

"Let's just say the light is on over here way too late at night. She says she's sleeping okay, but I have a hunch she's doing more worrying than sleeping."

Max buried the chilling alarm beneath a Mac the Knife scowl. "You got any idea what she's worrying about?"

"Delivery, I suspect. Last visit, she tap-danced around a lot of subjects, but she kept on coming back to that one."

Max narrowed his gaze. Jarrod didn't seem like the chatty type, so he had to figure the doctor had a point to make. Max decided to help him along. "Any particular reason she should worry?"

"Not so far, although I'd be a lot happier if she'd settle on a Lamaze coach and get herself enrolled in class." His mouth twitched. "Last I heard she was hoping it would be you. If you're not fixing to volunteer, be best to tell her now."

Max raked his hand through his hair. "This coach thing, how do I know I won't make it worse for her?"

"Not being there, that's what will make it worse." Jarrod gave him a hard look before walking out into the rain.

Chapter 8

Raine called at five to say she'd gotten tied up and would be late picking up the twins and their sloe-eyed big sister, Morgana, so Liza offered to feed them—and Max, too, if he'd keep the twins occupied. It was the first time she'd asked him to stay late. By the time Raine raced in to hustle her three into the car for a fast trip to the airport to meet their daddy's plane it was nearly seven.

"Poor Morgan. The twins have stored up two weeks of 'guess whats' for him." She laughed as she brushed back a wisp of hair. In deference to the heat, she'd coiled the thick mane into a haphazard coil at the top of her head. Here and there rebel wisps floated around her face, giving her a sultry eroticism that teased him almost to the point of pain. "Want some frozen yogurt? It's cookie-dough chip."

"I'll stick with coffee," Max said, then sucked in a breath when she leaned down to kiss him. Desire exploded, a hot blast in the gut. "I knew this was a mistake," he said as she danced away to open the fridge.

"I'll be good." She tossed the words over her shoulder as she retrieved the yogurt from the freezer. "You said you had nieces and nephews?" Liza asked as she scooped.

He hesitated, then nodded. He'd talked a lot about his family in those three days they'd spent together in the ski patrol hut. Mostly because Liza had a way of drawing him out. "Two nephews, two nieces. My older sister, Mary Janice, just had twin girls. The boys belong to my big brother, Pete."

"The brother who's the hotshot cardiac surgeon in San Francisco?" she asked before attacking the yogurt with a soup spoon.

"Used to be. He's in Seattle now, in the same office with my father and uncle."

She shot him a curious look. "Just how many doctors are there in your family?"

"Six, so far. Emma, the baby, graduates next year. She's planning to go into practice with Mom and M.J. when she finishes her residency."

"In other words you're the only rebel in the family."

"Like the man says, it's a tough job, but someone has to do it."

Her soft laughter warmed him in ways she'd never know. When she teased him about his frequent bouts of clumsiness, he didn't hurt quite so much. He didn't want to think about his life when she was no longer in it. He shifted restlessly, suddenly tired. "Liza, I haven't told my family about Boomer."

Liza concentrated on scraping the last of the yogurt from the carton. Slow and easy, she told herself. Let him deal with his demons in his own way. "Do you intend to?" she asked before lifting the spoon to her mouth. Glancing up, she caught a quick burst of heat in his eyes before his lashes came down.

"I don't know," he admitted, those powerful shoulders terribly rigid. "It's complicated."

Liza forced herself to look at him. The lines in his face seemed deeper. "I'd like him to know his father's family." She hesitated, then added softly, "Unless you don't want them to know me."

"My folks would be crazy about you both." Imagining the uproar in the big old house where he'd grown up had him smiling a little. "My mom would cry and then insist on taking you shopping for all kinds of baby junk. Dad would hug you till your ribs crack, then take Boomer to the country club to show him off to his golf buddies. As for my brothers, they'd have you suckered into a game of basketball before you'd even caught your breath."

"Sounds wonderful," she said, her breath catching. "And you? Would you be there, too?"

His jaw flexed, and his eyes went very dark. "Liza, you'll find someone—"

"To love me the way I deserve to be loved. Yeah, I know." She got to her feet, her back complaining as it took her weight. "I don't want someone, Max. I want you. But since that doesn't seem to be an option, I think I'd better start getting used to life without you."

"Liza—"

"It's all right, Max," she said before carrying her bowl to the sink. "I'm a big girl. My parents raised me to be independent, and I like it that way." She opened the dishwasher, methodically stowing the dishes one by one. "So thank you for your help with the children. Thank you for offering money. As of this moment all debts are paid. Boomer and I will take it from here, just the two of us."

"What the hell's that supposed to mean?"

She picked up a towel, then threw it down. "It means I'm asking you to leave and not come back."

His jaw dropped, then he turned white. "I said I was going to see you through this and I will."

"I don't want you. I don't need you. And most of all I won't let you think of my son as an obligation." She turned on her heel and stalked out. By the time she reached her bedroom she was shaking. This time she was the one who slammed the door.

* * *

Forty minutes later, after a good cry and a sooth-ing bubble bath, she was turning back the duvet on her bed when the door opened and he rolled toward her. His hair was tousled, as though he'd worked out some of his frustration by running those strong fin-gers though the shaggy thickness, and his shoulders were ramrod straight.

"I thought I told you to leave," she said, taking refuge in the anger that was wearing pathetically thin. Unfortunately it was all she had at the moment.

"I'm staying." He rolled to the other side of the bed and jerked back the covers. The street-cop ex-pression on his face dared her to object.

She folded her arms with as much dignity as her burgeoning stomach would permit and sent him a seething look. "What do you think you're doing?"

He met her look for look. "What the hell does it look like? I'm going to bed."

Surprise rendered her mute for an instant before she got her tongue unstuck. "Now wait a minute, Max Savage. This is my bed and my house. No one sleeps in my bed without my invitation."

He positioned his chair close to the bed, then set the brake. Only then did he glance up. "That's my child you're carrying, as you have insisted on re-minding me at least once a day for seven weeks now. According to Jarrod, you haven't picked a Lamaze coach, you're not sleeping well, and your mood is somewhere south of snippy, all of which are potentially harmful to the baby.''

She felt a stab of alarm before she reasoned it away. If Luke were truly worried, he would have said something. "I've picked a coach—"

"Yeah, me." He was daring her again.

She opened her mouth, then closed it. "Now wait a minute—"

His sigh was long-suffering. "Liza, I'm tired. My shoulder hurts like hell. Worse, it's a good bet I'm going to make a pathetic fool out of myself getting out of this chair and into this bed you're protecting so fiercely, so if it's all the same to you, I'd just as soon wrangle this out tomorrow."

She saw it then, the fatigue layered in the lines bracketing his mouth and furrowing his brow. The pain was there, too, visible when she looked past her own wildly swinging emotions. He insisted she needed help, but so did he. More, she suspected, than she had the experience to fully comprehend. Help she longed to give him. The question was, how much help could he tolerate before withdrawing completely?

"This isn't finished," she said, careful to keep her affronted look in place. "But you're right. It's better if we discuss it rationally, like two mature adults who respect one another."

He shot her a dark look before bending to slip off his moccasins.

"Are you planning to sleep in your clothes?" A jittery excitement was growing inside her at the thought of sharing a bed, even a celibate one, with him.

"I've done it before. Why? You worried I'll get your sheets dirty?"

"If you do, you'll wash them," she muttered, turning to plump her pillow.

"I can do that, too." With a fluid motion of muscle and lethal power, he stripped off the faded red T-shirt, baring the strong, sun-bronzed chest she'd mapped with her mouth and her hands a dozen times. Her mouth went dry, and desire burst in all the lonely places where he'd filled her.

He draped the shirt over the back of the chair, then gave her an impatient look. "If you're waiting to see how the cripple struggles out of his jeans, you're out of luck. That particular trick needs two hands."

"Go to hell, Max," she said slowly and distinctly.

His mouth quirked. "If that's supposed to be a curse, you're too late."

"If that's *supposed* to make me feel sorry for you, you're outta luck." It occurred to her that he might feel more comfortable transferring from his chair to the bed with the light out. She made a show of ignoring him as she gave her pillow another flurry of punches. Satisfied, she gave him a lady-of-the-manor smile. "I have sharp elbows and know how to use them, so keep on your own side of the bed."

"Don't worry, I'm not a restless sleeper these days," he muttered, his tone laced with a wry humor that stunned her.

Heart stuttering, she leaned over and snapped off the bedside lamp. The room wasn't totally dark. Nothing really was in the city. But the shadows were dense enough to blur the outline of his body. Turning her back, she pretended to relax. In the silence she heard him take a deep breath. The mattress dipped suddenly, then sagged under his weight. He cursed under his breath as he dragged first one leg, then the other on to the mattress. Finally, after what seemed like an interminable amount of time, she felt him lie still.

"You can breathe now, Liza," he drawled, startling her.

"Don't push it, Savage," she muttered as heat flooded through her. "Just don't push it."

His rich, deep chuckle was almost as good as a good-night kiss.

Even before the threat had a name, Max came instantly awake, his mind scanning for trouble. It took a split second to orient himself, another to realize Liza was huddled in a tight ball on her side of the bed, mumbling brokenly in her sleep. She'd thrown off the sheet and lay with her arms wrapped protectively around the baby. In the gray haze of ambient light, her skin seemed as translucent as an orchid petal.

Careful not to startle her, he braced his weight on one hand and leaned closer. The scent that teased his senses reminded him of the fragile white flowers arching over her back gate.

"Liza," he whispered, his voice jagged in spite of his efforts to keep it soothing. "Wake up, sweetheart."

His hand shook as he closed it over her shoulder and gently eased her to her back. Slowly she opened her eyes to stare at him, her eyes dark pools in the hazy light.

"He was dying. Luke was trying, but..." Her voice broke, and she turned her face into his chest. His strained shoulder screamed a protest as he pulled her closer.

"It was just a dream," he whispered, stroking her back. "You and Boomer are fine."

"I'm so scared, Max," she murmured, her lips soft against his bare skin. "If anything happened to Boomer, I—"

"Shh. Nothing is going to happen," he whispered against the clean silk of her hair. "Jarrod's good. The best, according to people who should know."

He felt her smile. "He said you checked him out."

His face heated. "Yeah, well, I might have mentioned his name to some people."

"Like your family?"

"A man goes with what he knows."

She snorted against his chest, but she didn't draw away.

"Still mad at me?" he whispered against her hair.

"Yes," she muttered, raking his chest with her blunt little nails. "You make me crazy."

"Funny, I had the same feeling about you." He threaded his hand through her hair, lifting it, letting it fall. Breathing in the intoxicating mixture of scents that was uniquely Liza. "I dreamed about this. When I was in the hospital. The way your hair slips over my fingers, the smell of flowers and sunshine." He smiled. "It got me through some bad times, thinking about making love to you on that old army blanket, with the firelight dancing in your eyes as you looked up at me." His voice was raw, revealing more than he'd intended.

"I remember, too," she whispered, her breath tantalizingly warm against his chest. "The bath we took in half melted snow, and the way you dried me with your tongue." She drew back far enough to lift a hand to his mouth. "You were very, very thorough." Her finger traced a slow, seductive line along his lower lip. His already tense jaw clamped harder as hunger uncoiled in his belly.

"You tasted like rainwater," he murmured before dipping his head to kiss her. Her lips parted, and he thrust deep, tasting her. She moaned, her hands clutching his shoulders, frantic little claws as she pressed closer.

He shifted, afraid for the baby, silently cursing the awkwardness imposed by his lifeless legs. He'd never been with a woman as a paraplegic, never learned to compensate, to discover what he could do easily, what he could never do again. Even as he slipped his hand beneath the hem of the thin nightgown, he grieved over the lack of skill he brought her tonight.

His lady deserved the best, and he was far from that. And yet, now, this moment, her body was writhing beneath the slow slide of his hand over her satiny thigh. Soft moans came from the elegant throat that never failed to enchant him. Seductive, sultry sounds that wound around his heart. Gently, reverently, he pushed the clinging gown out of the way, then worshiped the beautiful curve of her ripe belly with his gaze first, then his mouth. Beneath his lips, the baby shifted. He felt a moment of alarm, and then emotion burst inside him.

"Oh, Liza," he choked. "I..." Biting back the words that he had no right to say, he kissed the spot where he'd felt his son move, felt him fling out a tiny fist. Pride and need burst like shellfire inside him, almost too powerful to comprehend.

"He's curious," she said, her voice shimmering with love.

He closed his eyes on an inarticulate prayer for

forgiveness before burying his face in her thighs. What he couldn't do with his body, he did with his mouth and his hands, opening her, stroking her, loving her until she was bucking wildly against him, her head back and hands clutching the pillow.

His shoulder ached. He blocked it out. He'd learned patience during the months they'd been apart and he gave it to her now, everything he knew, all the words he couldn't say, the promises he wouldn't make.

"Please, Max, oh, please," she begged, her voice a thread. The scent of her was on his hands, her hot need on his lips as he thrust his tongue deep. He felt her stiffen, reach, then explode. But he wasn't finished. Not yet. He started again, slowly, patiently, testing, stroking until she was tossing from side to side, begging. When he took over again, she screamed his name.

Drowsy and boneless, she snuggled against him. He waited, lying motionless, matching his breathing to hers. In spite of the scrambled signals that prevented his body from hardening, his loins burned with a jittery need that took all his willpower to resist.

Whoever said a man's sexual desire was only between his legs was dead wrong. His need for Liza was alive and prowling, as much a part of him as the beating of his heart and the rhythm of his breathing. It was her scent, only hers, he wanted to breathe in the night when he struggled to accept his fate, her skin he wanted to feel beneath his hand when he reached out for the comfort he needed so badly.

A long time later, well past the time he thought she'd drifted off, she lifted her head to look at him. "Did you mean it when you said you wanted to be my Lamaze coach?"

"I meant it."

"I accept—under two conditions. Number one, you let Boyd build a ramp for your chair. Number two, you stay here with Boomer and me until I deliver."

His lips curved in the first easy smile he'd had in months. His Gypsy might move like shadows dancing on water but she had the soul of a horse trader. "Yes on the ramp. No on staying. Not because I don't want to," he added when her eyes flashed. "But my exercise gear is at my place." Having Randall witness his struggles to master the braces was bad enough. Having her see him would all but destroy what little confidence he'd managed to salvage.

"Weekends then. And the nights when you don't have therapy the next morning."

It was a mistake. A bad one. A smart man would refuse. "Agreed," he heard himself saying. She kissed him before he could take back the words. And then, finally, as night slipped into dawn, they slept.

Chapter 9

Liza woke to find herself wrapped in the security of Max's strong arms, her naked body curled against his. A serene silence surrounded them, broken only by the distant music of birdsong. In the month since he became an almost permanent resident, she'd come to love the weekends, when they were alone.

Slowly she drew back until she could see his face. He was deeply asleep, his face relaxed. He'd made love to her well into the early hours, just as he'd done almost every night they'd spent together, easing her into sleep sated and relaxed. But whenever she tried to return the favor, he gently pushed her away. In spite of the pleasure he gave her, his bitterness over his imagined inadequacy as a man was always there in the back of those sometimes brooding gray eyes.

Enough was enough, she had decided finally, and took herself off to a private consultation with a neurologist Prudy knew. Not the one who had treated Max, Prudy had explained, which meant she was free to ask him anything and he was free to offer an opinion without the pesky patient-doctor relationship thing getting in the way.

The human body has a powerful need to reproduce itself, the grandfatherly physician explained. It was nature's way. Even badly damaged nerves can regenerate, if the conditions are right. Like adrenaline, sexual desire can do amazing things to the muscles and nerves. All it takes is the right partner with enough patience and determination, Dr. Benedict had said with a kindly smile.

As soon as she'd left his office, she had gone to Raine's bookstore, coming home with stacks of books on how to make love to a man, especially one who was disabled. Mornings were the best time, since a man often woke with an erection. Inching upward, she whispered the lightest of kisses over his hard mouth. He was awake instantly, his eyes alert, his muscles wired and ready. "Good morning, handsome," she murmured, her voice sleep-sultry and throaty.

"Sassy this morning, aren't we?" He kissed her

nose, then lifted her hair from her shoulders and let it slip through his fingers. "It suits you."

"I love the way your eyes go silvery when you're thinking about making love to me," she whispered, caressing his arm with light, slow strokes.

"I'm always thinking of making love to you."

"I know." She bent to nuzzle his shoulder. "You smell like bubble bath."

"Hard not to when you insist on dumping in half the bottle." He sketched slow circles on her back, just above the swell of her buttocks.

"I like the feel of all those luscious bubbles against my skin when I'm rubbing my breasts against your chest." She levered up to brush against him. "I need a good-morning kiss."

"Come to think of it, so do I."

She leaned down to tease his mouth with hers. "I like kissing you. I like touching you."

"I think I'm in trouble here," he murmured, already reaching for her. His mouth was hot, the growl in his throat desperate. Heart soaring, she clung, twining her arms around the hard ridge of shoulder muscle, her tummy pressed against his corded belly. The tip of his tongue caressed her pliant lips, teasing into her mouth, then withdrawing, while his hand worked magic on her body. She moaned, eager, impatient. She made an inarticulate sound, thought she cried his name.

He made a rough sound in his throat before drawing back. "Easy, wildcat," he soothed, his voice thick. "We have all the time in the world."

"Now," she insisted, a little frantic. "I want you now." Her hands were in his hair, tugging him closer. Her breathing was too rapid, little bursts of impatience, and she was trying to climb inside him.

She was ready, quivering. He touched her breast, and she gasped. He froze, his hand cupping her. "Sore?" His voice was a rough thread.

"No, I just can't seem to help myself when you touch me."

"Good." Lowering his head, he opened his mouth over the tip of her full breast. She gasped, her head falling back. She made an inarticulate sound, her hands buried in his hair. He stroked her then, smoothing his hand over her nipple until it went hard.

"You take my breath," he whispered, his voice taut. He held her close, his body terribly tense, and she knew he was thinking of all the things he couldn't do instead of the wonderful things he could.

"My turn," she whispered, pushing him against the mattress.

"Hey…"

"Hush," she ordered before lowering her mouth to his chest. Heat poured from him, bathing her face. Indulging herself, she touched the tip of her tongue to the flat male nipple buried in the dark hair. He jerked, his hands gripping her arms.

"Liza, don't. You just make me want things I can't have." His voice was thick and full of regret.

"Relax and enjoy the attention," she ordered, giving him a shove.

"Fine, you want to embarrass both of us, have at it." He sounded angry, and yet his eyes mirrored another emotion. Something hot and volatile and rawly male. Terrified yet exhilarated, she met the fierce heat of that tinderbox emotion with the slowest, gentlest of caresses. *Love a man the way he loves you,* one of the books had counseled. *What he gives is what he wants.*

He gave her an aching tenderness, and now she gave it back, her hands gliding over all the hard, angular planes and taut valleys of his face. Eyes closed, she explored him as her father explored the smoothness of the clay, smoothing, lingering until the tension left his jaw. But his mouth—that hard, proud mouth. A challenge and a delight. Lovingly, she feathered her touch over the stern compression of his lips, then bent to repeat the slow exploration with her tongue. His breath hissed in, and she gloried.

Satisfied, she moved lower, exploring his corded throat, the taut, strong muscles of his neck, the shoulders that sometimes bent under a burden that was nearly unbearable at times, but never bowed. For this she used her palms, sliding them with delicious friction over the densely packed muscle. His arms next, those massive biceps that had the ladies of the Brigade lusting when he went without a shirt. His skin was slick, his big chest rising and falling in harsh jerks, beyond the control of mind or will.

"You are so beautiful," she murmured, watching his eyes. They were nearly black, with violent undercurrents beneath the hard sheen.

"Is this little exercise in futility about over?" he demanded in a low, dangerous tone.

"Not a chance," she whispered, her voice thick with her own need. His eyes narrowed, and he reached for her, his intention to take over in his eyes. "I told you, I'm not finished," she said, shifting to loom over him.

Watching her, loving her for trying, Max fought to keep his mind clear, but kiss by kiss, stroke by stroke, she was enchanting him. Frustratingly aroused, yet utterly useless to thrust inside her the way he so desperately wanted, he felt every slow brush of her hand, every gliding swipe of her tongue. And he ached.

He closed his eyes, unwilling to witness her disappointment. This was agony beyond agony, a punishment he made himself bear because she thought she was giving him a gift. To endure, he shut down his thoughts, giving himself over to her. Her scent filled him, her touch healing. His breathing was raspy, his skin damp. In all the parts he could feel, his body responded in all the primal ways nature intended, preparing him to mate. In every way, that is, but the one that really counted.

"My beautiful warrior, so many scars." She traced the jagged tear along one hip. A brush with a crack head who'd come at him from the dark.

He was no warrior, he wanted to tell her, but he couldn't seem to form the words. Not when her hands were busy gliding over his ribs, her fingertips teasing his navel, dipping, stroking, trailing lower, toward the place just below his pelvis where sensation disappeared. He sucked in hard when he felt her fingers drifting over his sex.

His voice choked as he called her name, and then she was stroking him in the most intimate ways, her hands warm. He gritted his teeth, sick with the growing feeling of loss. The sudden tension that clawed him was familiar. A phantom memory, a... His breath hissed out, his heart jolting.

Liza knew the instant he realized his body was swelling under her hand. His eyes flew open, and something like shock shimmered there. And then they were glazing, his jaw white, his torso slab hard. "Oh, Liza," he whispered, bucking suddenly. "Don't stop, oh, don't stop. I...it feels so good." His gaze was on hers, dazed, desperate.

She straddled him, her hand a little clumsy as she guided him to her. He shuddered as she slowly lowered herself over him. His gaze burned, his breathing rapid. He moaned as she began to move.

Max felt the tension building, his blood humming in his head. Reality dimmed, and then he was struggling to move, desperate to feel the joy of release. He clutched her arms, forcing gentleness into his hands even as a wild need tore through him.

"Baby I can't...it's been so long."

The look she gave him was triumph, a woman in all her power. A goddess. Head thrown back, her hair rippling in the sun, she was magnificent. He felt the tension burst, and then he was carrying that vision with him as he tipped over the edge.

He stayed in her as long as he could, stroking her hair, her back, her shoulders, smiling when Boomer kicked him like the little champ he was going to be.

"You look very pleased with yourself," he murmured as she lifted her head from his chest to look at him.

"I am gloriously pleased with both of us," she murmured, her fathomless Gypsy eyes smiling drowsily into his.

"You are indescribably wonderful." He'd meant to tease but his voice broke, and feelings he'd never thought to have again tumbled out. "Oh, Liza, I don't have words to thank you."

"No need, dearest, darling Max. All I did is love you the way you love me. The hard part as getting past that massively annoying pride of yours."

He choked a laugh and tightened his grip. "I'm not that bad, surely."

"Worse." She nuzzled his chin. "But I love you anyway."

Closing his eyes, he breathed a prayer of thanks. "And I love you, too."

"Oh, Max."

"I...if you'll just give me some time to work things out, what you said, I want it, too. You and Boomer and me. A family." He was making a mess of it, but he must have said it right because suddenly she was crying and laughing and kissing him. He didn't deserve this, he thought as he kissed her back. But damn, he was happy.

Chapter 10

"Luke said Boomer has dropped. He thinks I'll deliver close to my due date." Liza shifted her awkward bulk slowly, trying to find a comfortable spot on the plank seat. It was a perfect summer Sunday, and Riverside Park was bursting with families enjoying themselves.

A few yards away, her neighbors were playing their unique version of softball. Invented by Morgan with a little help from Boyd, it employed a child-size plastic bat and a whiffle ball that rarely made it past second base, no matter who was batting. Today, it was the Randolphs and the MacAuleys against the Paxtons and the Jarrods—or more precisely, Luke. Still a little worn after a recent bout with the flu, Maddy had opted to join Liza in the stands.

"You sound worried," Maddy said, shifting a sleeping Oliver into a more comfortable position in her lap.

"More like nervously excited." She drew a breath flavored with the tantalizing scents wafting from a nearby barbecue pit. "Max has already driven the route twice, and he's been practicing getting himself and his chair into the car more quickly. He's got it down to three minutes, but Max being Max won't be satisfied until he can do it under two."

She shifted her gaze to the softball diamond, where Morgan was about to bat. Behind the plate Case was ragging him mercilessly about the pop fly he'd dropped, allowing Tory to race home from third to put her team ahead. Morgan had dropped it on purpose, of course, but he'd made it look good. Getting into the act with gusto, Raine and Luke had feigned disgust, threatening to boot him off their team until Morgana had raced over from her spot at first to give her daddy a comforting hug.

"You gonna bat any time soon, Paxton?" Max demanded from his umpire's spot behind Case. In past games, that had been Liza's spot, but since she'd gotten too big to crouch, she'd volunteered him, instead. He'd grumbled a lot, but in the end, he'd accepted.

"He's like a different person," Maddy said when she noticed the direction of Liza's gaze. "When I first met him, I though he was a lot older than thirty-four. Maybe because he was always so taciturn. Now it seems he's always laughing—when he's not pulling you into his lap for an outrageously sexy kiss."

Liza sighed. "He's getting feeling back in his thighs, Maddy. At the moment it's nonspecific, just a sort of pressure. But the nerves are alive."

"Oh, Liza, that's wonderful! He must be relieved."

"Let's say he is guardedly optimistic." She chuckled, her gaze turning his way again. He was wearing shorts and a tank top that outlined every powerful muscle. Her body lusted. "He's not ready to commit yet, but he will. I think he just needs to decide what kind of work he wants to do."

"Give it a ride, Pax!" Luke yelled from third where he'd taken an outrageous lead. Intending to do just that, Morgan swung for the fence—and missed, nearly corkscrewing himself into the ground in the process.

"Eye on the ball, Paxton," Maddy shouted, winning her a thumbs-up from her husband.

On the mound, Prudy went into her elaborate windup, then lofted one right over the plate. Morgan whacked it hard, sending the whiffle ball arcing toward the twins, who were running in circles with their gloves in the air.

Liza laughed as they collided.

"Run, Luke," Maddy shouted, jostling Ollie, who protested.

"This should be good," Liza exclaimed as Case crouched to block the plate, grinning in anticipation. Neither man gave an inch. The collision was bone-jarring, the two large men coming together like colliding freight trains. The impact sent Morgan and Luke crashing into Max, who was bending forward to watch the play.

The impact toppled his chair, sending him sprawling. "Oh, no," Liza cried, clutching Maddy's arm.

"He's all right," Maddy assured her quickly. "He's even laughing."

Liza felt nearly weak with relief when Max sat up to direct a cutting remark to Luke, who was inspecting his bloody elbow. It was only when Case righted Max's chair that she realized the impact had somehow snapped the axle on one wheel. Max's chair was useless.

Liza sat on the edge of the bed, one hand on her aching back, watching Max stuff clothes into a duffel bag. "Max, this is ridiculous," she pleaded. "Just because you needed a little help—"

"It's finished, Liza. I should have known better, but I…" His face twisted and he turned back to his packing. He'd called Randall as soon as Morgan had carried him into the house from the car, and the imposing giant had come right over with a temporary chair until Max's could be repaired. In contrast to the sleek design she was accustomed to seeing, this one was cumbersome and ugly, with arms that made it difficult for him to transfer easily.

"So that's it? Just because a friend had to carry you to and from the car you've decided you can't be a father to our son?"

"Can't and won't." He tossed the last of his underwear into the bag and zipped it up.

"You and your damn pride," she whispered, hugging herself, her pride ripped into pathetic pieces. She'd done everything but chain herself to his wrist to keep him from leaving her again.

"I've talked to Prudy. She'll be your coach during delivery." His jaw was tight, his eyes remote, but he had to work to keep his mouth from turning vulnerable.

"I want you. You promised—"

He slammed his fist on the arm of the chair. "Damn it, I can't. Don't you understand? When Morgan walked off the field with me in his arms like a helpless baby, I saw the way the kids looked at me. Like I was some kind of..." His voice broke, and he took a ragged breath. "I couldn't stand it if Boomer looked at me like that. It would flat out destroy me."

"The girls were scared, Max. They thought you were hurt, that's all."

"They were embarrassed, Liza. Tory still won't come near me." He slumped in the chair, looking more defeated than she'd ever seen him.

"Give her time."

"No, it's finished. I'm going home where I belong."

"Doesn't it mean anything that I love you?"

He gave her an impatient look. "It means everything, but it's not enough."

"It would be enough for me." She blinked against the sudden sting of tears. "I could handle anything if you were with me."

His mouth slanted, but there was bitterness in his eyes. "You're the strongest woman I know, Liza. And the bravest. I'll...I'll always be proud that you loved me." He glanced at the hand fisted on the arm of the chair. "You gave me back my manhood, and I'll always be grateful."

"I don't want your gratitude, damn it! I want you!" She lumbered to her feet and flung out her arms. "This is your home. You belong here, in this room, next to me when we put our baby to bed."

He winced, his expression tortured. "Let me go. Don't make this any harder than it already is." The pain in his voice seemed bottomless, as bottomless as the despair filling her. She knew then that she'd lost him.

"If that's what you want," she said, her voice shredded.

"It's what has to be."

She nodded, then cleared her throat. "Will you come when the baby's born? To see him?"

He shook his head. "I'm leaving Portland. I won't be back."

"And no forwarding address?"

"You have my attorney's name, and Luke has the family's medical history. I intend to tell my family about you and Boomer. If you want him to know them, I have no objection."

"Thank you for that."

He acknowledged that with a wry curve of his mouth. "Take care of yourself," he said, his voice thick. "And Boomer." His gaze caressed her belly for a long, poignant moment before lifting to her face. "Goodbye, Liza."

She stood silent and helpless as he lifted the duffel to his lap, then turned his chair and left her. This time she knew he wouldn't be back.

Chapter 11

Liza struggled to focus her bleary gaze on the lop-sided clay angel on the table next to the bed. It was the same focal point she'd used during the Lamaze classes she attended with Max. She'd chosen it because he'd made it for her during a dreary rainy day when the children were climbing the walls and she'd been fighting a headache. He'd bullied her into bed, then taken over the art lesson she'd planned. He'd turned out to be a lousy sculptor, but that silly little figure was as precious to her as her father's seascape.

Holding it, looking at it first thing in the morning and last thing at night, it had been her own private candle in the dark. A reminder that there was a won-derfully sweet, loving man buried under all that seething bitterness. During the lonely hours when she lay awake, aching for him, she clung to the hope that someday that man would find his way back to her. Now, however, even that hope had failed her.

Boomer was proving stubborn, just like his father. Instead of entering the world headfirst, he seemed determined to come in backward. Reluctant to perform a C-section unless absolutely necessary, Luke was hoping the baby would turn again. In the meantime, he was keeping a close watch on the fetal monitor. So far it was a stalemate between doctor and baby, while Liza felt her strength ebbing as her body shuddered with one contraction after another.

Dimly, she was aware of voices. Prudy's calm coaching. The brisk comments of the two nurses. Now and then, Luke's distinctive drawl. After humming steadily for hours, the monitor gave a muted buzz, and she struggled to focus on the blue screen. "What's wrong?" she managed to gasp between panting breaths.

"Might be the little guy's gettin' a mite tuckered," Luke answered, his face swimming into view. "We might have to help him along a little bit." He and Prudy exchanged looks, and alarm raced through her. It was like her nightmare, and suddenly she was terrified.

"Please don't let him die," she pleaded, fighting a sick terror. "Do whatever you...have to." Her strength failed her, and she sagged against the pillows.

Max, where are you? she cried silently, tears slipping from her brimming eyes to slide down her cheeks.

"You're doing fine," Prudy soothed, gently blotting her face with a damp cloth. "Just be strong a little longer."

Oh, God, she wanted to be. But she was so tired.

"Doctor?" The voice was sharp, penetrating where others had not. She struggled to focus through the escalating waves of agony. The nurse beckoned Luke closer. "There's a very…forceful man outside who insists on seeing Ms. Vargas," she said, looking peeved. "He's threatening to tear down the doors to the suites one by one until he finds her."

Liza's already straining heart thundered harder as her parched lips trembled into a grin. "That has to be Max," she whispered, and Prudy nodded.

"No doubt in my mind."

Luke turned to give Liza an inquisitive look. "Yes or no?"

Joy burst in her as she nodded. "Yes," she said through dry lips. "Definitely yes."

Maxwell Joseph Vargas Savage was barely twelve hours old and already he had wound his doting parents around his tiny little finger. At nine pounds, thirteen ounces, with his father's wide shoulders and long legs, he was the largest baby in the nursery. A real bruiser, had been Luke's comment when the baby had slipped into his waiting hands, perfectly formed and vigorous in spite of the prolonged labor.

Max had been her rock during the last pain-racked hour before Boomer had finally decided to make an appearance. Liza would never forget the look on his face when Luke had placed his son in his arms.

There had been tears in his eyes as he'd looked into the mottled red face that so clearly bore his stamp. He'd looked at her then, love and reverence mingling with the tears. In every way that mattered, they had become one. With a ceremony, without one, they were man and wife.

"He has your chin," Liza murmured drowsily, her gaze soft on the sleeping baby nestled in her arms.

Max's chuckle was seductively throaty against her temple. "Is that good or bad?"

"More like challenging, I suspect." She turned her head, her lips already parting for his kiss. It was gentle, just flavored with a promise of passion. "I still can't believe you're here."

His eyes clouded. "I nearly lost it when I showed up at your house and no one was there." He nuzzled her hair with his chin. "I think I scared Raine a little when she opened her door to find this madman sitting on his butt on her back porch, shooting questions at her like rapid fire in a shooting gallery."

Laughing softly, Liza toyed with the big hand rest-

ing on the baby's swaddled back. "She and Stacy
are going to take over the day care for a week or
two until I'm steadier on my feet."

"A month, minimum." His voice warned that argument would be futile. "After that, we'll see."

Lips curving in an utterly content smile, Liza nestled deeper against the bulwark of his chest. "You
could always take over."

"I could," he agreed, "but only until the fall se-
mester at Portland State."

"You're going back to school?"

"I figured if I passed the entrance exam, I'd give
it a shot."

Because her back was to him, she let her gaze
linger on the long, still legs bracketing hers. "Have
you picked a major?"

There was a brief silence before he said quietly,
"I thought I'd give medicine a try. Pediatrics. A guy
doesn't have to be able to walk to treat the little
ones."

Startled and pleased, she twisted to look at him.
His face was taut, his eyes troubled. "I think you'd
make a wonderful pediatrician," she said firmly

He gave her a crooked grin that didn't quite hide
a sudden vulnerability. "I might not be able to hack
it, Liza. It takes a lot of stamina to get through internship and residency. If I'm still in this chair—"

She stopped him with a long, tender kiss. They
were both a little dazed when it ended. "Max, think

about it. Do you really think residency and internship can possibly be tougher than handling a house full of preschoolers?''

His eyes cleared, then crinkled. Slowly his mouth relaxed into a smile and then into an endearing, lopsided grin. ''No, but you have to admit it's good practice,'' he said, his voice husky.

She felt sweet warmth blossom inside her. ''Practice for what, exactly?''

''Making babies.'' He leaned forward to kiss her again. ''If it's all the same to you, when you're ready, I'd like a daughter with her mom's eyes.''

She smiled, and her eyes filled with tears. ''Oh, Max. I do love you.''

''I love you, too.'' He took a deep breath, then pulled her closer. ''You were right about me, Liza. I couldn't see past my pride. It took me a couple of weeks of missing you to realize that nothing was as important to me as being with you. With my family.''

Her smile was dreamy as she snuggled her cheek against his chest. He felt something tear inside as her lashes drifted down. ''Sorry,'' she murmured, fighting off a yawn.

''Go to sleep, sweetheart,'' he whispered. ''Boomer and I will be here when you wake up.''

She gave a contented sigh and closed her eyes.

Epilogue

"Daddy's an old sleepyhead, isn't he?"

Still drowsy from making love to his wife of one year and five days, Max felt the bed dip, and then his son was climbing on his chest. He opened his eyes to find big round eyes the same gray as his peering at him.

"Dada!" Joey crowed, bouncing up and down on the diaper his mama had just fastened to his chubby bottom. Joey had been two days old when his parents had married in the birthing suite where he'd been born. All their neighbors had been there, including the kids.

"Hey, Boomer, give old dad a break here. He's just finished final exams and he's wiped slick."

"Aced them, too," Liza said before leaning forward to give him another blood-sizzling kiss. "My brilliant hero."

His grin felt crooked as he ran his palm over her sleek thigh. There were times in the past year when he'd wondered if a man could possibly be any happier. "You weren't saying that a week ago, sweetheart."

"A bride's entitled to be grumpy when her husband forgets their first anniversary."

"I didn't forget the anniversary. I just didn't know what day it was."

Liza loved the sheepish look that came over his face. "I'll forgive you because you were taking exams, but next year I expect a huge celebration."

"Okay, just as long as you don't expect me to take you dancing." He had sensation in his legs now, and almost free range of movement. He and Randall were still working on strengthening the muscles so that he could walk without the braces he hated.

"No, dancing is on the agenda for our third anniversary," she teased, grabbing Joey by the back of his shirt before he could topple off the bed. Hating to be restrained, their sturdy little son struggled and kicked. Laughing, she set him on his bottom next to Max's braces. Between the tendency Tilly had to chew on anything leather and Joey's teething, the cuffs had taken a beating.

"Are you all packed?" Max asked before stretching his arms overhead. Tomorrow they were driving up to visit his folks for a week. Even though the visits tended to be chaotic and exhausting, she adored being part of a big family.

"My things, yes. I still have Joey's things to pack. And you, my darling husband, need to pack your own suitcase."

"What the hell, some jeans and a coupla shirts, and I'm ready." He took her hand and laced his through it. The tenderness in his eyes brought a lump to her throat. "Have I told you lately how crazy I am about you?"

"Not since last night." She grinned. "Among other more erotic things."

"Yeah, like what?"

She leaned forward to repeat the more provocative phrases in his ear. He colored, and she laughed. "I still can't believe a man who blushes as easily as you do survived all those years on the streets."

He grinned, his eyes laughing. "You're the only one who can get to me like that, sweetheart." He tugged on her hand, pulling her down for another long kiss. "Okay, I'm ready for this special treat you promised to give me if I passed my exams."

She smiled serenely. "Close your eyes, first."

Max glanced at his son, who was playing with an elaborate dump truck Ollie Jarrod had given him for his first birthday. "Watch Mommy for me, okay? Don't let her dump anything on my head."

Joey looked up and laughed, showing off his mama's dimples.

"Eyes shut," she ordered sternly.

His grin a little crooked, he settled back against the pillow and closed his eyes. Liza took a moment to enjoy the relaxed look on the face of the man she loved more every day. In spite of the occasional black moments when his paralysis seemed to push him to the limits of his control, he'd been a wonderful husband, making her feel special and cherished. Tears flooded her eyes as she reached for the big hand still curled around her thigh. A frown crossed his face, but he kept his eyes closed as she pressed his hand to her belly. "Okay, you can open your eyes."

Confusion crossed his face for an instant before happiness flooded into his eyes. "You're pregnant?"

"Six weeks. I've ordered a girl this time."

"Come here, you," he whispered, pulling her down. The kiss he gave her was tender and so full of love she thought she would burst.

"Dada!"

Breaking off the kiss, they both looked at their son, who was standing by the weight bench, looking tremendously pleased with himself. For several weeks he'd been pulling himself to his feet, but he hadn't quite figured out what to do next. "Hey, tiger, lookin' good," Max said, grinning.

Joey laughed, then lifted both chubby hands.

Sticking out his chin, he screwed up his face in concentration and took a wobbly step. Liza started to leap from the bed, only to have Max stop her. "He needs to do this on his own," he said, his gray eyes dark with pride.

"What a big, strong boy," she praised around the thick lump in her throat. "Mama is so proud of you."

Grunting, Joey took another step then another before sitting down hard on his rump. He looked stunned, then broke into frustrated tears.

"Now you can pamper him," Max said, releasing her.

A quick cuddle and soothing words soon had him laughing again. "How about we go make pancakes for Daddy?" she said before kissing the tickle spot in his neck he'd inherited from his daddy. He giggled, and she stood, shifting him to her hip.

"Dada," Joey said, pointing.

Turning, she saw that Max was standing by the bed with only his forearm crutches supporting him. Sweat stood on his face, and his jaw was locked tight. "Can't let my son show me up." He grated the words when her anxious gaze found his.

Holding her breath, she waited while he straightened his back. His hands whitened on the grips of his crutches, and the muscles of his arms bulged as they took most of his weight. Concentration glittered in his eyes as he struggled to move one leg, then the other. He took three steps toward the foot of the bed before he half-fell, half-sat on the mattress. In spite of the sweat pouring from him, his grin was pure male triumph.

"What a big, strong boy," she whispered, her voice husky. "I love you very much."

His eyes turned soft. "I dare you to come here and say that, wife," he said, holding out his hand. Two seconds later she was in his arms with their son wiggling between them. As he tightened his arms around his family, Max buried his face in his wife's hair. For the second time in his adult life he cried. For joy.

* * * * *

Dear Reader,

Without question the one person in my life who has influenced me the most is my mother. In her gentle, loving ways, she taught me how to cook and sew, run a household on very little money and to be thankful for the small, everyday joys of life. From her I learned how to be a lady and respect myself as a woman. I learned the love and devotion it takes to make a marriage work, and most importantly, the vital role a woman plays in making a home a warm and blessed place for the whole family.

As for being a mother myself, there is nothing as precious or rewarding as having a child. And through the years, I have tried to give my son the same tender love and firm guidance my mother gave me.

I hope you enjoy reading how Caroline's life is fulfilled when she becomes a mother to baby Nick. And on this Mother's Day, whether you're a mother, wife, daughter, sister or friend, you deserve to be applauded. Because I happen to think it's more than just a day to remember mothers. It's a day to celebrate being a woman.

Wishing you much love and happiness,

Baby on Her Doorstep
Stella Bagwell

To my wonderful mother, Lucille, for raising all five of us
and managing to stay young and beautiful in the process!

Chapter 1

"Oh! Oh, Lord!"

The words rushed out of Caroline Pardee as she stared at a baby swaddled tightly in several receiving blankets. The baby was in a basket pushed up against the bottom of her door. The basket was green, oblong and plastic. A thin cotton blanket was draped over the top. Only the baby's face and a small patch of black hair could be seen peeking out from a fold of blanket.

"Oh, you tiny thing! You precious little thing!"

Her hands shaking, Caroline opened the door of her rather isolated home—Caroline liked her privacy—then carefully carried the basket inside. Although it was spring in New Mexico, the weather was still cool and unpredictable. Thankfully, Caroline had turned on the heating system before she left for work this Saturday morning, and the rooms were warm.

How long had the baby been out in the cold? she wondered frantically. It could be suffering from hypothermia. Trying not to panic, she hurried to a long couch.

"Why, you're only an infant," she whispered in shock as she lifted the newborn into her arms. "Where have you come from? Who do you belong to, little one?"

The baby made a soft mewing sound as Caroline began peeling back the blankets. To her relief, the child felt warm to the touch and was perfectly formed. On further examination, she discovered her unexpected guest was a boy with a soggy diaper.

With the baby cradled snugly to her breast, she glanced helplessly around the cozy living room. Caroline had never been married, much less been a mother. She did have nieces and nephews, but they were well out of the infancy age, and had never visited her home in Santa Fe. There was nothing in the house to care for a baby!

Turning to the basket, she used one hand to rifle through the tumbled blankets and was further surprised to discover a small diaper bag.

Quickly, with the baby cradled in one arm, she sat on the couch and searched the contents. There were six disposable diapers, one plastic bottle filled with formula and a separate packet of dry formula to be mixed at a later time with water. But more importantly there was a sealed plastic baggy containing several papers, one of which appeared to be a birth certificate.

Swiftly she scanned the document. Nicolas Ruy Garcia. Seven pounds, two ounces. Twenty inches in length. Born five days ago in Albuquerque. Mother—Pamela K. Ashby. Father—Joseph L. Garcia.

Caroline skipped over the remaining information on the certificate as the last name rolled over in her mind. Joseph Garcia. It was so familiar! Where had she seen that name?

Her green eyes flew wide open. Her neighbor! The mailbox with that name stood next to hers at the intersection of dirt roads down the mountain. Whoever left the baby on Caroline's porch must have intended it to go to her neighbor's house!

From time to time, she'd seen the man from a distance as he walked along the road. She'd guessed him to be in his early sixties, and from his slow, hunched gait, she'd decided his health was poor. Other than that, she knew nothing about the man. He never had any visitors that she'd seen. Nor had she ever met him driving in and out on the road. He was a recluse.

The idea put a wry twist on her lips. Apparently

the man was healthier and more sociable than she'd imagined.

Caroline glanced at the baby boy nestled in the crook of her arm. His eyes were open, staring at her. A bluish brown for now. But Caroline figured later on they would turn much darker. Maybe brown or even black. One tiny fist waved and wobbled toward his sweet little bow of a mouth.

Already he was a handsome boy, and her heart clutched at the idea of some woman abandoning him. Caroline had wanted a child of her own for so long, she couldn't fathom a woman giving up this precious baby to anyone for any reason.

Her mind whirled to the father. What in the world was Joseph Garcia going to think about this little bundle? Probably deny he'd ever seen a Pamela Ashby in his entire life. Obviously the man was avoiding his responsibility as a father. Otherwise, little Nicolas wouldn't have been left on a doorstep. He'd be snug in his own home with two loving parents.

The baby suddenly let out a wail, and the sound jerked Caroline to the problems of the present.

"Poor little Nick is wet and hungry," she crooned as she laid him out on the couch to deal with his diaper. "I'm going to fix you up, sweetheart, and then we're going to see about getting you to your daddy."

Minutes later, halfway through the warmed bottle,

Nicolas fell asleep. Caroline placed him on the couch and covered him carefully with a light blanket before she reached for the thick phone book on a shelf underneath an end table.

She thought about calling the sheriff's office. Abandoning a baby was no doubt a felony. But in this case, information had been left with the child, and she didn't want to get anyone into serious trouble when this might just be some sort of mix-up between the parents. And since it appeared as though the father was her neighbor, it would be quicker and easier to let him handle the whole matter.

Garcia was a common name in Santa Fe, and it took her several moments to find a Joseph with the right address.

Her fingers trembled nervously as she punched in the number. How was she going to put this to the man? He might not even know he had a child!

The questions flew out of her head as she heard the phone being picked up on the other end of the line.

"Hello."

"Is this—Joseph Garcia?"

"Yes. Who is this?"

His deep voice, clipped, with a faint Mexican accent, didn't sound old or sickly, she thought. But voices could sometimes be deceiving. "This is your neighbor, Caroline Pardee. I'm the last house. Above you. On the cliff."

There was a long pause, then he asked, "Is something wrong?"

"Uh—no. Not exactly." She glanced at the sleeping baby, then rolled her eyes toward the beamed ceiling above her head. "Do you think you could manage to come up to my house? Do you have a vehicle?"

"I suppose I could manage," he said with puzzled amusement. "Are you having car trouble?"

"Er—no. This is something—it's terribly personal. I can't explain on the phone."

He let out a rough breath. "Look, Mrs. Pardee—"

"It's miss," she quickly corrected. "And before you say no, I realize you're not in the best of shape, but I promise the trip up here will be worth the effort. Even in the rain."

"Are you sure you have the right man, lady?" he asked after a moment.

"Oh, yes. Please come as quickly as you can. I'll be waiting."

Five minutes later Caroline heard a vehicle in the driveway and hurried to the front door, but the caller standing on her threshold was not the man she was expecting.

"Can I help you?"

The man's dark eyes slid over the woman standing before him. A riot of red, curly waves surrounded her face and tumbled around her shoulders. Her skin

was white, her eyes as green as wet clover. Even
with her forehead puckered into a frown, she was
the most exotic-looking woman he'd ever seen.

"Are you Caroline Pardee?"

"Yes."

Though her face was incredibly beautiful, he
found his eyes slipping along the slender curves of
her body. Her dress was russet colored and made of
something soft and clingy. A heavy gold chain in-
dented the material between the thrust of her breasts.
As his gaze appreciated their round fullness he felt
his body react with a sudden surge of interest.

"I'm Joseph Garcia. You phoned me."

Shocked, she stared at him. This wasn't the Joseph
Garcia who walked the road between her house and
his! This man was—young and extremely virile.
"Oh. Oh, I—"

"You do remember calling me?" he interrupted.

She quickly let out a long breath. "Yes! Certainly!
I was just—expecting an older man."

His chiseled lips twisted into a dry semblance of
a smile, and Caroline realized she must sound totally
crazy.

Pushing the door wide, she gestured for him to
enter the house. "I'm sorry if I'm not making much
sense. Please come in and perhaps we can get to the
bottom of this."

Joseph stepped past her and into a small living
area. It was warm, quiet and simply decorated with

a southwest flavor. Gauging from the thick walls, low ceiling and wooden plank floor, the structure was old and original and would be worth a small fortune on the real estate market.

"To be honest with you, Miss Pardee, I don't have the faintest clue to why you asked me up here. I've only been back here for about a month, and I realize it might seem amiss to you that I haven't introduced myself, but neighbors usually aren't neighbors anymore."

She shut the door behind her and came to stand in front of him. He was tall, particularly for a Mexican-Indian of this area. She was forced to tilt her head in order to look at his coarsely hewn features. Thick black hair was cropped closely to his head and waved ever so slightly to one side. His eyes were also black, and as he continued to look at her, Caroline could feel a rush of heat all the way from her toes to the roots of her hair.

"I didn't realize—" She stopped, moistened her lips by pressing them together, then tried again. "The Joseph Garcia I knew was an older man. Grayheaded. Slightly humped."

"That was my father. He died six weeks ago."

Caroline felt like an utter fool. For the mistake and for reacting to this man in such a carnal way. "Oh. I'm sorry. I didn't know. We-er, didn't socialize," she tried to explain.

His nostrils flared as he drew in a long breath.

With it came the sweet scent of her musky perfume. Joe couldn't help thinking how the sultry fragrance matched her appearance. "Why did you want to see my father?"

She pushed nervously at a wave of red hair pestering her right eye. "Well, I thought it was him I needed to see, but now—it obviously must be you."

He stared at her, waiting for further explanation. Deciding there wasn't any way to put it in words, Caroline motioned for him to follow her to the front of the couch.

"You have a baby," he stated, his gaze slanting to her. There was no wedding ring on her hand, and she had announced herself as a Miss. "You're a single mother?"

Shaking her head, she walked to the end table and picked up the plastic bag containing the documents she'd discovered in her earlier search. "I think you should read these."

Caroline handed him a folded document, and as he quickly read, she watched shock spread across his dark face.

He lifted his head and looked at her. "Is this some sort of joke?"

Caroline shrugged her slender shoulders. "You tell me. All I know is when I came home from work, the baby was on my front porch in a basket."

"Oh, sure, lady," he drawled sarcastically.

"Can't you come up with something more original than that?"

Her lips compressed to a tight line. She didn't like to lose her temper with anyone, but this was hardly a time for sarcasm. "Look, Mr. Garcia, my first inclination was to call the sheriff, but I thought you might want the chance to deal with the matter without the authorities stepping in. But—"

His black eyes narrowed with skepticism. "Do you know Pamela?"

"I've never spoken to the woman in my life," she answered. "And all things considered, I'm not certain I'd want to."

He opened his mouth to speak, but Nicolas interrupted with a loud yell of protest. Caroline went to the couch and picked up the baby.

"Poor little darling," she crooned softly while gently rocking him in her arms.

"What's the matter with him?"

She glanced at Joseph Garcia. His legs were planted apart, and his hands were resting at either side of his trim waist. When she'd first opened the door, her initial impression was that he was a big man. Now she could see just how broad and thick his shoulders were beneath the long-sleeved cotton shirt he wore. His legs were equally impressive, the thighs straining the worn fabric of his jeans. It was too easy for Caroline to imagine this man siring a child. Just the idea filled her face with renewed heat.

"He probably hears his father trying to disown him," she said in a clipped voice.

His jaw like granite, Joe once more studied the birth certificate in his hands. It was dated, notarized and appeared to be legitimate. And he was listed as the father! But how could that be? Pamela had been on oral contraceptives, or so she'd assured him more than once.

The baby was a major shock to the man, Caroline decided as she studied his rigid features. Which could only mean he couldn't have had much of a relationship with the mother. "Is it possible this baby could be yours? Were you intimate with this woman?"

Joe was thirty-eight years old. He didn't think there was anything that could make him blush, but Caroline Pardee's question was filling his face with ruddy color.

"Do you think that's any of your business?"

She rolled her eyes. "Since the baby landed on my porch I think I have a right to some answers."

He grimaced. "All right. It is possible."

"You didn't know the woman was pregnant?"

Staring at the baby, he shook his head. "No. I haven't talked to her in months. Not since I left Fort Bliss."

Caroline's brows lifted at this bit of information. "She was a servicewoman?"

"No. I was a serviceman."

"Was?"

"I'm retired. Twenty years."

He looked too young to have spent twenty years in the military. She inclined her head toward the plastic bag he held in his hand. "There's a sealed envelope in there with your name on the front. Perhaps you better see what's inside," she suggested.

The baby continued to fuss. While Joe read the contents of the envelope, Caroline offered Nicolas the remaining formula and was relieved when he began to nurse hungrily.

Stunned, Joe walked to the first armchair he spotted and sank into it. "This is—unbelievable."

"What is it?" she asked.

Even though his mind was spinning with everything he'd just read, he couldn't help noticing Caroline Pardee was holding the baby as though she already loved it. But that was the natural way with a woman, he'd heard. Instinctively maternal and loving. No matter if the child was born from her own womb. So why had Pamela deserted this little boy? Then again, why had his mother deserted him all those years ago?

"This is a document stating she's turning the baby over to me. Full custody. His mother has signed away all legal rights to the child."

Caroline's heart cringed. "Why?"

Joe's head jerked one way and then the other. "She doesn't want him. She thinks giving birth to him is enough payment on her part. She's marrying a rich businessman, and neither one of them want to be bothered with a child.''

Caroline had been expecting the mother's excuse to be lack of money, not love of it. The idea made her green eyes glitter with anger. "That's—that's obscene! She must be the coldest woman on earth!''

"The only thing cold about Pamela was her heart.''

Caroline pinned him with a disgusted stare. "And isn't it just like a man to overlook that part of the anatomy.''

His expression turned to a glare. "I wasn't looking for a wife,'' he muttered.

Her brows arched even higher. "Then what were you doing with a woman like her?'' she asked. With a disgusted groan, she quickly shook her head. "No. Don't answer that. It's obvious what you were doing.''

Joe didn't know why this woman's remarks were getting to him. He'd never been too interested in what any female thought of him or his morals. He was a man's man. His own man.

"What do you want, Miss Pardee? My apology for being human?''

Her chin lifted to a frosty angle. "I don't need your apology. But this innocent baby does. He didn't ask for any of this.''

She was right, and as his gaze dropped to the child

snuggled against her breasts, Joe's resentment was suddenly replaced with bewilderment and a strange pull of attraction toward this redhead with a tart tongue.

"I'm not even sure the baby is mine," he said. "She wasn't interested in a serious relationship and neither was I. We really didn't spend that much time together before we called it quits."

Caroline's gaze drifted to Nicolas. It was so very hard for her to imagine something so precious not being created out of love.

"Apparently it was enough time to produce this little guy."

Desperate for some sort of proof, Joe left the chair to join her and the baby on the couch. Caroline was instantly aware of his hard body only inches away and the faint masculine scent that emanated from his clothes and hair. Everything about him was male and everything inside Caroline was reacting in a way that secretly shocked her. "Do you think—does he look like me?"

The slight quaver in his voice was an odd contrast to his big, tough appearance. Caroline suddenly felt herself softening toward the man.

"Well, his hair is black and his complexion is dark like yours."

She carefully studied the baby's face, then lifted her searching gaze to Joseph Garcia's stern, chiseled features. His wide forehead was set over a pair of incredibly dark, hooded eyes framed with thick black brows and lashes. His nose was on the large side, the lips beneath more full than thin. Yet it was the squared strength of his jaw and chin that gave his face character. He had the look of a man who could take a hard hit and still remain standing.

"Babies usually change in appearance after the first few weeks, but right now I'd say he has your stamp on him. Do you have any sort of birthmark he might have inherited? Why don't you look?"

Before he could answer, she extended the wrapped bundle to him. His response was to look at her as if she was offering him a bomb.

"I couldn't."

She frowned with impatience. "Why?"

He heaved out a breath as he looked from her to the boy. "I've never held a baby. I don't know how."

Caroline opened her mouth to scold him, then quickly shut it. She didn't know this man or what his life had been like. He might not be from a large family like she was.

"You've never been around children?"

"No," he said gruffly. "There aren't any children in the army."

"What about brothers or sisters?" she prodded.

"No. Just me. And growing up here didn't give me many neighbors."

Somehow his admission didn't surprise her. The

mark of a tough loner was stamped all over him. And the idea that he didn't have anyone close tugged greatly at Caroline's heart.

"Well, I think you need a quick introduction to babies," she said gently. "Nicolas is going to require a lot of care."

His dark eyes were once again filled with disbelief. "You're not expecting me to do it, are you?"

Smiling faintly, she leaned forward and pressed the infant into his arms. "Be careful to support his neck and head. He can't do it for himself right now."

Joe could truthfully say there wasn't much in life that unsettled him. For years he'd turned green young men into fighting machines. He prepared them for battle, taught them how to face fear and death. Still, that could hardly compare to nurturing a tiny, dependent child.

He positioned the baby in the crook of his big arm like a piece of fragile glass, then glanced from Nicolas to Caroline. "He's so little. And helpless."

A strange ache suddenly filled Caroline's heart. Not only for the child, but also for the big man holding him. "And so very precious."

Carefully, Joe brought his hand to the baby's head and touched the soft black hair. It was thick and stuck out in unruly spikes. Dark eyes stared at him.

"He has a dent in his chin. Like mine."

Caroline couldn't stop her gaze from slipping to

Joe's face. Everything about him was tough, striking. "Yes. I noticed."

His expression suddenly defensive, Joe glanced at her. "But that doesn't mean he belongs to me. Pamela might have been seeing some other guy."

"She named you the father. She's given him to you. That has to mean something."

"Maybe she's mistaken."

It was as though he wanted this to be a big mistake, Caroline thought. "If it's so important for you to know he carries your genes, you could always do a paternity test," she suggested. "But if I were you I would simply take him and love him and feel very blessed. No matter if he were of my blood or not."

Groaning, he quickly thrust the baby into her arms. "Look, Caroline, I—I'm not heartless, but I'm just not cut out for fatherhood. I can't be a daddy to this baby."

Her mouth fell open. "First of all, Nicolas is going to grow quickly. In no time at all, he'll be a little boy in school. He's going to need you! Not just now or then, but through his whole life!"

Joe left the couch and began to pace around the small room. "I never planned on being a husband, much less a father. I don't know the first thing about it!"

Maybe he had never wanted a family, but he'd obviously needed human contact with the opposite sex. Which was, after all, perfectly normal. He was a red-blooded male in every sense of the word. Still, she wanted to believe there was more to this man than a night of casual sex now and then.

"You knew all about getting him here," she couldn't stop herself from reminding him.

Joe stopped in his tracks and stabbed her with a hard glare. "That's the second time you've pointed that out. What's the matter with you, anyway? Do you have something against sex? Is that why you're not married or don't have a child of your own?"

Caroline did her best not to flinch at his questions. She wasn't a prude. She had given herself to a man before. But only because she'd believed she'd been in love with him. Not until later had she discovered he wasn't the solid, dependable man she'd thought him to be. The brief relationship had taught her a painful lesson about men and sex and love.

"I'm not married because I haven't yet found a man I want to live the rest of my life with. As for sex—" she paused to draw in a bracing breath "—I think it shouldn't take place unless it's done with love."

For one split second, Joe almost threw back his head and howled with laughter. But something on her face and in the way she clutched the infant to her breasts stopped him. "You'd better wake up, Miss Pardee. We're living in a cruel world. Life isn't all flowers and romance and love as you'd like to think."

"Caroline," she corrected. "You called me Caroline before. Why go back to Miss Pardee? Especially now that you've decided to be frank with me."

Joe didn't remember calling her by her given name, but then the past half hour she'd been more rattling to his senses than being under live gunfire.

"All right, Caroline, I am going to be frank. I don't have any business with a baby. I don't know the first thing about taking care of one. And I don't have any desire to learn. I'm a working man. A baby just wouldn't fit in my schedule or my life—or anything."

Still holding Nicolas, she stood and walked over to within a few scant inches from him. "I thought you said you were retired."

She was standing so close he could see the fine pores in her porcelain skin and a faint pulse beating at the base of her throat. Her nearness was like a drink of wine, warm and hard to resist. "I'm thirty-eight. I don't plan to sit on my a—my rear for the rest of my life just because I'm no longer a drill sergeant. I'm starting a new job next week with the DOC."

Her heart suddenly sank. Which was silly. It was nothing to her if this man was planning on becoming a lawman. "The Department of Corrections?"

He nodded. "Training prison guards, deputies, policemen."

The relief she felt was enough to leave her knees

weak, and she wondered what could be happening to her. It wasn't normal to get this stirred up over a stranger. "Then you're not planning on wearing a badge yourself?"

A curious frown puckered his brow. "No. Why?"

Feeling like a foolish schoolgirl with her first crush, Caroline quickly glanced away from him. "No reason. I just wondered."

Unwittingly, he reached out and touched her arm. It was smooth and warm, and the softness tempted him to slide his fingers back and forth against her skin. "There is a reason," he said more softly. "Tell me."

Did he really care what she'd been thinking? she wondered. Or was he simply getting back at her for all the personal questions she'd asked him?

Slowly, she forced herself to look at him. "My father was the sheriff of Lincoln County, New Mexico, for thirty-five years. He's a wonderful dad and I love him with all my heart. But all the while I was growing up, I was scared each time he walked out the door. I'd go to my room and cry because I was afraid someone would shoot him and I'd never see him again. I'd hate to see little Nicolas go through the same thing."

Clearly her concern was for the baby's sake, but Joe couldn't help wonder what it would feel like to have a woman like Caroline care about him. "I'm not going to be a lawman," he murmured.

Caroline tried to remember she had a baby in her arms and she'd only met this man. But all she could think about was the feel of his hand and his dark eyes sliding slowly over her face. "I'm glad. Because you are going to be Nick's father."

She stated it as a fact. As though she wouldn't allow him any other choice. Joe couldn't recall meeting a more headstrong woman than this beauty standing in front of him. But then he hadn't exactly gone out looking for her type. He'd always preferred women who were content to let him call the shots.

"I followed my superiors' orders for twenty years because that was my duty as a soldier." His lips suddenly twisted with cocky certainty. "But I'm no longer a soldier, and you're sure as hell not my superior."

If any other man had talked to her in such a fashion, she would have been furious. But Joe was different. He made her *feel* different. "What about your duty as a man?"

Her calmly spoken question gouged him as nothing else could. He turned and walked across the room to a tall, arched window. The view looked down the mountain toward his house, the place his father had lived out the last years of his life. Joseph Senior hadn't been the best of fathers, but he had tried in his own way. Was that all this woman was expecting of him?

"Maybe I'm just a sorry bastard. Did that ever

occur to you? Maybe Nicolas would be a lot better off with someone else, a family who wanted him.''

Although he was a few feet away from her, Caroline could see his painful swallow and the wretched shadows in his eyes. No matter if he wanted her to believe otherwise, he was a decent man.

''Perhaps you're right. You could always give him up for adoption. There's thousands of childless couples who would consider Nicolas a gift from God.'' She placed the sleeping baby on the end cushion of the couch, then, after making certain he was warmly covered, she walked over to where Joe stood at the window. ''I think the first thing you need to do is get some legal advice. You can't be certain the papers that arrived with Nicolas are valid. Do you know a lawyer here in Santa Fe?''

He grunted. ''I don't know a lawyer anywhere. I've never had a need for one.''

She sighed. ''Well, several people in my family work in law. As I told you earlier, my father is a retired sheriff. My brother is a Texas Ranger, my cousin is the present sheriff of Lincoln County and his wife is a judge there, also. I'm sure one of them can give me some advice as to what sort of legal procedures you need to take next.''

He turned from the window to face her. ''We don't need—I mean I don't necessarily need to do anything about him tonight, do you think? He doesn't appear to be harmed, and if I am really the father I don't have to report to anyone that I have my own child.''

She mulled over his words. "No. Put that way I don't expect you do.''

He crossed the room to the couch, and as he stared at the sleeping baby his expression turned regretful. "I suppose if I don't keep him he'll go to a state orphanage.''

Caroline couldn't bear to think of the newborn in such a place and instantly decided she would do everything in her power to prevent it.

"Yes. Then more than likely he'll be sent on to a foster parent. But like you said, Nick might be better off with one of those than with you.''

He shot her a tired look over his shoulder. "Don't try to use reverse psychology on me. It won't work.''

"Reverse psychology?'' She laughed with disbelief. "I was serious. If you don't want Nick, it would be disastrous for both of you if you attempted to raise him. I happen to think he deserves better.''

"You think being wanted by someone is all that matters in this world?''

"It's all that matters to me.''

His gaze slipped over her luscious curves silhouetted by the stormy sky beyond the window. No doubt she'd been wanted by many men, and he was half afraid he was becoming one of them. But that wasn't the sort of wanting she was referring to. Caroline Pardee was talking about love. Something Joe knew nothing about. As for wanting a woman with his heart, needing her for a lifetime, he'd never gotten that close, that vulnerable before. He couldn't do it. He'd watched his father grieve himself to death over a broken marriage. He had no intention of making the same mistake.

"I've got to go," he muttered, then before Caroline could open her mouth, he was out the door and gone.

Chapter 2

"Mom, it's just like you finding Adam and Anna on the porch of the Bar M! Only this baby is a newborn! Isn't it the most unbelievable thing you've ever heard?"

"Are you sure you didn't have too much wine with supper, Caroline?"

From the sound of her voice, Caroline could tell her mother didn't know whether to laugh or cry, and she could certainly understand why. More than thirty years ago, Justine had found twin babies on the porch of her family ranch, which she later discovered were her half siblings. Hearing her daughter had found a baby of her own must seem like an incredible coincidence.

"It's true, Mom. I can't tell you how shocking it was when I looked down and saw a tiny baby in a basket!" she exclaimed, then because her mother had been a nurse for thirty years, she went on to assure her that Nicolas appeared to be in perfect health.

"That's good," Justine said. "Now what about the authorities? Have you contacted them?"

"Uh—no. You see, this is different than when you found Adam and Anna. I know who this baby belongs to. I have his birth certificate."

"You're joking! What kind of idiot would set themselves up to be charged with child abandonment?"

"The mother. She thought she was leaving the baby on the father's doorstep. He's my neighbor, and I guess she got the houses mixed up or something. Anyway, he didn't know anything about the child until I called him."

"Oh. Then he's already picked him up?"

Caroline tamped down a sigh as she recalled the look on Joe's face when he'd handed Nick back to her. "Not exactly. The baby is still here with me."

"With you! Why hasn't he come after him?"

Caroline sighed. "He did come up here to the house. But—well, to put it plainly, Mother, Joe is in a state of shock. He doesn't know what to do yet."

"Joe? He's the neighbor who's supposedly the father?"

"Yes. Joseph Garcia."

"Well, your father could advise you about the legal part of this, but he's not home right now. You might call Ethan and Penny."

"I will," Caroline promised.

"So what's this man like, honey? I don't like the idea that you might be getting mixed up in something ugly."

There wasn't anything ugly about Joe Garcia, Caroline thought. In fact the man was just too damned tempting for her own good. "He's not a weirdo or anything. He's retired from the army."

"Dear Lord, this sounds more and more like your grandfather's story. An older man having an affair with a young woman. Don't tell me he's married, too."

Caroline rolled her green eyes. "No. He isn't married. And he isn't an older man. He's only seven years older than me. Next week he's taking on a new job with the DOC here in New Mexico."

"Hmm. Sounds like you learned a lot about the man in one short visit. Did you like him?"

Caroline knew exactly where her mother's thoughts were headed. Her parents had expected her to marry a long time ago. Instead, she'd thrown herself into her career as a jewelry designer. Not because she'd planned things that way. It had just slowly happened as one boyfriend and then another and another had been checked off her list.

"Mom, one of these days I will find Mr. Right."

"There is no Mr. Right or Mr. Perfect out there, Caroline. When you take a man into your heart you have to take his flaws along with him. Otherwise you're going to be living the rest of your life alone."

Caroline glanced at the sleeping infant on the opposite end of the couch. For so many years she'd imagined herself with a husband and children. But she wasn't going to marry just for the sake of having a family. She had to be in love. Deeply in love, the same way her parents had been for more than thirty years. And that just hadn't happened yet.

"I know you and Dad think I'm too picky. But I want what you two have. I'm not going to settle for less."

Justine sighed. "Well, tell me more about the baby's father. Is he handsome?"

Caroline didn't really want to think about Joseph Garcia's looks. Everything about the man had disturbed her. "He's not exactly handsome. I guess striking would be a better word. Along with tall, massive and rock hard."

"Is that last part describing his body or his attitude?"

Caroline sighed. "Both."

"Then maybe he shouldn't try to keep the baby. He might not have fatherly instincts. Not all men do, you know. And if he's spent practically all of his adulthood in the army, he probably is a tough man.

He might not know anything about families or babies.''

"He admitted he didn't. And he went on to say that Nick needs two parents.''

"Then the man isn't stupid. It sounds as though he wants to do what's best for the child.''

"Yes," Caroline agreed, but her mother hadn't seen Joe when he held the baby in his arms. She knew he'd felt something and she believed if he'd only give himself a chance, he'd be a good father. "But right now, I'm not sure what to do. It's a cinch he's not coming back tonight. And I have nothing here to care for the baby. I don't see any choice but to drive into the city and do some shopping.''

"Oh, there are other choices, Caroline. You could take the baby to his father and forget the whole matter. Or you could call the state welfare department, and they'll send someone out to get the baby.''

"No! Never!" she responded fiercely. "I'm not going to let this child be treated like an orphan when he isn't! His daddy is going to come to his senses. I'm going to see to it!''

Caroline's outburst must have stunned her mother. Silence hung in her ear for a long time, then Justine said, "All right, since you're so set on this, the only thing I can say is be careful.''

Caroline arched her brows at her mother's warning. "Careful? Of what? All I'm going to do is babysit for a few days while Joe Garcia has time to adjust to becoming a father. There's nothing dangerous in that.''

"Maybe not. But meanwhile, you might just become very attached to that little boy, Caroline. And if you do, it will be painful when you're forced to give him up.''

Caroline realized her mother was right. Only a few hours had passed since she'd come home and discovered Nick on the doorstep and already she was getting used to him being in the house. Every few minutes she found herself leaning over the child, staring in wonder at his precious face.

"I'll just have to take that chance. I have to do what I feel is right,'' she said, then quickly told her mother goodbye.

The rain had fled with the sinking sun, and broken clouds skidded quickly across the dark skies over Santa Fe. On the drive up the mountain, Caroline glanced in the direction of Joe Garcia's house. Lights were on in the small stucco, but she didn't stop or let up on the accelerator. She wasn't going to beg the man to love or need his child. He had to come to that conclusion on his own. And right now she had more things to worry about than a stubborn, retired drill sergeant.

From the moment she'd lifted Nick out of the laundry basket, she'd felt a connection, a bond that went far deeper than a woman attending to a helpless child. Nicolas had come to her for some reason. In her heart she believed an angel had brought him to her doorstep and it was truly her job to love and nurture him as her own child.

Minutes later, her heart nearly stopped. A pickup was parked near her carport, and one glance at the man inside told her it was Joe.

By the time she parked her car, he was waiting a few steps away. His muscled arms were folded, his long legs planted firmly apart.

Even though her dad and brother were brawny men, she'd never found herself physically drawn to tough guys. A man's intellect was the thing that stimulated her. Or so she'd always believed. But there was something about Joseph Garcia's powerful body that set her pulse pounding.

"Where have you been?"

The question hit her the moment she swung her legs to the ground. Vexed by his demanding attitude, she quickly countered, "Where do you think I've been?"

"To the authorities."

The spurt of anger she'd felt at him quickly died. He'd been worried. "No," she assured him. "I've been to the store. Nick needed several things."

She climbed out of the car, then leaned inside to unbuckle the baby carrier from the car seat.

"Where is he?"

The barked question made Caroline want to ask

him if he really cared. But she held her tongue. The man had come back tonight. And whether or not he realized it, his being here said he cared at least a little.

"He's right here. Where else would he be?" With the baby carrier firmly in her grip, she eased out of the car and turned to face him.

"I didn't know," he replied. Actually, when Joe had decided to return to Caroline's house, he'd been stunned to find her and the baby gone. All sorts of scenarios had rushed through his head. In the main one she'd gone to the local police or the child welfare agency. He'd been telling himself it would be okay if she had. Someone had to take care of the baby. He couldn't. Yet he felt immense relief that the two of them were safely back and nothing had changed for the time being.

"The trunk is full of bags," she told him as she headed into the house. "Would you carry them in for me? I want to get Nick out of this damp night air."

Joe was amazed to find several shopping bags filled with diapers and formula, and all sorts of blankets, bottles and clothes. He even spotted the head of a little brown teddy bear sticking out of one sack.

Before he could ask himself what it all meant, he gathered the bags in both arms, shut the trunk lid and entered the house through the side door she'd used.

Joe found himself inside a warm, brightly lit kitchen. The vague scents of chicken and spices lingered in the cozy little room, making him realize he'd not eaten since lunchtime.

After placing the bags on a small wooden dinette table, he glanced around him. Bright colors seemed to be everywhere. Yellow and orange printed curtains partially covered the windows. Cooking pots in red porcelain enamel hung on one wall by a heavy-duty gas range. Above the sink two clusters of dried chilies swung from an arched enclosure between the pine cabinets. Nearby was a pot of yellow daffodils, and across the way, on a wide window ledge, red geraniums spilled over a huge terra-cotta pot.

The kitchen was not anything like the drab work space in his father's home. Seeing this room made him wonder if Caroline ever cooked for friends or a man. He had no idea what she did for a living, but she appeared to be financially secure and then some.

"Where's the bassinet?"

At the sound of her voice, he turned to see her entering the kitchen. She'd changed into a pair of black jeans and a thin white sweater. Her vivid hair was gathered in a barrette atop her head and tumbled down her neck in a cascade of wild curls. The sight of her left him feeling as if the wind had been knocked from his chest.

"What's a bassinet?"

She gave him a patient smile. "A little woven

basket on wheels that makes a portable bed for the baby. I'm sure I loaded it in the trunk.''

"It probably slid to the back. I'll go look.''

In less than two minutes he was back with the bed in hand. ''Where do you want me to put it?''

"In the living room for now.'' She went to the gas range and reached for a percolator that matched the red pots. ''Would you like coffee? I'm going to make a fresh pot.''

"I hadn't planned on staying long.'' In fact, one look at the sexy sight of her made him forget why he was here in the first place.

"It will perk in just a few minutes,'' she assured him while thrusting the pot under the tap.

He'd be a fool to get cozy with this woman, but he was already here, and coffee was innocent enough. ''All right. I'll go set this up for you.''

Moments later, she joined him in the living room. He was screwing the rollers into the legs of the bassinet. On the couch, Nicolas was squirming and waking. The sight warmed her, and she realized that having Joe in the house made her happy. Way too happy.

Sensing her presence, Joe glanced over his shoulder to see Caroline standing a couple of steps behind him. A faint smile curved her full lips, and he tried to remember a woman from his past who'd affected him as much as this one. But there wasn't any.

"You went to a lot of expense," he said, "for a child who isn't yours."

Nicolas was beginning to feel like her child, which Caroline knew was dangerous. But how could she stop herself? No more than she could stop herself from looking at Joe and wondering what it was like to be the object of his affection. Heady, no doubt.

She cleared her throat and said, "The expense was nothing. I want Nick to be safe and comfortable. For as long as I have him," she forced herself to add.

Joe wanted to ask how long that would be, but he wouldn't let himself. If he did, the whole issue of what to do with the baby would start all over again, and he couldn't deal with that tonight.

Straightening to his full height, he motioned to the white bassinet. "I think this thing is ready."

"Thanks. I'll get the sheets and blankets. Thankfully I found a set that was pre-washed."

She left for the kitchen, and as he watched her swinging hips disappear from sight, the baby let out an unhappy squall. Joe glanced over to see a pair of tiny fists flailing the air.

He didn't know why babies cried, and even if he did he wouldn't know how to make them stop. Whatever was wrong would have to wait until Caroline returned.

Nicolas let out another lusty yell and then another. Joe ventured toward the couch to see if he could spot what was wrong, but the only thing evident to him was an angry red face.

"What's the matter, trooper?"

The moment he spoke, the baby stilled. Encouraged, Joe sat down on the cushion next to him and leaned closer. The tiny boy smelled of powder, and his dark hair had been slicked to one side with baby oil. Just to look at him filled Joe's chest with an odd pressure.

"If I didn't have any teeth I'd probably be crying, too," he said to the baby.

Nicolas whimpered, and instinctively Joe reached out and brushed the pads of his fingers against the child's cheek. It was warm and incredibly soft, the skin already tinged golden brown. And as he studied the baby, he couldn't help but wonder how his own father had felt when he'd first looked at him. Proud? Scared? Or just downright overwhelmed?

As for Joe's mother, she'd cared nothing about her offspring. By the time Joe had turned two, she'd left town and never bothered to come back.

"The way you're frowning, it's no wonder Nick's crying."

The sound of Caroline's voice pulled Joe from his somber thoughts, and he turned his head to look at her. "Why *is* he crying? What's wrong with him now?"

She quickly covered the bottom of the bassinet with a sheet printed with happy ducks and geese.

"Crying doesn't necessarily mean something is wrong. That's his only way of communicating. He's trying to tell us he's wet or hungry or uncomfortable or lonely."

"How can a baby get lonely? He's not old enough to talk and socialize."

"No. But he knows when he's alone. He needs to feel your touch and hear your voice to be reassured he hasn't been abandoned."

Joe had to believe the woman knew what she was talking about. Only moments ago Nick had quieted when he'd spoken to him. "If you've never been married or had a child of your own, how do you know so much about babies?"

The question made her glance at him, and as her eyes locked with his, she felt a rush of heat sting her cheeks. Everything about the man reminded her she was a woman who hadn't dated in a long time, much less been made love to.

"I don't know everything about them," she admitted. "But I learned from my nieces and nephews. Unfortunately none of them live here in Santa Fe."

She folded a thick blanket and placed it at the foot of the little bed, then tucked the teddy bear to one side. "What about you?" she asked. "Do you have any family around here?"

"No."

"Where are they?"

He glanced at the baby and was amazed to see he

was drifting back to sleep. "I told you before. My father is dead and I don't have any siblings."

"What about your mother?"

His cynical snort brought Caroline's gaze to his face. "She cut out when I was two. I don't remember much about her."

Caroline's brows lifted. "Cut out? You mean she left?"

Bitter resignation twisted his lips. "And was never heard from since. I guess she'd had all of me and my father she could stand. From what he and others said, she ran off with a local musician. She fancied herself as a singer and was always dreaming of becoming a big country music star. Obviously that didn't happen."

Drawn by his story, Caroline went to stand in front of him. "Did your dad remarry and give you a stepmother?"

His caustic laugh ripped at something inside Caroline.

"After Dolores, Dad didn't care much for women. He spent the rest of his life alone."

Caroline shook her head with sad regret. "Then you know what it's like to grow up without a mother?"

His dark gaze was full of conviction as it leveled with hers. "Yes. And I don't want that for Nick. I don't want it for any child."

He didn't want to be married, yet he didn't want

Nick to be motherless. Maybe she was crazy to think she could change his mind about keeping the baby, Caroline thought. "Well, at least you had your father," she reminded him. "Was he good to you?"

Joe shrugged one shoulder. "He didn't mistreat me, if that's what you mean. As for being a good father, I don't know. He made sure I understood right from wrong, that I got an education and learned how to take care of myself. But he was a quiet man who kept his feelings to himself. I never really knew if he loved me or just more or less accepted me as his responsibility."

Caroline gently eased down on the cushion next to him. "Can't you see what's happening, Joe? Nick has already been deserted by his birth mother. He can't lose both of you!"

Grimacing, he leaned forward and propped his elbows on his parted knees. "I sure as hell know he didn't need Pam for a mother. She doesn't have the material for it, if you know what I mean." He let out a rough sigh. "Frankly, I'm surprised she didn't terminate the pregnancy. But her family has money. Quite a bit of it, and I don't figure she wanted to be written out of the will by going against their religion. Even if she is going to marry a rich man."

Everything about Joseph Garcia was tough. His deep voice, his muscled body, even his black eyes were hard. Yet there was something about the man that drew Caroline as nothing had before. Somewhere inside him there was a soft spot. Maybe it was hidden. Maybe he didn't even know he had it. But she would find it. Somehow. Some way.

Unable to stop herself, she reached out and placed her hand on his forearm. The touch brought his face around to hers, and her heart took off in a mad gallop.

"My family has quite a bit of money, too," she told him. "But that wouldn't motivate me to give up a baby. Nothing could."

His dark gaze slipped over her face to settle on her lips. "The why of it doesn't matter anymore."

Where he was concerned, the why of things mattered too much, Caroline thought. "Why did you come back tonight, Joe?"

For you. For the baby. Because I'm a fool and I couldn't help myself. To Caroline, he murmured, "I don't really know."

Her fingers tightened ever so slightly on his arm. "Well," she said softly, "whatever the reason, I'm glad."

The touch of her hand, the sweet scent of her hair and skin, the honesty on her face were all working Joe's senses, quietly tugging him toward her.

"I'm not so sure you should be."

Her brows lifted and then her lips parted to ask him what he meant. But she never had the chance.

Suddenly his head dipped down to hers, and his face was so close she could see the pores in his skin, the chocolate brown flecks in his eyes and a tiny chip on the edge of his front tooth.

"You're the most enticing creature I've ever seen," he whispered roughly.

Something inside Caroline quivered with need as he thrust one of his big hands into the hair lying against the side of her neck. "But I'm not the mother of your baby." She felt the odd need to remind him.

His lips twisted in a purely sensual way. "Would you like to be?"

A soft gasp rushed past her lips, and then he was kissing her, drawing her into the circle of his arms, and all she could do was let him.

Chapter 3

The odd notion flitted through Caroline's mind that she was being kissed, really kissed, for the first time in her life.

The pure male scent of him filled her nostrils as the lazy inspection of his warm lips urged her to lean into him and open her mouth. She did so without thinking, and as he deepened the contact between them, her hands fluttered to his shoulders, then latched onto their solid strength.

Joe groaned, and Caroline's head reeled.

Then, without warning, a loud hissing sound exploded from the kitchen. The interruption was such a shock to Caroline's muddled senses, she jumped back from Joe as though he'd touched her with a bolt of electrical current.

"The coffee!"

She leaped to her feet and rushed to the kitchen. The percolator was boiling over onto the gas burner, dousing part of the blaze and filling the reflector pan with coffee and grounds.

With a loud groan, she quickly shut off the gas and reached for a sponge. Her hands shook as she mopped at the hot liquid, and her breaths were coming and going in rapid spurts.

Caroline didn't know what had come over her. Never in her life had she done anything so impulsive or reckless. She'd been kissing Joe as if he were her lover. And she didn't even know the man!

"What's wrong?"

His voice caused her to jerk as if she'd been shot. Drawing in a much-needed breath, she dared to glance over her shoulder at him.

"The coffee boiled over. That's all. It's nothing. I have it under control now." But not herself, she thought wildly, as her eyes collided with his. Her cheeks were on fire and her head was still full of the scent of him. The imprint of his lips continued to burn upon hers.

She stepped to the sink and rinsed the sponge. When she turned, Joe was standing right in front of her.

He inclined his head toward the stove. "I'm sorry about the mess, Caroline. But as for the kiss—"

He moved closer, and she felt herself melting inside as his hand reached out and touched her hair. "Well, I'm not going to apologize for the kiss."

Her brows lifted, and eventually she managed to get out one weak word. "Oh."

The corner of his lips curled upward, and Caroline was reminded all over again of the warm possession of his mouth on hers. It was crazy how much she wanted to kiss him again.

"It was nice," he said. "Too nice to be sorry about."

She heaved out the breath she'd been holding for the past five seconds. "Do you make a habit of kissing women you hardly know?"

His expression was suddenly a little sheepish and a whole lot frustrated. "No. Contrary to what you're thinking, I'm not a womanizer. You just happen to be very beautiful, Caroline. And you were so close I couldn't resist. That's the only excuse I can give you."

She couldn't be angry with him. It would be hypocritical after the passionate way she'd responded to him.

"I guess these past few hours we've both been under...unusual circumstances," she said quietly.

His hand dropped from the curls on her shoulder. "Would you like for me to go?"

The question caught her off guard, and for a moment all she could do was stare at him. She'd not thought of asking him to leave. In fact, ever since he'd kissed her, she'd been incapable of thinking about much at all. That should be enough to convince her to send him packing back down the mountain. She shouldn't be attracted to Joe Garcia! He wasn't looking for love or marriage. It would be disastrous to fall for him when there could be no future in it.

But Caroline had to forget about herself for a moment and think about Nick. He needed his father, and as far as she could see, she was the only connecting link between the two.

She moved to the stove and began to wipe up the remaining mess. "There's no need for you to leave," she said as casually as she could manage. "I can forget the kiss—if you can."

"I don't want you to feel threatened by me."

She closed her eyes. He didn't make her feel threatened. At least not in the way he was thinking. But he had shaken her badly. A kiss wasn't supposed to do that much to a woman. "As long as you promise not to repeat that...performance in the living room, we'll get along fine."

"All right. I promise. Hands off," he told her.

But as Joe watched her fetch cups and saucers from the pine cabinets, he wondered if he'd suddenly lost his mind. How was he going to forget about kissing Caroline Pardee when it was all he could do to keep from walking across the kitchen floor, taking her into his arms and doing it all over again? Just looking at her fired his blood.

She must have accepted his promise because she turned and gestured toward the small dining table. "If you'd like to sit, I'll serve the coffee."

"What about Nick? Will he be all right by himself?"

Caroline was pleased and not entirely surprised he'd thought about the baby before himself. He was that sort of man. He just didn't know it yet.

"Don't worry. I'm going to put him in the bassinet and move him in here."

She left the kitchen and in a matter of moments returned with the little portable bed.

"He's still asleep," she said, leaning over the baby and making sure the blankets were tucked around him. "I think he'll be out for a few hours now."

Joe didn't know how she could know such a thing. And he didn't ask. If he kept popping questions about the little guy, she was going to get the idea he was interested.

Caroline filled their cups and offered him cream and sugar. After he'd taken a seat and stirred a dollop of half-and-half into his cup, she asked, "Have you eaten this evening?"

Food had been the last thing on Joe's mind. "No."

"I have a few leftovers in the fridge. It won't take a minute to heat them in the microwave."

Joe couldn't believe she might actually care if he was hungry. Especially after the way he'd kissed her. Damn it, that had been one of the more stupid things he'd ever done in his life. But then, she'd more than kissed him back, he argued with himself.

"I don't want to put you out."

She gave him a brief smile as she started toward the refrigerator. "My mother says when a woman feeds a man she's also nurturing his soul."

His gaze slid over her curved bottom as she bent to search the refrigerator shelf. "Have you fed many men?"

"Not really."

"Why is that?"

The question was out before Joe could stop it. But damn it, he was intrigued with the woman. And not just because she'd found baby Nick on her doorstep. No matter where he might have met up with her, he knew she would have turned his head. Even though she wasn't his type, her beauty and sensuality were too much for any man to ignore.

A plastic container in hand, Caroline headed toward the microwave. "My parents say it's because I'm too picky. I think it's because I'm too smart."

No doubt she would expect a lot from a man, Joe thought, like a nice, secure home and money to support her life-style. But more than those things, she would want his deep abiding love—the very thing Joe refused to give any woman. The idea helped to remind him that she was a woman who would always be off limits to a man like him. Still, that didn't stop him from looking or wanting.

"You're a successful woman. I'm sure you're happy the way you are."

His statement had her glancing at the sleeping baby, then back to him. She was happy. She loved her job and she was very proud her gallery had turned out to be a success. She had many friends and a host of relatives who loved her. But a husband and child were missing in her life. The two things that would make her life full and meaningful.

"Success doesn't keep you company," she said.

Joe couldn't believe the woman ever lacked male company. But then maybe her standards were so high she couldn't find a man to match up to her wants.

The bell on the microwave dinged. Caroline carried a plate of chicken and rice and warm tortillas to the table and placed it in front of him.

He glanced gratefully at her, and as his eyes met the soft shimmer in hers, something warm and strange pierced the middle of his chest. The feeling startled him, and he quickly dropped his gaze to the plate of food.

"Thanks," he said gruffly.

"You're welcome," she replied.

She sank into the chair at his right elbow and picked up her coffee. As she sipped, she wanted to ask him again why he'd come back to her house. She'd been shocked to see him parked in the drive. But perhaps it was even more of a surprise that he was still here, sitting at her table, eating. Maybe he'd come back because of her. Or it could have been because of the baby. Whatever the reason, he'd cared enough to come, and that was all that really mattered.

"Do you miss being in the army?" she asked. "You must, after devoting twenty years of your life to the service."

He glanced up from his plate, and she felt her breath catch in her throat as his dark eyes took their time searching her face.

"Getting used to civilian living is taking some doing," he admitted. "But that part of my life is over. It's time to start a new one."

"What was it like? Being a soldier for all those years?"

Pam or any of the women he'd encountered through the years had never cared about his career or his feelings toward it. His twenty years of dedication to the service had meant nothing to them. To think Caroline could really be interested in his life touched him in a way that left him feeling oddly vulnerable.

His eyes on his plate, he said, "It was rigid. Disciplined. Routine."

She placed her cup on its saucer. "I've never known a military man before. My family are all ranchers and lawmen. That's what their fathers before them were, so I guess that sort of life was bred in their genes."

She came from a family where tradition meant something, where parents and grandparents and generations before were known and remembered. Hell, he didn't even know where his mother had come from, much less where she'd gone, Joe thought.

"Where does your family live?" he asked her.

"Down in southern New Mexico in Lincoln County. Except for my brother, Charlie. He's a member of the Texas Rangers and lives near Austin." She picked up her mug, took another careful sip and watched his hands as he ate. They were big, strong hands, the color of rich coffee, the backs sprinkled with black hair. Nick would always be safe in those hands. Somehow she was sure of it. As for a woman, well, Caroline figured making her feel safe would only be a part of what those hands could do.

"Was your father a military man?"

"No. He was a mechanic."

"Then how did you come to be in the army?" she asked curiously.

Joe never talked about himself. His life wasn't

anything to brag about. And no one really seemed to be interested, anyway.

"You'd only be bored if I told you. My life is nothing special."

Her soft smile was full of encouragement. "Why don't you let me be the judge of that?"

Her words, coupled with the tender expression on her face, were Joe's undoing. With a sigh of resignation, he reached for his coffee.

"Well, if you really want to know, after I graduated high school I needed some sort of job so I wouldn't be a burden to my father anymore. And the army was a quick way to get a career going."

Caroline tried to imagine how it would feel to think of herself as a burden to her parents. She couldn't. Her parents had always made her feel loved and special and wanted.

"Why did you think you were a hardship on your father? Did you give him problems while you were growing up?"

"I never did anything to anger my father. But I knew it was my fault he was so unhappy."

Her eyes suddenly misted over as she imagined the heavy weight he must have carried around in his heart. Maybe he was still carrying it. For some reason she didn't understand, she desperately wanted to ease it, to take away all the pain and loneliness he'd ever felt. "How could you make him unhappy? You were his son."

His features tightened. "That's right. *I* was the reason my mother left my father. Dolores didn't want a squalling brat tying her down. And Joseph never got over losing her. He spent the rest of his life just going through the motions, getting him from one day to the next."

It was on the tip of Caroline's tongue to tell Joe he wasn't the reason for his father's sad existence, it was Dolores's selfishness. But she kept the thought to herself. She didn't want him to think she was getting personal.

You are getting personal, Caroline. You've been getting personal with the man ever since he first walked through the door.

Trying to shake off the little voice of warning, she glanced at his brooding face. "So you believed leaving home and your dad behind would make him happier. Did it?"

He shrugged and returned his gaze to the nearly empty plate before him. "No. Not really. But at least the old man didn't have to work as hard. And eventually I was able to help him retire."

"That must have made you feel good."

His gaze lifted to her face, and his heart squeezed at the compassion he found in her eyes. "A little," he murmured.

"Maybe Nick will care about you like that someday."

He didn't want to think about the sleeping baby

in the bassinet growing up to love or need him. He didn't want to think about anyone loving or needing him. That was too much of a connection for Joe.

He took a sip of coffee and quickly changed the subject. "So why do you live in Santa Fe and not in Lincoln County with your family? Don't you get along with them?"

Caroline laughed softly. "I get along with all my family. So well that I want to drive down to the ranch more than I should. As for living here in Santa Fe, it wasn't intentional. Several years ago, I happened to come up here to sell a few pieces of jewelry and from the first moment I saw the city, I guess you'd say I was enthralled. Like the old saying goes, it truly is an inspiring place for writers and artists."

Surprise flickered across his face. "You sell jewelry for a living? I figured you were some sort of money investor or something like that."

As Joe watched the corners of her lips curve with amusement, he wondered why she had to be so beautiful, so damned desirable. If she hadn't been, then maybe he could have walked away the first time and forgotten all about her and the baby.

She said, "I would never have the urge or the nerve to play with other people's money. As for the jewelry, selling it is a part of what I do. But I also design it. Southwestern-style pieces with copper and silver, turquoise, coral and marcasite. That sort of thing."

"I don't mean to sound critical, but that kind of jewelry can be found on every street corner from here to the border of Mexico." He placed the fork on his empty plate and pushed it aside. "Do you make money at it?"

"At first I didn't," she admitted. "But I'm an artist. I also paint and sculpt, and thankfully, after a while, people began to take notice of my work. Now I have my own gallery and even an assistant. I also sell other artists' works on commission."

Entranced, Joe watched her push the thick swathe of red curls from one ear and lean toward him. Her musky scent once again floated to his nostrils, and as his eyes drifted to the moist curves of her lips, he wondered if she thought he was made of iron or if she was deliberately testing his word.

"See this little coyote?" she asked, touching a forefinger to the copper figure dangling from her ear. "I made these earrings a long time ago, but they're a good example of my work."

Joe forced himself to look at the wild creature etched in copper rather than her soft skin and tempting lips. "He looks authentic. You do beautiful work," he murmured.

Caroline suddenly realized she was too close as the odd glitter in his eyes beckoned her to lean even closer and press her cheek against his warm brown skin. For a moment she almost gave in to the urge, but common sense forced her to finally tear her eyes away from his and ease back in the chair.

"Thank you. Maybe you could come by my gallery sometime. It's not far from the Palace of Governors in old downtown."

The space she'd purposely put between them sobered Joe somewhat, but the craving to touch her lingered, making it difficult to concentrate on her words. "What's the place called?"

"The Red Mesa."

One corner of his lips cocked upward as his eyes slowly meandered over her face. "Maybe I will come in and look around sometime. My walls could use a bit of dressing up. But I doubt I could afford your work."

Or her, he thought ruefully. No doubt she was used to having plenty of money and the social standing that went with it. She was artful, classy and successful, a world apart from his simple life. That was something he needed to remember every time he got the urge to kiss her. Which was too damn often for his peace of mind.

With a shake of her head, Caroline shot him a provocative smile. "I promise not all the pieces are pricey. And I'm a woman who will bargain."

Yeah, but just how far would she be willing to drop her price for him? Joe wondered. Not nearly far enough, he figured.

A few feet away the baby began to squirm and

whimper. Joe was suddenly reminded of exactly why he was sitting in Caroline Pardee's kitchen and why, more than likely, she'd given him the small supper and conversation. It was all for the baby. It was her way of softening him into thinking he needed the boy on a permanent basis.

"You said he'd sleep for hours," Joe reminded her.

As Caroline rose to her feet, she gave him a rueful smile. "That tells you how much I really know about babies."

She crossed the short space to the bassinet and quickly checked Nick's diaper. "Dry and clean. He must be hungry again."

She removed a can of formula from one of the sacks and went about filling a bottle. Suddenly, the domestic sight of her at the counter and the baby in his bed made Joe more than uncomfortable. Caroline was a pleasure to look at, but if a stranger were to walk in, the three of them would appear as a family. Mother, father and baby. And he didn't belong in the picture.

He said, "It's time for me to go."

Caroline glanced over her shoulder to see him rising to his feet. "Why don't you stay and give Nick his bottle?"

He looked at the baby, whose face was growing redder by the minute. Nick needed someone to love and care for him. Someone like Caroline Pardee. Not

Joe Garcia. He didn't want anyone to depend on him for emotional support. He was much better at the physical world.

"I don't know anything about feeding a baby."

"Maybe it's time you learned," she suggested.

Frowning, he moved toward the door. "Even if it turns out that Nick is really mine, I just don't think I could ever be a daddy."

Caroline could see arguing with him tonight would get them nowhere. It was clear he hadn't yet accepted the idea that he'd fathered a child, much less that he could be a daddy to one.

"Well, until you can come to some sort of decision, you don't have to worry about Nick," she said gently. "I'll be here to take care of him. For as long as is needed."

Her unexpected words caused him to pause. With his hand on the doorknob, he glanced at her. "You can't care for a baby and do your work, too."

She placed the bottle in the microwave. "Right now, Nick is more important to me." *And so are you,* she wanted to add. The notion was scandalous. She'd only met the man this afternoon. But already she cared about his life. She wanted him to be happy.

He let out a rough sigh, then raked a hand through his short, dark hair. "Right now I can't tell you what's going to happen. I don't even know when I'll be able to tell you."

A few hours ago his comments would've disgusted Caroline. But she knew a little more about Joe Garcia, and she realized he was a man who didn't know what it felt like to be loved or wanted or needed. From all that he'd told her, he'd never had much of a family. He didn't understand how important he was to little Nick. Or how much the child would enrich his life.

"I can wait on you," she assured him.

He shook his head with disbelief. "Why are you doing this?"

The baby whimpered louder. Caroline picked him up, then turned a smile on Joe. "Do you believe in angels, Joe?"

The unusual question made him stare at her in complete bewilderment. "Angels? What have angels got to do with anything?"

She carried the baby to where he stood, one hand on the doorknob, apparently ready to bolt at any moment. "Do you believe in them?" she repeated.

"I hadn't really thought about it. I believe in God, so I suppose I do."

"Good. Then you'll understand when I tell you I believe an angel brought Nick to my door."

A scowl puckered his forehead. "That's a crazy notion. Pam must have left the baby. Or someone did the job for her."

Shaking her head, Caroline said, "I don't mean an angel drove the vehicle and placed Nick on the porch. It probably was your ex-girlfriend or someone she knew. But an angel directed her or him to this house—*my* house. For a special reason.''

He wasn't going to argue with her. He wasn't an overly spiritual man, but he'd always believed God was ruling his fate. And until now, fate had made it pretty clear to him that he wasn't meant to have a family of his own.

''And what is the reason, do you think?''

She was relieved he wasn't laughing. ''To make sure Nick will always be loved and cared for.''

What would he have done if he'd discovered the baby on his doorstep? Joe asked himself. More than likely he would have called the child welfare agency. But Caroline was making him think and feel things about himself and his life that he'd never felt before. Maybe *she* was the angel.

''Look Caroline, I—''

Shaking her head, she said, ''You don't have to say anything, Joe. Just go home and get some rest. Before I go to bed, I'll call my cousin Penny. She's a judge. She'll be able to tell us what we need to do about the papers we found with Nick and so forth. I'll let you know what she says.''

Nodding, he opened the door, then looked at her. ''Will the two of you be all right tonight? Alone, I mean.''

Her heart burgeoned at his awkwardly spoken question. ''We'll be fine,'' she assured him. ''I've lived alone for years now. Surely I can handle a little guy of this size.''

He tried to smile, but he'd never had much practice at it and his lips felt odd as they stretched against his teeth.

"Good night then."

As Caroline looked at his roughly hewn features, she realized she didn't want him to go. Having Joe in the house made her feel like a woman. Something she hadn't felt in a long time.

But she couldn't ask him to stay. He'd think she was coming on to him. And maybe deep down she would be. Lord knows, she couldn't get that kiss out of her mind.

"Good night, Joe," she murmured, then before she could stop herself, she rose on tiptoe and kissed his cheek.

Surprise flickering in his eyes, he reached up to touch the moist spot her lips had left behind. "What was that for?"

Her cheeks flamed with color. She was never this forward with men. She couldn't even remember the last time she'd felt such a physical reaction toward a man. She'd kissed Joe twice and was already thinking about doing it again. "To thank you. For caring enough to come back tonight."

He did care. He didn't want to, but he did. He cared about the baby cradled in her arms. And he was beginning to care about Caroline in a way that was scaring the hell out of him. He wanted to see her smile—and know he'd put it there. He wanted her to be proud of him. Proud of Joe Garcia.

"You don't know what you're doing," he said roughly, then before she could guess his intentions, he bent his head and covered her lips with his.

The kiss lasted only seconds, but it was more than long enough to sizzle every nerve ending in Caroline's body.

"You weren't supposed to do that again," she whispered huskily. "You promised."

His lips twisted ruefully as he gazed at her. "You're the first woman I've ever made a promise to, and now I've already broken it. That ought to tell you the kind of guy I am."

He wanted her to view him as worthless. He wanted her to regard him as not fit to be a husband or father. But most of all he wanted to believe it of himself, and that was the thing that filled Caroline's heart with tears.

"I know what kind of guy you are, Joe," she said softly. "And one of these days, you're going to know it, too."

There was yearning in her eyes, and something else that challenged him to prove her right.

But she wasn't right, he thought sadly. He was a loner. An ex-sergeant who knew how to face combat, but nothing about being part of a family.

"I'll see you later," he muttered, then quickly stepped out the door before he was tempted to reach for her one more time.

Chapter 4

More than two hours later, Caroline had finally managed to reach her cousin on the telephone. After she explained the whole story, the judge's first impression was exactly what she wanted to hear. Caroline sighed with relief. "Penny, you can't imagine how much better it makes me feel to hear you say that. It would be awful to have Joe finally accepting this child and then have him taken away on some legal technicality."

"Well, Caroline, you do understand that without seeing the documents I can't be certain of their authenticity. That's why I want you to meet with Bradley. He's a very good lawyer, and because he's a friend, I know I can get him to see you on short notice."

"Thanks, Penny. You're wonderful for helping me like this."

"That's what family is for," she said brightly, then in a more serious tone, added, "I hope everything works out for the child."

"It will. I'm going to see to it," Caroline said with fierce conviction.

The two women visited briefly about the family before Caroline eventually thanked her cousin once again, then told her goodbye.

She had to call Paloma and let her employee know she wouldn't be coming in to work at the gallery for a few days.

The woman's drowsy voice answered the phone on the first ring. Caroline quickly apologized. "I'm sorry, Paloma, did I wake you?"

"No," the older woman assured her. "I was just lying here reading. But it is getting late. Is something wrong?"

Caroline drew in a deep breath and let it out slowly. So much had happened since she'd left the gallery this afternoon. Her whole world had suddenly changed. When she wasn't holding Nick in her arms, she had to keep reminding herself it wasn't a dream. She really did have a baby in the house!

"Nothing is wrong. But I do have something to tell you. First of all, do you think you can manage to look after the gallery without me for a few days?"

"Of course. I hope you're going home to the Pardee Ranch. You could use a nice long visit with your family. You've been working too hard this past year.''

Caroline had been working hard. But that was the gist of her life. And work helped to fight the loneliness that ate at her late at night when she had time to think and wonder if she was going to live the rest of her life as a barren old maid.

''Actually, I'm not going anywhere. But something has happened—well, I don't know how to tell you other than I have a baby here with me. I found him on my front porch today after work. He's five days old and he's absolutely gorgeous.''

She could hear the older woman scrambling to sit up.

''But what was he doing on your porch? Who does he belong to?''

Caroline quickly explained all that had happened and ended with how she'd promised Joe to care for the baby until he could make some plans. And how the baby stirred strong maternal instincts in her. ''One of these days I'll find a man for myself and we'll have a child together, Paloma.''

''Maybe you think you've already found him.''

Did she? The question brought Joe's tough image to her mind. She'd never been so physically attracted to a man in her life. Just the memory of his scent, his taste, the feel of his strong arms around her made her shiver with longing. Yet it wasn't just the tangible things about him that had drawn her so swiftly to him. When he'd talked about himself and his life, she'd found herself hurting for him, wanting for him. But to dream she could have a future with the man was another matter.

"Don't worry, Paloma, Joe isn't the marrying kind. I'd be a fool to set my sights on him. Now I'd better go to bed and get some sleep before the baby decides he wants to eat again."

She quickly told the woman good-night, then hung up the phone before anything more could be said. Between her mother and Paloma, she'd had enough warnings about Joe Garcia and broken hearts. What did the two women think? That she'd taken one look at the man and catapulted head over heels in love with him?

Things like that didn't happen. No more than babies were left on doorsteps.

The sun dawned clear over the Sangre de Cristo Mountains. From his chair on the small stone patio, Joe could see fingers of pink light creeping toward the roof of Caroline's house. Only one side of the structure could be seen from this vantage point. The rest was sheltered from view by juniper, tamarack and cottonwood trees.

He'd never paid much attention to the house before. When he'd returned to Santa Fe, his father had been in the hospital, dying from heart failure. Since

his death six weeks ago, Joe had been too busy settling what little there was of his father's estate to
notice the neighborhood. Now his every waking
thought was on the house above him.

Joe placed the empty coffee cup beside his chair,
then closed his eyes. They were tired and gritty from
no sleep, but his brain refused to shut down long
enough to allow his body to rest.

From the moment Caroline Pardee had called him,
his world had changed. Learning he had a son had
shaken him. Yet little Nick was only a part of the
reason for the jumble of emotions tearing through
him. The woman had gotten inside him somehow.
He couldn't forget her touch, her taste or the sight
of her face as she'd talked about the baby needing
him.

Hell, no one had ever needed Joe Garcia. He'd
been a damn good drill sergeant. But many men
could have come along and taken his place. His father had never appeared to need him. Down through
the years the old man had rarely contacted Joe for
any reason. As for his mother, it was very clear she'd
never needed or wanted a child in her life.

*What are you going to do, Joe? Be like Dolores?
Ignore your responsibility, shun your own child?*

Joe opened his tired eyes, and once again his gaze
traveled to the house on the cliff above him. Caroline
believed he could be a good father, but she didn't
understand that he was from bad stock. She didn't

realize he'd been better off without a mother like Dolores, and that little Nick would have a far brighter life without him around.

He glanced over his shoulder at the sliding glass door that led into the small house. Maybe he should go inside and telephone her right now. Get it all over with and end this torture. The best thing he could do would be to hand the baby over to the child welfare department and let them place him in a home with two loving parents.

His jaw set with determination, Joe rose from the lawn chair and hurried into the house. The telephone was in the kitchen on the wall. He snatched it off the hook, then cursed as it dawned on him that he didn't know Caroline's number.

He slammed the receiver down, reached for the directory and quickly flipped to the P's. Pardee was near the top of the page. He didn't bother to jot the number down. Instead he repeated it to himself, drilling it into his memory as another part of his brain rehearsed the words he would say to her.

You're a loser, Joe Garcia. If you try to raise Nick you'll make him a loser, too. Why don't you be honest and tell her that?

The taunting voice inside him wrung another curse from his lips. He'd always thought of himself as a strong man. The army had taught him to make quick decisions and stand behind them. He'd never doubted his ability as a soldier. But being a father was a job he'd never planned for himself. He wasn't prepared for the role. He couldn't do it. He *wouldn't* do it.

Just as his hand inched toward the telephone, Caroline's soft smile drifted before his eyes, and the warm weight of the baby in his arms came back to him. Caroline would hate him for the rest of his life if he gave up the baby. So would the boy when he got old enough to understand his father had turned his back on him. Strange how much he didn't want to disappoint either one of them.

The telephone shrilled, and he jerked as if he'd been shot. Who could be calling? The only people in town he knew were his boss and a couple of old acquaintances.

"Hello," he barked.

"Joe? Is that you?"

His heart stilled at the sound of her voice. She sounded so good to him. Too good. "Caroline. Is something wrong?"

"I was just about to ask you the same thing."

"Why?"

"I'm not used to people biting my head off when they answer my call."

He closed his eyes and thrust his fingers through his rumpled hair. She didn't need to know thoughts of her and the baby had kept him awake all night. "Nothing is wrong. I just haven't had enough coffee yet this morning."

"Oh. Well, the reason I'm calling, Joe, is to let you know I talked to my cousin, the judge, last night. She's arranged for us to meet with a lawyer tomorrow so he can inspect the birth certificate and other papers we found with Nick."

"She couldn't tell you anything more concrete?"

"Not without looking at the papers firsthand. But her initial opinion is that the custody of the baby is rightfully yours now."

He swallowed, then grimaced as strange emotions knotted once again in his throat. "I see. I wonder if she could tell me if the child is really mine?"

Caroline sighed. "You're not going to start that again, are you? Anybody with a good eye can see he's the spitting image of you."

Without even realizing it, one corner of Joe's mouth lifted in a cockeyed grin. "Yeah," he admitted. "I guess you're right."

"I know I'm right," she said, then added softly, "about a lot of things."

The sudden urge to see her, touch her, suddenly overwhelmed Joe. He squeezed his eyelids tightly shut as he fought against the needs she evoked in him.

"Joe? Are you still there?"

"Yes."

"I was wondering...you are planning on going to the lawyer's office with me, aren't you?"

He'd already accepted the fact that Nick was his

child. Before he could make any decisions regarding the baby, he needed to know Pam was legally out of the picture. "I have to report in to my new job tomorrow morning, but I'm only scheduled to stay until noon. I'll pick you up at one."

"I'll be ready."

Joe could hear a smile in her voice, and the notion that he'd pleased her lifted his troubled spirits.

"And speaking of time," Caroline went on, "I'd better hang up and get ready for church. Services start in less than an hour."

His eyes popped open. "You're going to church? What about Nick?"

"I'm taking him with me," she answered easily.

"But he's...isn't he too tiny to be out? He might catch something."

"Flu season is far past, and the weather is warm and beautiful."

"But what if he starts crying?"

"I'll have a bottle with me. Besides, the priest says the noise of children is a welcome sound in the house of God. But if you'd like to come along and make sure he gets through the service okay, you're welcome to come with us."

Joe could just imagine the stir that would cause among the congregation. Acquaintances of Caroline would probably view the three of them as a soon-to-be family. But even worse, Joe might be tempted to think of them as a family. His family.

"No," he said abruptly. "You're going to have enough explaining to do as it is."

"There won't be any explaining. I'm simply going to tell everyone the truth. I'm baby-sitting for a friend," she said.

He could hear Nick in the background. The baby's cry was deep and lusty. The perfect voice for a drill sergeant, he thought ruefully. But he didn't want Nick to be a serviceman. He wanted him to be something unique and special. Something he couldn't be.

"I didn't realize I was your friend," Joe said before he could stop himself.

When Caroline replied, he could hear another smile in her voice. It did something strange to Joe's heart.

"Of course you are. Don't you want to be?"

He wanted to be more, damn it. So much more. But fate wasn't going to give him a woman like Caroline. Any more than it had given him a set of loving parents or even one grandparent. Caroline was out of his league. She was from rich stock with high values. He wouldn't fit. Even if he dared to try.

"I'm honored to be your friend, Caroline."

There was a long pause, and he could hear the baby fussing again.

She said, "I'll talk to you later. Nick's having a fit. Bye."

Joe slowly replaced the receiver on its hook, then sank into a nearby armchair.

So much for telling her he couldn't be a daddy, he thought with self-disgust. The moment he'd heard her voice he'd melted like a pat of butter. But it would be different the next time they talked, he promised himself. Before they went to the lawyer's office, he had to convince her he couldn't be Nick's father. There wasn't any point in her thinking he could be.

Joe didn't know he'd been asleep until a light knock on the front door jerked him awake.

Bleary-eyed, he pushed himself out of the armchair. Since moving into his father's house, he'd had very few visitors. And all of those had been old acquaintances of Joseph's, who'd come by after his death to pay their respects. He couldn't imagine who might be calling on a Sunday afternoon.

Before he opened the door, he raked his fingers through his hair, then wiped a hand over his face. A fresh growth of beard made a raspy sound beneath his hand. It wasn't like him to be unshaved and dressed in rumpled jeans. Especially at this hour of the day.

The caller knocked again, and he opened the door. Caroline was standing on the small porch, the baby cradled in her arms. The sight of the two of them squeezed something in the middle of Joe's chest.

''What's wrong?''

Not waiting for an invitation, she stepped past him

and into the house. "You do always expect the worse, don't you?"

Most of the time, he thought. If a person always anticipated the worst, he was less likely to be disappointed.

"Well, I wasn't expecting to see you." He glanced at his watch. More than two hours had passed since she'd telephoned.

She walked to the middle of the small room, then turned to face him. She was dressed in a sea-green dress that fluttered around her legs and exposed her slender arms. Her hair was pulled into a mass of fiery curls atop her head. She was the most beautiful person he'd ever seen, and the urge to have her back in his arms, to taste her lips again was so strong he ached from it.

"I realize I should have called, but since was I driving right by on my way home from church it was easier to stop by and issue you an invitation for lunch. Or maybe I should call it an early dinner. It will be a couple of hours before I have anything cooked. Have you eaten yet?"

He'd consumed a pot of coffee and two jelly sandwiches. His stomach was gnawing. But dealing with his hunger would be easier than being in the same house with her, he thought. Caroline already had too much effect on him. And he didn't want to be a changed man.

"Just because you're taking care of Nick doesn't

mean you have to concern yourself with me, Caroline. I've managed to feed myself for a long time now."

Instead of putting her off, his words seemed to amuse her. Her brows lifted, and the corners of her lips tilted in a tempting little smile. "Really? I thought the army fed you for twenty years."

"They did. But I know how to fend for myself in the kitchen. And wherever else is needed."

Caroline glanced around the living room and the part of the kitchen she could see from where she was standing. Everything was spotless. The floors were so clean you could use them for a dinner plate, and if there was any dust in the place she'd have to use a magnifying glass to find it. But the rooms were stark and sterile. The miniature image of a soldier's barrack. She couldn't bear to think his heart, his life were equally barren.

"I hate eating alone," she told him. "It would be nice to have your company."

"I'd rather not." He made himself say the words before the pleasure of being with this woman overtook him and forced him to change his mind.

The tiny smile on her face deepened. "Why? Afraid of my cooking? Or just afraid?"

Her taunt caused his dark eyes to narrow, and as Caroline studied his rugged face and hard body, she knew she'd never met a more sensual man in her life. Everything about him reminded her she was a woman.

"Afraid? Of what?" he asked softly.

She glanced at the baby, then back at him. "Me. Or little Nick. Or maybe the both of us."

He stepped closer, as though determined to prove her wrong. "Why would I be afraid of either one of you?"

Caroline's senses were suddenly enveloped by his voice, his male scent and the nearness of his body. Like a haywire clock, her heart raced fast, then slowed to a heavy thud. "Because I..." She stopped, pressed her dry lips together, then tried again. "Because you don't want to like either one of us."

He took a step closer, and then his finger was touching the tender skin beneath her chin. Her green eyes glimmered with unspoken messages as they met his dark, probing gaze. Almost from the first moment she'd laid eyes on the man, she'd wanted him, and since then the feeling had only intensified.

"From the time I was a small child, I've learned not to like anyone or anything too much," he said quietly. "Because eventually you're going to have to give them up."

"Like your mother?"

His jaw tightened. "Like my mother. My friends in school. My buddies in the army. My father. Everyone leaves for different reasons."

"Not everyone," she murmured.

His nostrils flared ever so slightly as his fingers climbed to the soft curve of her cheek.

"In my world they do," he said, then his gaze dipped to the sleeping baby in her arms. Nick's rosy cheek was pressed lovingly against her breast, and Joe had the sudden image of yet another child feeding at her breast. And that child was also his. His and Caroline's.

Dear God, was he going crazy? He wasn't the marrying sort. Not now. Not ever. Quickly, he stepped away and jammed his hands into the back pockets of his jeans.

He cleared his throat, then asked in a rough voice, "What time do you want me to be there?"

Like a rainbow, joy beamed through her. She couldn't stop a wide smile from spreading across her face. "Two will be fine. But you can come sooner if you like."

She left without giving him the chance to refuse, and once she had driven away, Joe sank into the nearest armchair and dropped his head in his hands.

What was the woman thinking? Couldn't she see the way he lived? He didn't have wealth. There was nothing in this house, not even one photo to suggest he was a family man. So why did she want his company? Did she have the idea she could change him into something he wasn't?

Lifting his head, he scrubbed his face with both hands. Maybe he was good-looking in a rough sort of way. He'd never had much trouble finding female company on a short-time basis. But Caroline wasn't like those women. She didn't just look at a man's face and body. She wanted to see his brain, his morals, his heart. Those were the things important to her.

Well, maybe she should have a good look at those things inside him, he thought grimly. Then she could see for herself that he wasn't cut out to be anything more than what he'd always been. A man alone.

Chapter 5

Nick, there isn't any reason you should cry," Caroline crooned to the baby as she buttoned him up in a tiny checked shirt. "You're only going to a day care. Not to a doctor with a nasty old needle. Even though we will have to start getting your immunization shots soon."

Nick suddenly shushed his whimpers. Caroline's hands paused on the last button as she gazed at his precious little face. Paloma and her mother had been right. She did already think of this baby as hers. When she pictured his future, she was there with him. And Joe.

A tiny groan of fear slipped from her throat as she lifted the baby from the bed and pressed his head into the curve of her neck. It was almost time to leave for the lawyer's office. Joe would be driving up any moment now.

Joe. Each day, each hour, the man was growing more and more important to her. Which was reckless, she knew. Joe didn't want love or marriage in his life. Yesterday, they'd shared an enjoyable dinner together. They'd talked and even laughed. But she could tell he was being careful not to get too close to her, and his distance had disappointed Caroline a great deal.

After he'd gone home, and all through this morning, she'd kept reminding herself she'd be a fool to let herself hope Joe might eventually love her and make her his wife. She needed to get her head out of the clouds. But for the first time in her life, she couldn't control her feelings. Good or bad, she couldn't stop herself from wanting the man.

Sighing, she glanced at the baby. "Your daddy loves you, Nick. He doesn't realize it just yet, but I know he does."

But would or could he ever love me? she asked herself. If he took the baby and walked away from her, how could she ever go back to her life as it had been before? Joe had already taken root in her heart. She could never be happy marrying someone else.

Joe arrived promptly at one. After they dropped Nick off at a day care run by a trusted group of ladies from Caroline's church, he headed the pickup truck onto the main loop of highway heading into the city.

While he negotiated the fast-paced traffic, Caroline glanced at his profile. Even wearing a pinstriped dress shirt and dark trousers, he was still the image of raw masculine power. The idea sent a shiver of heat straight down her spine.

"Have you ever loved a woman?"

His dark eyes momentarily left the highway to search her face. "Why are you asking me such a thing now?"

Her face full of heat, she did her best to shrug in a casual way. "I don't know. I guess I've been thinking about Nick's mother not wanting him and wondering how that made you feel."

"I was never in love with Pam or any woman. I guess the only person I've ever loved was my father. But that didn't mean anything to him."

The sourness in his voice was enough to show how much Joseph Garcia's lack of attention had hurt him.

"You said before that he lived in his own private world. But maybe that was because he didn't know you loved him."

He shot her a sharp glance. "Why wouldn't he have known? I was his son. His own flesh and blood."

Smiling wanly, she nodded in acquiescence. "You've always believed he raised you because it was his responsibility as a father and not because he loved you. Has it ever occurred to you that he might have thought the same thing about you? That you blamed him for not being able to provide you with a mother and you were being a good son to him just out of a sense of duty?''

He snorted then slanted an anguished glance her way. ''Why are you always trying to make me think about such things?''

''Because you need to understand that Nick doesn't want to be thought of as responsibility. No more than you did.''

Her point taken, he decided it would be safer to move on to something else. ''You like having Nick around, don't you?''

A soft smile tilted her lips. ''I adore having him around. I've always wanted children.''

''A woman who looks like you should have been married years ago.''

Her gaze once again slipped over his rugged features. He'd stopped being a stranger to her a long time ago. When she looked at him it was easy to imagine him as her husband and the father of her children. And she realized with a start that the physical longing she'd felt for him at the very beginning had somewhere along the way turned into much more.

''What's the matter? Do I have grease on the side of my face or something?''

Caroline blushed and quickly turned her attention toward the busy traffic ahead of them. "No. I'm sorry if I seemed to be staring. I was…just thinking about some things."

He didn't press her to explain, and Caroline was relieved. This wasn't the time to tell him she was falling in love with him. The very word would send him running like a scalded cat. And right now she had to put the baby's needs before her own.

Two hours later, as they stepped from the lawyer's office, Caroline had to stifle the urge to shout with joy.

"Isn't it wonderful, Joe? Nick is legally yours."

Joe opened the vehicle door and handed her onto the bench seat. "It's a relief to know Pam no longer has any rights to the child. She could have never been a mother to him." *Not like you,* he couldn't help thinking.

After making certain the documents concerning Nick were legal, the lawyer had talked with Pamela Ashby. The woman had made it clear she wanted nothing to do with Nick's future. Now that the custody of the baby was clear, Caroline wondered if Joe was any closer to a decision about his part in the boy's future. But she bit back the urge to ask him. This was a joyous day, and she didn't want to spoil it.

"Is there anywhere else you'd like to go before

we leave town?'' he asked as he slid behind the wheel.

The question surprised Caroline. She'd expected him to make a straight shot for home and end the outing with her as quickly as possible.

''Would you like to see my gallery? It's not far from here. And I promise not to twist your arm and make you buy anything.''

He glanced at his wristwatch, and Caroline said, ''Usually it stays open until five, but I told Paloma she could close early today to tend to some errands of her own.'' With a tempting little grin, she added, ''I'll give you a private tour.''

Joe let out a silent groan. Just what he needed, he thought, to be totally alone with the woman. There wouldn't be the baby or anyone to distract him. He didn't know how the hell he could resist her. Still, he could see how much it meant to her, and he was quickly realizing it was next to impossible to deny her anything.

''Okay,'' he agreed. ''Point the way.''

A few minutes later Joe found himself inside a small shop that was sandwiched between an antique store and a dress boutique. Shades were pulled on the front windows, so the bustle on the busy street and sidewalk were hidden from their view.

A skylight sent a shaft of oblong light through the middle of the darkened room. At the edge of the shadows Joe waited while Caroline went to the light switch.

Seconds later, lights flickered on from every direction, and Joe glanced curiously around him. Along the back wall was a long glass showcase filled with a large assortment of jewelry displayed against swathes of black, burgundy and copper-colored velvet. On the opposite walls were numerous paintings, mostly southwestern pieces. Bronze and pewter sculptures of cowboys, Indians, pioneers, miners and cavalrymen were displayed throughout the room on shelves and small tabletops.

Caroline made a sweeping gesture with her arm. "This is the Red Mesa," she said proudly. "It's small. But I always went by the old adage of quality before quantity."

The room was tastefully decorated, but not too formal to make a person uncomfortable. It was like her, Joe thought. Warm, inviting and beautiful.

"You must be very proud. I don't know much about art, but this all looks like excellent work to me."

She moved toward him, and Joe's breath momentarily hung in his throat as her hand closed over his forearm.

"Would you like to see where I work?" she asked softly.

Joe couldn't help himself. He wanted to know anything and everything that had to do with her.

"Sure," he murmured.

She led him to a narrow door at the back of the room. Once they were through it, Joe found himself inside a tiny studio illuminated by a row of skylights.

"When I'm not dealing with customers, this is where I spend most of my time," she said.

Several easels were sitting at odd angles around the room, and in one corner all sorts of paints and brushes were stacked on an old wooden table. One long work counter was piled with vises and tools. At the nearest end was a piece of copper just beginning to take the shape of a horse. Joe stepped forward for a closer look.

"Obviously you do more than jewelry and paintings."

"Sometimes. But designing jewelry is my first love."

Her first love. But had she ever really loved a man? Had she ever felt that desperate craving he was beginning to feel for her?

Turning, Joe found her standing only a step behind him. There was an all too inviting look on her face, and before he could think about it, he placed his hands on her shoulders and drew her closer. "Earlier you wanted to know if I'd ever loved a woman. Now it's my turn. Is your work all you've ever really loved or has there been a man?"

Never one that made me feel like you, she wanted

to say. Aloud, she asked, "Why do you want to know?"

The open neck of her dress exposed part of her shoulders. He couldn't stop his fingers from sliding gently against the smooth skin or keep his gaze off the tiny cross nestled in the valley between her breasts.

"You've showed me this much of your life. I'm curious about the rest."

Her heart thudded wildly as she felt the warm caress of his gaze on her face, her throat, her breasts.

"There have been a few men in the past that everyone thought were a perfect match for me. They were all successful, intelligent and caring. But I couldn't make myself feel the sort of love a marriage needs to survive."

"Maybe you were expecting too much."

She had to force herself to breathe as the urge to kiss him clamped a hold on her senses. Lifting her hand to his cheek, she murmured, "I expected to look at his face and be intoxicated. I expected the touch of his fingers to thrill me. That's not asking too much."

His eyes glittered as they came to rest on the moist curve of her lips. "You're confusing sex with love."

Her brows lifted to a mocking arch. "And you'd know the difference?"

A few days ago he wouldn't have. But Caroline

had made him see there was much more to a woman than the warm pleasures of her body.

"I can show you the difference," he answered huskily.

Her lips parted with another question, but he didn't give her time to get it out. He gathered her against his chest, then ducked his head and placed his lips over hers.

No matter his motives, she couldn't resist him. Rising on tiptoes, she opened her mouth and welcomed the warm invasion of his tongue.

Groaning deep in his throat, Joe pulled her toward him until her breasts were flattened against his chest and her thighs pressed his.

Her hands fluttered against his shoulders, then curled around the warm column of his neck. He lifted his lips just long enough to let her drag in a breath, then hungrily captured her mouth all over again.

Time and reason fled his mind as the warm softness of her body took control of his senses. Tasting her lips, holding her in his arms wasn't nearly enough. He wanted every part of her. He wanted to feel the heat of her passion surrounding him, lifting him to paradise.

Somewhere outside the building he heard the bang of a car door and then the dim sound of voices. Thankfully, the distraction was enough to bring him to his senses, and he slowly lifted his head and put her away from him.

"Looks like I broke my promise again," he said huskily.

Still gasping for breath, Caroline pressed her fingertips to her burning lips and lifted her eyes to his. "What promise?"

"The promise not to kiss you again."

Kiss her! It felt like he'd just made slow, passionate love to her! "You were supposed to be showing me the difference between sex and love. Which was that?"

Joe wanted to believe it was only sex. He couldn't admit to her or himself that his heart had kissed her, too.

"You figure it out," he said gruffly, then grabbing her by the hand, he headed them both toward the door.

"Where are we going now?" she asked.

"Home. Don't you think it's about time?"

It was about time for a lot of things, Caroline thought. It was especially time to make it clear to Joe how she felt about him, and home was the perfect place for that.

"Let me lock up and I'll be ready," she told him.

Thirty minutes later Joe parked beside Caroline's carport. Between them on the bench seat Nick was fast asleep and had been ever since they had picked him up from the day-care.

"Do you need help getting inside with the baby?" Joe asked.

She looked at him, and a needy ache settled somewhere deep inside her. Kissing Joe in the studio had jolted more than her body. She could see that hours or days with him would never be enough. She would always want to be near him.

"I don't need help. But I will need company for supper tonight. I can't celebrate by myself."

His brows lifted in question. "Celebrate? What's the occasion?"

She smiled at his bewildered expression. "Why, Nick being legally yours, of course. Surely you're happy about that."

Obviously Caroline was happy. And Joe had to admit it was a relief to know Pam could never enter the boy's life.

"I suppose I am," he conceded.

She smiled again, and as Joe caught the tenderness in her green eyes he felt something in his gut twisting tighter and tighter. With each hour that passed, he wanted this woman more. If he was smart, he would tell her to find a deserving home for Nick, then walk away from this place. They were both too good for the likes of him. But the willpower to end his time with them was weak.

During their meal, clouds rolled in and the house

grew cooler. While Caroline cleaned away the dishes, she asked Joe to build a fire in the fireplace.

She joined him a few minutes later, and the piñon was snapping with cheery flames.

"The fire feels nice," she said as she placed a tray with two mugs on the table in front of the couch. "Come have coffee with me before Nick wakes and wants his bottle."

He sank onto the cushion next to her. "You think he'll wake up soon? He's been asleep for a long time. Ever since we came from the lawyer's office."

"That's what all babies his age do. Sleep and eat. But in a few weeks he'll begin to stay awake for longer periods and take more notice of things around him." A wistful smile crossed her face as she glanced toward the bassinet. "In no time at all he'll start rolling over and sitting up. Teething and walking and talking and turning into a little man." She turned to Joe and pressed one of the coffee's mugs into his hand. "That's when your patience will be tested."

From the very beginning Caroline believed Joe could be a father to Nick. He didn't understand why, but her confidence filled him with a sense of self-worth he'd never had before. "What makes you keep thinking I can be a father?"

Her eyes were serious as they caught and held his. "Because you know what it's like not to have a good parent. You know all the things you needed and missed when you were a boy and you won't make those mistakes with Nick.''

He desperately hoped she was right. Because deep down, he was beginning to see that he couldn't let Nick go. He wanted his son. But even more, he wanted him to have a good home. To give him one, Joe probably needed a wife who would also be a dedicated mother to the boy. But a man couldn't always have everything he needed.

''I've made plenty of mistakes down through my life, Caroline. I might make them with Nick.''

She reached over and placed her hand on his. ''We all have.''

Joe didn't know how such tiny fingers could fill him with such a massive need. ''I want to do what's right for my son.''

''You will,'' she said softly.

All during supper Joe had desperately been trying to forget about their kiss in the studio, but every time he looked at her, he wanted to do it all again and more.

Quickly, he placed his mug on the coffee table. ''I think I'd better be getting home,'' he said.

She caught him by the forearm. ''Why? It's still early.''

His lips twisted. ''Time has nothing to do with it.''

Her eyes searched his. ''You're afraid of wanting me, aren't you?''

Groaning, he looked away. "Hell, yes," he muttered. "And so should you be!"

Yes, she probably should be afraid, Caroline thought. Inviting Joe into her life was risky. Especially when she knew he didn't want any of the things she wanted. Marriage and a house full of kids. But she couldn't ignore her heart, and it kept telling her to love him.

Placing her mug beside his, she moved closer. "Earlier this evening in the studio, you didn't answer when I asked you if you were showing me sex or love."

Unable to meet her gaze, he studied her small hand pressed into his flesh. "What did it feel like?"

Her soft laugh was like a kiss in the dark.

"Both," she said.

His eyes snapped to hers. "You don't know what you're talking about! I don't know how to love a woman."

She leaned forward and slipped her arms around his neck. "Maybe I should teach you."

The invitation was too much for Joe. He pulled her onto his lap and eased his lips over hers in a slow, coaxing kiss.

"This is sex," he whispered as he nibbled a trail across her shoulder. "Just a man wanting a woman."

She let out a tiny groan of pleasure as his teeth bit gently into her earlobe. "And a woman wanting a man."

Just hearing her say she wanted him turned Joe inside out. What would it feel like to know she really loved him? Yet he didn't want to know. It would be too much pleasure to lose.

"Caroline."

Her whispered name caressed her cheek as his hands roamed her back and meshed in the wild tangle of curls on her shoulders.

The baby's cry was faint at first. Caroline wasn't sure she'd heard anything. Her heartbeat was throbbing in her ears like a pagan drumbeat, muffling the sounds around her. But she heard it again, louder this time, and she realized Nick was letting them know he was awake and hungry.

Joe heard the baby at the same time and slowly lifted his head from Caroline's. Once her gaze managed to focus on his face, she could see it was taut, his eyes drowsy with desire.

With a rueful smile, she said, "Your son has terrible timing."

Joe was thinking it had been more like perfect timing. One more kiss and he wouldn't have been able to stop.

Easing her off his lap, he said, "Maybe you'd better check on him."

At the bassinet Caroline quickly changed Nick's soggy diaper, then carried him to the couch.

"Will you hold him while I go heat a bottle?"

She was asking, not demanding, and that made all

the difference in the world to Joe. "What do I do if he cries?"

Laughing softly, she placed the baby in the cradle of his big arms. "You don't have to do anything. He's just telling you he's hungry."

In the kitchen, she quickly went about warming a bottle in the microwave while trying to ignore the heavy, tingling ache in her breast and between her thighs. But it was impossible to push aside the longing Joe had evoked in her, and when she returned to the living room to see him cuddling the baby to his chest, her feelings only intensified.

Joe was content to hand Nick over to Caroline for his feeding. She carried him to a nearby wooden rocker, and the tiny boy nursed hungrily as she rocked, the chair creaking gently.

Minutes ago, with her lips clinging to his and her arms wound tightly around him, Joe had wanted her desperately. His body was still hard with desire. Yet as he looked at her now with the baby feeding at her breast and the glow of the fire outlining the soft profile of her face and hair, something was tugging at him, pulling at the deepest part of him. It had nothing to do with sex, as he'd wanted her to believe.

Joe wasn't sure how long he'd been sitting there watching the two of them when she finally rose from the rocker and put the baby back to bed. He figured it must have been several minutes, because the bottle she placed on the coffee table was empty and the logs in the fireplace had burned low.

She sank onto the couch beside him and reached for his hand. ''I doubt he'll wake until two in the morning now.''

Anticipation knotted his throat and sent his heart into a heavy thud. ''I...really am leaving now. I have to.''

Her fingers tightened over his as her eyes sought out his dark ones. ''Do you want to?''

''No.''

At the huskily spoken word, she tilted her lips into a provocative smile. Then she was leaning toward him, pressing her cheek against his. ''Good,'' she whispered, ''because I don't want you to go.''

''Caroline, I can't give you what you want. Or what you even need. I—''

The tips of her fingers upon his lips shushed the rest of his words, then with her hand on his, she urged him up from the couch. ''I happen to think you can.''

The bedroom she led him to was small and only a few feet from where Nick lay sleeping. The glow from the fire shed enough light to see a four-poster bed and part of a dresser along one wall.

The bed was tall and covered with a calico quilt. When she stepped away from him to turn down the covers, Joe could see the sheets and pillowcases were edged with crocheted lace. The sight reminded him this was a real home. Not just a house or motel room. This was a special place, and she was an uncommon woman.

"I don't belong here, Caroline," he said as she turned to him.

Her fingers reached for the buttons on his striped shirt. "How do you know?" she asked huskily.

"I just know."

As the buttons parted, she pushed the fabric away from his chest, then pressed her palm against the rapid thud of his heart.

"Do you worry this much when you're with other women?"

He groaned then caught her face between his hands. "In spite of Nick, I'm not a playboy. And—God help me—I've never been with a woman like you."

"Oh, Joe. Joe," she whispered fervently. "Don't you know I've never been with a man as special as you?"

She pushed his shirt off his shoulders and then he took over, his shaking hands peeling away her little pink sweater and the skirt full of roses. Delicate lace covered her breasts and the alluring vee between her thighs.

As he unfastened clasps and slipped his thumbs beneath elastic, he was acutely aware of the rough skin of his hands snagging like a rasp against the baby softness of hers.

When she stepped out of the scrap of panties, then stood before him, Joe's breath caught in his throat. Her breasts were full and firm, the nipples pale pink and puckered with excitement. Her waist narrowed to a circle he could probably span with his hands, and far below her belly button, a fluff of red curls hid that most intimate part of her.

"You're too beautiful, Caroline. Too beautiful," he said with anguished need, and then his head dipped and his mouth opened over one breast.

The touch was all it took to send Caroline's senses shattering with need. She hardly knew when Joe shed the rest of his clothing, then laid her back against the pillows.

His kisses were taunting, teasing, heating her blood while his hands gently explored the curves and hollows of her body. Several times he stopped long enough to look into her eyes, and each time Caroline's heart surged with so much longing she was certain it would burst.

And when he finally joined their bodies, she was desperate to hold him to her, to cherish every part of him before the night was over. But all too soon their desire turned to raw, clawing need. Sweat slicked their bodies, and their cries of release mingled in the quiet bedroom.

Long minutes passed before Joe realized he was slumped over Caroline, who was struggling to regain her breath.

Quickly, he rolled onto his back, but kept one hand possessively on her breast. "I didn't mean to squash you," he said.

She turned her head toward him, and a tender smile tilted her lips. "You didn't," she said, then with a tiny groan of pleasure, she rolled over and propped the upper part of her body against his chest. "Are you all right?"

His lips twisted wryly. "I'm supposed to be asking you that, aren't I?"

She chuckled softly, then pushed her fingers through his thick black hair. "I am more than all right. Now that you're here with me. Like this."

Her face was bare of makeup, her hair a wild tangle of red curls on her white shoulders. Her beauty was natural and deep. Yet it was the moist shimmer in her green eyes and the yearning beneath that jerked on Joe's heart.

"I...never meant for this to happen," he said truthfully. But oh, Lord, how could he regret it, he wondered, when just the touch of her hand on his face was giving him a slice of heaven.

"I know you didn't." She smiled as she slid her fingers along his jaw and down to the faint indention in his chin. "Neither did I. But—" Her eyes connected with his. "Oh, Joe, do you know how I feel at this moment?"

He couldn't answer. There was a lump of emotion

in his throat, choking him, frightening him with its intensity.

She scooted closer, and the silky weight of her breasts sliding provocatively against his chest sent a shaft of fresh heat through his loins.

"No man has ever..." She stopped, shook her head, then murmured against his lips. "I've never felt this way with a man."

"It's because you're happy about little Nick." He tried to reason it away.

She tilted her head far enough to look at him. "Happy. Oh, yes, I am happy, Joe. And not just because of Nick." With a blissful sigh, she snuggled her head in the curve of his shoulder. "You know, I have to admit my parents have been right about me. I have been picky about men. But I knew if I kept waiting I would eventually meet a special man like you."

He caught her hand as it wandered over his chest and lifted it to his lips. "I'm not special, Caroline. I've never been anything but a soldier. I'm years older than you and—well, I'm just your everyday average Joe."

"Hmm. My everyday Joe. I like the sound of that."

Before he could tell her that wasn't exactly what he'd meant, her lips began pressing tiny kisses at the corner of his eye, down his jaw and along his chin.

By the time she reached his mouth the only word he could get past his lips was her name, and he whispered it over and over as she built another raging fire inside him.

Chapter 6

Dawn wasn't far away when Joe woke from a light sleep. A moment or two passed before he realized he was in Caroline's bed and her warm body was curled up beside him.

He turned his head on the pillow and studied her sleeping face. She was an incredibly beautiful woman on the outside, but at this moment Joe wasn't seeing that part of her. He was remembering the generous way she'd given herself to him. So sweet, yet so full of fire. Full of love. And he'd lost himself in her. Totally lost himself.

Joe had always scoffed at the idea that making love to a woman was altogether different than having sex with her. He couldn't imagine what more there could be than physical pleasure. But tonight, for the first time in his life, he'd made love to a woman. And it scared the hell out of him.

In a few days Caroline would wake up and realize he wasn't at all what she wanted or needed and then she'd be gone from his life. And he wasn't about to spend the rest of his life like his father. Grieving for a woman he couldn't have.

Caroline woke to Nick's cry rather than a lazy kiss from Joe. She hadn't known what to think when she'd found him gone from the bed and the house. She tried to tell herself that he probably had things to do before going off to work, but deep in her heart she suspected that greeting the morning in bed with her was just too much bonding for the man. But she had to keep hoping that what they'd shared would eventually bring him back and keep him here.

Caroline was finishing Nick's bath when a knock sounded on the back door. She wrapped the baby in soft terry, went to answer it and found Joe on the doorstep.

She pushed the door open for him to enter the house. "Good morning," she said.

Joe hadn't known how she would greet him this morning. Especially after the way he'd left without a word. He mostly expected her to be angry. He certainly wasn't expecting to see the warm smile that was on her face, and it made him feel just that much more of a bastard.

"Good morning," he replied.

She said, "I was just finishing Nick's bath. Have you had breakfast yet?"

"Yes." He tried to keep his eyes from traveling over the luscious curves hidden beneath her blue silk robe. He couldn't let himself fall under the spell of her body again. Not if he planned to have a sane conversation with her.

Caroline went to where the baby lay on the table. "There's still coffee left in the pot on the stove if you want to help yourself," she offered.

He walked to the two of them and gazed at the baby, who was looking around with wide, bright eyes. His little fist made wobbly jerks in the air. Already, Joe could see change and growth in him.

"He seems to love having water on him. Maybe he's going to be an Olympic swimmer," Caroline said with a laugh. "Oh, and look, Joe, his navel clamp fell off. He's nearly all healed. I'm going to save the clamp so that—"

Joe glanced at her and saw her head was bowed, her gaze on the plastic object in her hand.

"What's wrong?"

"Nothing," she answered quietly.

Quickly, she went about drying Nick, then rubbing him with baby oil.

"You were about to say something else." He pressed her. "Do you see something wrong with Nick?"

Her eyes full of shadows, she looked at him. "No.

He looks perfect. It's just that—I keep forgetting. Nick is your baby.''

She handed the navel clamp to Joe. ''Here, you should have this. Not me.''

''Caroline, I've never been one to save sentimental things.'' Hell, he'd never been sentimental over anything. Until now. ''You keep it.''

She shook her head. ''No. I don't think that would...well, be a good idea.''

She pressed the clamp into his palm, then turned to Nick.

Joe drew in a deep breath and decided it was time to get himself a cup of coffee.

As he searched for a mug in the cabinets, he said, ''I've been doing a lot of thinking since I went home this morning.''

''I'm glad.''

He cleared his throat and wondered why he couldn't rid himself of the suffocating pressure in his chest. ''Yeah. I've decided that I can't give Nick up. He's my son. And I want him. I don't know anything about being a father, but I'm going to try like hell to raise him right.''

She closed the last snap on Nick's shirt, then looked at Joe. Her heart was beating fast in her throat, and though she desperately wanted to smile and let him know how proud she was of him, she couldn't. All of a sudden something about the expression on his face left her terribly frightened.

''And you will raise him right, Joe. I know you

will.'' Without saying more she carried Nick into the living room and placed him in the bassinet.

Joe forgot the mug and followed her. ''Are you angry with me?''

Still trying to calm the fear in her heart, Caroline turned to face him. ''Angry? No. Of course not. I'm just thinking. Wondering about the rest of your plans. When do you want to take him home with you?''

Earlier, as he'd paced through the rooms of his house, Joe's decision had seemed cut-and-dried. Simple and easy. But now that he was facing Caroline, he knew this was the hardest thing he'd ever done in his life. She loved little Nick. He didn't want to separate her from the baby. And yet they couldn't keep on like this. Like the three of them were a family. In the long run, it would only cause more pain. She'd leave him at some point, and he didn't want to be hurt by that. He didn't want Nick hurt.

''I suppose I'll take him this morning.''

The air rushed out of her lungs as though someone had hit her. ''And what about us, Joe? What about last night? Are you... Did it mean something to you?''

He bent his head and closed his eyes. He had to. It was too painful to go on looking at her while his mind replayed the passionate way she had made love to him. ''It did mean something to me, Caroline.''

She walked to where he stood in the middle of the

room and pressed her palms against his chest. "But not as much as it meant to me," she murmured.

He lifted his head, and pain knifed through him as he glimpsed the wounded look in her eyes.

"I'm sorry, Caroline. Not that we made love. I couldn't be sorry about that. But I've been telling you all along that I'm a loner. If you thought I wanted something more—well, I'm sorry."

All this time she'd heard him insisting he didn't want a woman on any sort of long-term basis. But her heart had ignored his words and listened instead to his kisses and the warm urgency of his hands on her body. What a little fool she'd been.

"I guess ever since little Nick arrived I...it's changed me," she told him. "I suppose I started thinking things that, well, otherwise—"

She turned her back to him and bit hard on her lip as tears threatened to fill her eyes. "A baby is a symbol of hope and joy. And love. I guess I was swept away with all of that for a while."

Swept away. That's why she'd taken him to her bed, Joe thought. Otherwise, she would have never looked at him twice. Much less made love to him.

He let out a heavy breath. "I realize I can never repay you for all the things you've done for Nick. And for me. Without you I would have probably turned my back out of fear and lost my son forever."

She swallowed the fiery ball of tears in her throat. "Oh, it wasn't me, Joe. You were always going to keep Nick. It just took the fact a little while to settle in on you.''

She drew in a bracing breath, blinked, then turned to face him. ''I hope you'll let me see him from time to time.''

His gaze fell to the middle of her chest. ''I'd like to say you can see him any time you want. But I...don't think that would be a good idea. Not because of Nick. But because of us and what happened last night.''

What did happen? she wanted to ask him. She'd given him her heart, her very soul. Now he wanted to shut her out. Forget her.

''Why?''

His insides were quivering. Even his hands were trembling. Nothing in his life had ever shaken him, and the realization only proved how much power this woman had over him.

''Because if we're together it would only happen again.''

''Would that be so bad? I thought you were pleased. I mean, I'm not a very experienced woman. If I—''

Groaning, he reached out and caught her shoulders. ''Oh, Lord, Caroline. It isn't that! You're the most beautiful, desirable woman I've ever known. The problem is I want you too much.''

Her heart was pounding with love and dread as she met his anguished brown eyes. ''That's a problem?''

"Hell, yes. I made love to you last night without a thought about birth control. I already have one child born out of wedlock. Do you think I want two?"

Suddenly it was all coming together and making sense to Caroline. He wanted her in bed. He just didn't want her in his life. Especially as a wife or the mother of his child. Yet she couldn't be angry with him. He'd never led her on. She was the one who had led herself.

"No. I don't expect you would want that to happen," she said, her voice husky with tears.

He dropped his hands, and Caroline turned and walked to the bassinet.

Nick was still awake, and as she bent over him and placed a kiss on his soft cheek his dark eyes followed her.

"Goodbye, my little precious. Your daddy will take care of you now," she whispered, then before Joe could see the tears on her face, she hurried to the bedroom to pack the baby's clothes.

"How are you doing?"

At the simple question, Caroline glanced up from her work to see Paloma standing beside her. She didn't know how long the other woman had been in the work room at the back of the gallery. But then her mind had been in another place. More than a week had passed since Joe had walked out of her life. She was still numb with pain.

"The pendant is finally taking shape," she told Paloma, "but I haven't decided about the edging around the stone. I don't think copper lace would look right. It needs to be something more bold. What do you think?"

Paloma grimaced. "I think you are miserable."

Caroline sighed. She'd tried not to mope or let her misery show in front of her friend. She didn't want Paloma to know she'd been a fool and allowed a man to break her heart. "That doesn't tell me anything about the pendant."

"Forget the jewelry," Paloma gently scolded her. "What are you going to do about Joe and the baby?"

Her eyes wide, she swiveled to face the older woman. "I'm not going to *do* anything. Joe doesn't want me in his life. Or the baby's."

"But you love them."

Her heart squeezed with pain. She'd always wondered how it would feel to really love a man, and now she knew. She should have known that once she finally fell in love her feelings might not automatically be returned.

"I'm not going to beg Joe to reconsider his feelings. He made his choice."

Paloma frowned. "Who said anything about begging? Talking might be enough."

What good would talking do? Joe had made himself very clear. He didn't want a wife or even a lover. He wanted nothing else to do with her.

"Joe's already done his talking, Paloma."

"Yes, but have you? Does the man know how you really feel about him?"

Caroline silently groaned as the memory of making love to Joe flashed through her mind. In the most intimate possible way, she believed she'd shown him what was in her heart. But apparently he hadn't seen or cared. To him, they had shared nothing more than a night of sex.

With a shake of her head, Caroline turned to the workbench. "Yes, he knows, and that's all I have to say about it, Paloma. Besides, I think I heard the doorbell. Maybe you'd better see if we have a customer."

That evening, in Joe's little adobe house, Nick wailed at the top of his lungs.

Joe smoothed the tabs of the diaper in place, then snapped up the legs of the terry pajamas. "Okay, son, you have clean, dry clothes. You've just had a bottle. What more do you want? Conversation? Entertainment?"

Propping the baby against his chest, he aimed the remote at the television. A commercial flickered onto the screen.

"Look, Nick, it's a dog and a little boy like you. Well, almost like you. You'll be that size one of these days. And I'll get you a dog if you'll quit all this crying. You won't grow very fast if you keep wasting all this energy."

Nick continued howling. Joe sat in the recliner and

placed the baby against his shoulder. As soon as he began to pat his back, Nick burped loudly, and the crying stopped like the flip of a switch.

Caroline had reminded him several times that Nick would have to be burped after he took a bottle. Joe had remembered until this evening.

But his mind wasn't exactly clear and sharp. In his whole life he'd never been through a more miserable week. Not because he'd been caring for Nick. Dealing with the baby's diapers and bottles and crying spells hadn't been all that hard. He was learning and managing. And his new job with the DOC was a breeze compared to the rigid training classes he'd put his troops in the army through.

It was Caroline who was occupying his thoughts. He missed her. Not just for odd moments throughout the day, but from morning until night the emptiness never left him. Just to glance up the mountain toward her house put a fierce ache in his heart.

But she didn't need him hanging around, ruining her life. She was better off without him and Nick. She could get on with running her gallery and eventually she would find that special man she wanted.

He eased Nick away from his shoulder and dabbed the milk from the corners of his tiny mouth. Joe was amazed at how much his love for his son had grown these past few days. Already he felt fiercely protective toward the little tyke. In the mornings on his way to work, Joe didn't want to leave him at day-care. In the evenings, he couldn't wait to pick him up.

Like Caroline had said, Nick was a gift from God. She had also been right about Joe needing the child. And he thanked her, more than she could ever know, for making him see just how much.

He rose from the chair, walked to the glass patio doors and looked up the mountain toward her house. A light was on in one of the rooms. Probably the kitchen. Was she eating alone? he wondered. Had she been thinking about him these past few days or already turning her life to other things?

Groaning inwardly, he glanced at Nick, who was cradled in the crook of his arm. "Looks like we're going to have to move, son. Some place north of town. Away from Caroline. I'm not going to stay in this house like your grandfather did and grieve for more than thirty years for a woman I can't have."

But you could have had her Joe. She took you into her bed. She made love to you.

Hell, there hadn't been any love to it, Joe mentally argued. A woman was no different than a man. She didn't have to feel love to go to bed with him. If his mother hadn't proved that, then Pam certainly had.

But was Caroline that kind of woman? he asked himself. She'd claimed to need love for sex. Had she been honest with him? One thing he knew for certain, she would never abandon a baby or child of any age. But that didn't mean she would stick with a man. Especially a man like him.

With that sobering thought, Joe quickly turned from the glass doors and the beckoning light in Caroline's house.

Caroline glared at the ringing telephone. She was trying to read. She wasn't in the mood to talk to anyone. But the ringing persisted until she was forced to lift the receiver.

"I was beginning to think you weren't home," a female voice said.

"Hello, Mom."

"You sound cross. Should I hang up and call some other time?"

Caroline drew in a weary breath. A little more than a week ago, she'd phoned her mother and told her Joe had taken the baby home with him. Somehow Justine had picked up on her daughter's misery and guessed Joe was the reason. After that, Caroline hadn't bothered to deny she was in love with her neighbor.

"No. I'm not cross. I was just...distracted when you called."

"Hmm. Well, I guess there's no need to ask how things are going. I can tell by the sound of your voice. You still haven't talked to Joe?"

Caroline swallowed painfully. "Mother, I don't want to go into this. I'm trying to forget the man."

"Why? You've been waiting for years for the right man to come along. Now you want to forget him?"

Caroline rubbed the ache that was building in her forehead. "What makes you think Joe is the right man? You haven't even met him."

"That's true," Justine conceded. "But he has to be wonderful. Or you would have never fallen in love with him in the first place."

"I've got a news flash for you, Mom. Your daughter isn't perfect and lately she's been behaving very foolishly."

"The only foolish thing you've done is not telling Joe that you love him."

As far as Caroline was concerned, not declaring her love to Joe was the only thing that had saved her from complete humiliation. The night she'd given herself to him, she'd carefully avoided using the word *love*. She'd been afraid of scaring Joe off before he got used to the two of them being together.

Being together. Dear Lord, she'd been an idiot. She'd been so besotted with the man, she'd actually believed he'd been touching her with love.

"Then I guess I'll just have to go on being a fool because there's no way I'm going to tell the man anything."

Justine groaned with disappointment. "Caroline, you have to tell him! Otherwise you're going to have very deep regrets."

"He wouldn't believe me. Anyway, he'd think I was using him to be close to the baby."

"If you're half the woman I think you are, you could convince him otherwise."

The tears in Caroline's eyes suddenly spilled over. She dashed them back with her hand and sniffed. "Oh, Mom, would you and Dad mind if I came home for a few days? I think…being on the ranch would help me get myself back together."

"Of course we won't mind, honey," Justine said gently. "We always love to see you. I just hope you're not coming down here in order to run away from Joe. Because that won't help."

Her mother was right. Caroline could run to the ends of the earth, and Joe would still be right there in her heart.

"I'm not, Mom. I'm just hoping one of these days I'll quit hurting and I'll be able to think back to my time with Joe and baby Nick with nothing in my heart but fond memories."

The evening sun was warm, the breeze gentle as Joe pushed the stroller down the red dirt road. Nick didn't seem to mind the little bumps along the way. In fact, the baby was always contented when he was out of doors.

Never in his wildest dreams did Joe think he would one day be pushing a baby stroller. Much less have the baby inside it be his own. But since he'd returned to Santa Fe his life had changed drastically. He was a father now. He felt totally different than the drill sergeant who'd barked endless orders at young army recruits.

In a little more than five minutes Joe reached the

intersection and his mailbox. On his way home from work, he'd forgotten to stop and collect the mail. Fetching it had given him an excuse to exercise and give Nick a ride in the fresh air.

His box sat beside Caroline's. Each day Joe read her name and like every other day for the past week and a half, he fought the urge to look up the mountain toward her house. Looking only made his ache for her worse, and he was getting sick and tired of hurting. Sick and tired of wondering how things might have been if he'd been brave enough to trust her with his heart. To love her.

You already love her, Joe. When are you going to realize that?

Cursing the little voice in his head, he pulled the stack of mail from the box and quickly shuffled through the flyers and envelopes. Junk mail and bills. That was all Joe ever received. He didn't correspond with friends or relatives. He supposed he'd never been that close to anyone.

Suddenly his hands stilled as his eyes rapidly scanned a long white envelope. It appeared to be a personal letter, the stamp mark from Albuquerque. A return address was written in the corner, but no name.

Who the hell, he wondered as he ripped open the back flap. Maybe it was money from an old army buddy. Heaven knows, he'd lent plenty down through the years.

Joe stared in stunned disbelief at the single sheet

of paper in his hands. They wanted his baby! His son!

The handwritten letter was short and frank and signed by both parents of Pamela Ashby. But they couldn't take him, Joe mentally shouted. Even they admitted that.

Quickly he scanned the brief paragraphs once again. Lorna and Bill were highly upset with their daughter. They hadn't known of her intention to give the baby up and would have done everything in their power to stop her if they had been aware of her plans.

Joe read.

We accept that as the father of the baby you have the legal say-so of his welfare. However, from the information Pam has given us, we understand you are single and never wanted to have a family. We do want the child and we think it would be in his best interest if you would allow us to raise him in the manner we see fit. After all, you've been a single, military man for twenty years, you couldn't know about caring for a baby. Moreover, we have the financial security to make sure his future opportunities are the very best, where your funds are no doubt limited.

We're sure that after you've had time to consider our request, you'll see the benefits of allowing us to have the baby. Not only for his sake, but yours, too. You would be a free man again, without the burden of raising a child.

The Ashbys closed the letter with their telephone number, address and a last line saying they would be expecting to hear from him soon.

With a strange feeling in his heart, Joe slowly folded the letter and placed it and the rest of the mail in a holder on the back of the stroller. Then he carefully picked up Nick and cradled the boy in his arms.

The baby was awake, his brown eyes searching curiously for a shape to latch onto. Joe lifted Nick's tiny hand and smiled as it curled trustingly around his big finger. This was *his* son. Nothing and no one would ever change that fact. Joe would raise him as he saw fit. And he'd do a hell of a better job than the Ashbys had with their own daughter, and a damn sight better than his parents had with him.

You will be a good father, Joe. I know you will.

Like a ray of sunshine bursting through the clouds, Caroline's words surged through him. He studied his son's face and felt the warm weight of his helpless, tiny body against his arm, and was overwhelmed with love and gratitude and hope.

"Until this moment, I didn't understand, Nick. I didn't know just how much Caroline had done for me. And you. She made me see how much I love you and need you. She made me see I'm a man worthy of being a father. Even a husband."

His gaze flew up the mountain, and his heart

pounded loudly in his chest. Could she forgive him? he wondered. Could he make her see just how much he loved and needed her, or had he waited too long?

Caroline was packing a suitcase when the doorbell rang. She'd not heard a car announcing the arrival of a caller, and the unexpected sound caused her to start.

She dropped a cashmere sweater into the open case and hurried to the front door.

"Who is it?" she called.

"It's me. Joe."

Joe! Suddenly her heart was in her throat, beating at such a frantic pace, she felt almost faint.

After fumbling with the knob, she finally managed to swing the door wide. The sight of Joe standing on the threshold with Nick cradled in his arms was so astounding, so achingly familiar that tears stung her eyes.

"Hello, Caroline. May we come in?"

If she'd possessed an ounce of sense, she would have never opened the door in the first place. Even now, she should send him packing down the mountain. But the past week and a half she'd ached for him, fought with herself to keep from picking up the phone or turning her car toward his house. Now that he was here, she couldn't turn him away.

She pushed open the screen and gestured for him to enter the house. She peered beyond the sheltered entrance to the front yard.

"I don't see your truck," she said in a bewildered voice. "Did you walk all the way up here?"

He stepped past her, then stopped. "I pushed Nick in his stroller."

She shut the door, then turned to face him. A wan smile lifted one corner of her lips. "So Nick has a stroller now?"

Joe grinned sheepishly. "Yeah. He really likes the thing, and I've discovered it's mighty handy when we go out."

Caroline knew she was staring, but she couldn't help it. She didn't know why he was here or how long he would stay, and her eyes were starved for the sight of him.

"Would you like to lay Nick down? It looks like he's asleep."

Joe's gaze slanted over her slender figure. A powder-blue cotton dress skimmed her waist, then flared in a circle around her ankles. The round neckline dipped temptingly low, giving him just a hint of creamy cleavage. Raw hunger gripped him, and he had to force himself to breathe.

"I think I should. Would it be okay to put him on your bed?"

Nick was still tiny enough to fit quite easily on the end of the couch or the chair, but Caroline didn't point that out. Her mind was spinning with more important things. Like why he'd suddenly appeared after telling her things between them had to be all over.

"Of course," she told him, then motioned for him to follow her into the bedroom.

The moment Joe stepped through the door, memories flooded through him, stirring his body with heated longing. But those thoughts were instantly forgotten as his eyes caught sight of the suitcase lying open on the bed.

"Are you going somewhere?"

After a long pause, she answered. "To Hondo. To the Pardee Ranch to visit my parents."

Joe placed Nick on the calico quilt, then, grim-faced, he turned to her. "For how long?"

Her mangled heart was crying for her to reach out and touch him, but her brain forced her to remember all the pain he'd put her through.

She glanced away from him and drew in a long breath. "I'm not sure. Maybe a few days. Maybe a few weeks."

He scraped a hand through his black hair. "I don't want you to go, Caroline," he said slowly.

Her eyes jerked to his face. At the same time her mouth formed a perfect O of astonishment. "Don't you think it's a little late to ask me to consider your wants?"

After a glance at the sleeping baby, he took hold of her upper arm. "Let's go out to the living room. I have something to tell you."

She allowed him to lead her out of the bedroom but broke free of his grasp once they were near the couch. "Is that why you're here, Joe? If it is, then why couldn't you have telephoned?"

He made a frustrated sound. "Because what I have to say—" He shook his head, then moved across the room. "Maybe I should start by showing you something."

Her brows puckered with confusion. Caroline watched him step out the front door, then seconds later step inside carrying a long white envelope.

"What is this?" she asked as he handed her the single sheet from inside.

"Just read it. I want to see what you think."

Caroline read each line carefully. By the time she'd gotten to the end, she felt sick. "This is disgusting! It's insulting to you as a man and a father!"

"I know."

Her brows lifted with disbelief as she watched a smile curve his lips. "Then why are you amused?"

"I'm not amused. I'm happy."

Her head swung. He wasn't making sense. Or maybe she wasn't. Caroline was so shaken by the sight of him she could hardly think, hardly remember she should be loathing him instead of wanting to smother his face with kisses.

"Happy?" She waved the letter at him. "Something like this makes you happy?"

He stepped closer, and her heart pounded even harder.

"Yes. Because it made me see what you've done to me, Caroline."

Her cheeks filled with heat as the night they spent together whirled through her mind. She hadn't done anything except love him, want him with every pore of her body. "I haven't done anything to you. Except—except—"

"What?" he urged.

She dropped her head and squeezed her eyes tightly shut. "Except try to love you," she murmured huskily. "But you didn't want that."

Groaning low in his throat, he moved even nearer and curled his hands over her shoulders. "I did, Caroline. I wanted it very much. I still do."

Her green eyes were shadowed with doubts as she looked at him. "No. Don't even say it. I don't know what you're wanting, but it's not me. You made that quite clear, Joe. You took little Nick and walked away. You said you didn't want us to be together. I've accepted that. So leave me alone."

His throat tightened as he realized the pain he'd caused her. "I can't, Caroline. I know I hurt you. And I know I don't deserve your love or your trust, but I'm asking you for it anyway."

His fingers were warm and rough against her skin, evoking memories so hot and sweet it was all she could do to keep from flinging herself against his broad chest.

"Why?"

He released another heavy breath. "You're not making this easy."

"No. You don't deserve easy."

"Maybe I don't. Maybe I'm not worthy of you or Nick. But I happen to believe I am."

Desperate to keep him from breaking down her defenses, she turned and moved to the opposite side of the room.

"That's quite a switch," she said flatly.

Joe went to her and slipped his arms around her waist. As he bent his head and pressed his cheek next to hers, the flowery scent of her perfume filled his head and he wondered how he'd survived these past days without holding her, hearing her voice, seeing her smile. He'd been crazy to think he could live without Caroline in his life.

"I realize I'm asking a lot," he murmured. "Two weeks ago, even a week ago, the idea of me being a father or a husband scared the hell right out of me. But not now."

She tried to swallow the ball of tears in her throat. "I'd be a fool to think you were any different from the day you walked out of this house."

Slowly, he turned her to face him. Her lips quivered as his thumb and forefinger hooked her chin and lifted her green eyes to his.

"A few minutes ago, when I first opened that letter, I—I was infuriated that the Ashbys had the gall to ask for my son and to question my ability to father him. And then it suddenly hit me just how much I had changed since I met you. Before, I would have agreed with them. I probably would have handed baby Nick over to them, thinking I couldn't give him what he needed.''

"Oh, Joe," she whispered with anguish.

A rueful smile touched his lips. "You see, Caroline, all of my life I never knew what it was like to love or be loved. I didn't know what having a family really meant to a man. Or a woman. And all these years I believed I'd only be asking for trouble to try to be anything more than a soldier, a loner. But you gave me the confidence to believe in myself. You made me find the courage to be a father. And a husband. Though that part took a little longer," he added sheepishly.

She shook her head as hope and joy mingled with lingering doubt. "If it took a letter from the Ashbys to open your eyes, then I'm glad they had the audacity to send it. But what if you'd never gotten that letter, Joe? I haven't seen or heard from you in days and—"

Before she could finish, he was pressing kisses on her cheeks, nose and forehead. "Letter or not," he said, his voice rough with need, "I couldn't have kept avoiding what was in my heart. This past week and a half has been hell. I don't ever want to go through anything like it again."

A groan slipped past her lips as she pressed her cheek against his chest. "Oh, Joe, since you and Nick left I've never been so miserable. I thought you didn't love me. After that night we spent together, I was convinced sex was all you wanted from me."

His arms circled her and crushed her against the length of him. "That night, for the first time in my life, I learned what it was like to make love to a woman. You pretty well shook me up, Caroline. But I'm not running anymore. I'm here to stay." He eased her head back and cradled her face with his palms. "Will you forget about packing and marry me?"

Wild joy was suddenly pumping through her veins, but she kept her expression carefully guarded. "You think I love you, Joe Garcia?"

His brows arched and his fingers trailed down the side of her neck. A provocative grin twisted his lips. "If you don't, you damn well better learn to love me. Because you're stuck with me, woman."

She couldn't stop the smile that was quickly spreading across her face. It lit her green eyes as she stood on tiptoe and brought her lips close to his. "If that's the case, I will marry you. But I won't unpack."

He looked at her quizzically. "You still want to go to your parents' ranch?"

She nodded as she slipped her arms around him and snuggled closer. "If you'll go with me. A little Catholic church has been there in the valley for nearly two hundred years. Our Lady of Guadalupe is where all of my mother's family, the Murdocks, get married or christen a newborn. I'd like to become your wife there and have Nicolas's christening, too."

"We'll go tomorrow."

His urgency sent a thrill of joy bubbling inside

her. "Sounds like we're not going to have a long engagement," she said with a soft laugh.

"Hmm. Forget the engagement," he whispered. "We're going straight to the real thing."

She closed the last fraction of space between their lips and for long, long moments he kissed her with all the aching emptiness he'd felt the past days.

When he finally lifted his head and smiled at her, Caroline was breathless and trembling and so filled with happiness she thought she would burst.

"You know," she murmured, "when I found a baby on my doorstep, I didn't realize I was going to find the man I'm going to love for the rest of my life, too."

He grinned. "Maybe the angel that brought Nick to your doorstep brought me, too. I don't know. But one thing I'm sure about is an angel is going to keep me here. A redheaded angel with green eyes and soft, creamy skin and…"

His words trailed away as his lips began a slow descent to her chin and neck and the valley between her breasts. When he lifted her in his arms and carried her toward the couch, she glanced in the direction of the bedroom.

"Do you think Nick is going to sleep for a while?"

Joe chuckled. "He wouldn't dare interrupt his parents now."

Nicolas Ruy Garcia slept peacefully the rest of the night.

* * * * *

Want surprises? Adventure? Seduction? Secrets? Emotion?

All in one book?

You've got it!

In June 2000 Silhouette is proud to present:

SENSATIONAL

This special collection contains
four complete novels, one from each
of your favorite series, and features some
of your most beloved authors...

all for one low price!

Sharon Sala—Intimate Moments
Elizabeth Bevarly—Desire
Sandra Steffen—Romance
Cheryl Reavis—Special Edition

You won't be disappointed!

Available at your favorite retail outlet.

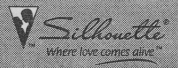

Silhouette®
Where love comes alive™

From bestselling author

ANNETTE BROADRICK

comes her most compelling novel yet....

SONS OF TEXAS
Callaway Country

An earth-shattering explosion…a mysterious call to
duty…the woman he'd never forgotten. They all
beckoned rugged Clay Callaway—one of the last
of the family's bachelors—home to Texas. But his
tempestuous reunion with his childhood sweetheart
was more threatening than any danger he'd *ever*
faced in the line of duty….

When the Sons of Texas ride,
adventure, intrigue—and passion!—
forever become the legacy of Callaway Country.

Available in May at your favorite retail outlet.

Silhouette®
Where love comes alive™

Multi-*New York Times* bestselling author

NORA ROBERTS

knew from the first how to capture readers' hearts.
Celebrate the 20th Anniversary of Silhouette Books
with this special 2-in-1 edition containing her fabulous
first book and the sensational sequel.

Coming in June

IRISH HEARTS

Adelia Cunnane's fiery temper sets proud, powerful horse
breeder Travis Grant's heart aflame and he resolves to
make this wild *Irish Thoroughbred* his own.

Erin McKinnon accepts wealthy Burke Logan's loveless
proposal, but can this ravishing *Irish Rose* win her
hard-hearted husband's love?

Also available in June from
Silhouette Special Edition (SSE #1328)

IRISH REBEL

In this brand-new sequel to *Irish Thoroughbred*, Travis and
Adelia's innocent but strong-willed daughter Keeley discovers
love in the arms of a charming Irish rogue with a talent for
horses...and romance.

Where love comes alive™

Visit Silhouette at www.eHarlequin.com   PSNORA